Opal

The Twelve Horizons of Charlie
Book Three

MELODY ANNE

D1607568

Published by Falling Star Publications
Editing by Karen Lawson and Janet Hitchcock

Author's Photos

This is Renita and me in Texas. I met Renita at the VERY beginning of my career. She messaged me one day after reading my new book and we began talking. It's been an amazing friendship from that moment on. I wanted this pic for the Texas book because she took me all over the Lone Star State including to the Alamo. I thought I was going to die in Texas it was so hot, but it's one of the funnest trips I've taken. Love you woman!

Books by Melody Anne

Romance

BILLIONAIRE BACHELORS
*The Billionaire Wins The Game
*The Billionaire's Dance
*The Billionaire Falls
*The Billionaire's Marriage Proposal
*Blackmailing the Billionaire
*Runaway Heiress
*The Billionaire's Final Stand
*Unexpected Treasure
*Hidden Treasure
*Holiday Treasure
*Priceless Treasure
*The Ultimate Treasure

BABY FOR THE BILLIONAIRE
*The Tycoon's Revenge
*The Tycoon's Vacation
*The Tycoon's Proposal
*The Tycoon's Secret
*The Lost Tycoon
*Rescue Me

THE ANDERSON BILLIONAIRES
*Finn – Book One
*Noah – Book Two
*Brandon – Book Three

*Hudson – Book Four
*Crew – Book Five

THE TWELVE HORIZONS OF CHARLIE
*Diamond – Book One
*Sapphire – Book Two
*Opal – Book Three
*Emerald – Book Four
*BloodStone – Book Five – Coming Spring 2022

BECOMING ELENA
*Stolen Innocence – Book One
*Forever Lost – Book Two
*New Desires – Book Three

TAKEN BY THE TRILLIONAIRE
#1 Xander – Ruth Cardello
#2 Bryan – J.S. Scott
#3 Chris – Melody Anne
#4 Virgin for the Trillionaire – Ruth Cardello
#5 Virgin for the Prince – J.S. Scott
#6 Virgin to Conquer – Melody Anne

SURRENDER SERIES
*Surrender – Book One
*Submit – Book Two
*Seduced – Book Three
*Scorched – Book Four

UNDERCOVER BILLIONAIRES
*Kian – Book One
*Arden – Book Two
*Owen – Book Three
*Declan – Book Four

FORBIDDEN SERIES
*Bound – Book One
*Broken – Book Two
*Betrayed – Book Three
*Burned – Book Four

HEROES SERIES
*Safe in his arms – Novella
*Baby it's Cold Outside
*Her Unexpected Hero – Book One
*Who I am with you – Book Two – Novella
*Her Hometown Hero – Book Three
*Following Her – Book Four – Novella
*Her Forever Hero – Book Five
*Her Found Hero – Book Six – **Coming May 2022**

BILLIONAIRE AVIATORS
*Turbulent Intentions – Book One (Cooper)
*Turbulent Desires – Book Two (Maverick)
*Turbulent Waters – Book Three (Nick)
*Turbulent Intrigue – Book Four (Ace)

TORN SERIES
*Torn – Book One
*Tattered – Book Two

7 BRIDES FOR 7 BROTHERS
#1 Luke – Barbara Freethy
#2 Gabe – Ruth Cardello
#3 Hunter – Melody Anne

ANDERSON SPECIAL OPS
*Shadows – Book One
*Rising – Book Two
*Barriers – Book Three

*Shattered – Book Four
*Reborn – Book Five

TRUTH IN LIES
*One too Many – Book One
*Two Secrets Kept – Book Two – Coming May 2022
*Three of a Kind – Book Three – Coming August
    2022

Young Adult / Fantasy

PHOENIX SERIES
*Phoenix Falling – Book One
*Phoenix Burning – Book Two
*Phoenix Ashes – Book Three
*Phoenix Rising – Book Four

PROLOGUE

T HEY TELL US the definition of insanity is to do the same thing over and over again while getting the same results. I've decided I must be insane. I think anyone who's in love is actually insane. How foolish is it for us to trust another person with our heart?

That's a great question to ask. Normally, we learn that once is enough. We go through the trauma of falling in love and we give that person our heart. Then when it inevitably gets shattered, the person who took it will always keep it—or at the very least keep half of it. There are no take backs.

We don't get a choice in this. We can demand it back, but they still keep our heart. Even if we meet someone else, which is very likely, the person who first took our heart refuses to let it go. The person we might meet at a later date will make us laugh, make us cry, give us pleasure, and might even give us snippets of true happiness. But no matter what this future person does, they can't hold a heart we no longer possess, a heart we've already given away. It's a simple reality.

How sad is this for the ones who choose to love us? How sad is this for ourselves? I've given my heart away already and though Bentley is gone, he took it with him to the grave. I believe what is meant to be will happen no matter how hard we try to fight it. I believe my ache will never end.

I also firmly believe that no matter what, I'm going to hurt people in my life, and they will hurt me. Why? Because love is selfish, and love will always find a way no matter how many roadblocks we throw at it. Circling back to the definition of insanity, am I crazy, or do I still believe in love? I'm not sure I can answer either way. It might be as basic as accepting that I'm both crazy and want to believe in love.

Stephy and I walk up to the incredible 1895 Fort Worth Tarrant County Courthouse. I stop and stare at the huge pink granite castle in front of me. I give Stephy a look that makes her instantly laugh. I roll my eyes and wait her out. It takes several moments.

"I should've gotten you a tiara," she gasps in between giggles.

"This looks like a dang castle," I tell her.

"I honestly didn't look at pictures so I had *no* idea what the place looked like."

"This is supposed to be a simple ceremony to a man I don't know. There's nothing romantic about it, and it's only a job," I insist.

"Well, except you're starting this one off as a fairy tale right from the start in your very own princess castle. He must be prince charming," she tells me.

"Do *not* get any romantic ideas, Stephanie Lawrence. I will murder you. I'm doing this, but it's not going to be anything more than a marriage contract to help the man out. I don't know why I agreed. I think I was drunk."

She laughs harder. "Then maybe you should stay permanently buzzed because I love the girl willing to marry a stranger. She's a ton of fun."

"That's so not going to happen."

I begin walking forward. What in the world am I doing right now? I've accepted a marriage proposal from an ad in a paper. Ugh, sadly, for the most part, I'm okay with this. Why? Because I'm not drowning my sorrows in what could have been. Instead, I'm nervous and wondering what the next adventure will be like.

Stephy and I chat as we make our way to the third floor of the historic courthouse. I'm getting closer to the man I'm about to marry—a man I've never met. I start to giggle.

"What?" Stephy asks.

"I wonder if someday we're going to look back at this and realize how crazy we are, or if we're going to simply shrug and say it was all an adventure."

Stephy is laughing with me. "We're going to decide to have no regrets at all. We can live life in a box or we can love the hand we're dealt. Bentley is smiling from heaven and laughing at our adventures."

"I'd like to think so."

The elevator doors open, and we step out. He's here. As the man looks up and our eyes meet, I have no doubt whatsoever this is *him*. This is the guy I'm about to marry. His eyes laser in on mine, and I falter in my steps. I've known what to expect, and I've seen his picture, but a picture doesn't do the man justice.

He begins to move forward, his long, muscled legs striding with confidence in his worn cowboy boots. He's wearing dusty jeans, and a fitted button-down blue shirt. His old brown leather Stetson looks as if it never comes off his perfectly shaped head. He's breathtaking with his light grey eyes and chiseled jaw.

I feel an instant ping of attraction that makes me stumble on my next step. This isn't supposed to happen. What have I gotten myself into?

"Charlie?" he asks. It's a question but it's pretty obvious who I am. Just as I've seen him, he's seen multiple pictures of me.

"Yes, you must be Colby." I want to add that the pictures truly didn't do this man justice.

"Yes, ma'am." He takes off his hat and tips it, making both Stephy and me giggle. "Are you ready to get married?" This makes me laugh harder. Oh my gosh, there's no turning back now.

"I guess so," I tell him. "This is Steph."

"It's good to meet you, Steph," he says as he holds out his hand. She shakes it while beaming at him.

We all turn and walk up to the window. It goes very quick after that. Within fifteen minutes, we're pronounced man and wife by a bored looking judge in a small room with zero character to it. At least the room doesn't resemble a castle. There's no kiss, no words of love, just a quick ceremony performed by a judge who stamps a paper and declares us husband and wife.

I'm silent as the three of us walk down the staircase, and I don't take my first real breath until we step out of the courthouse. We are halfway down the outside steps when Stephy reaches into her pocket and pulls something out. Then she tosses whatever it is into the air over the top of us.

"Congrats!" she yells as seeds come flying down on us.

Colby laughs as I try to dodge the birdseed. I glare at Stephy.

"Come on you two. We just had a wedding. You're acting as if we're leaving a funeral."

It feels like a funeral. I'm not sure I'm glad I've done this. It seemed fine at the moment, but now that we're here, I'm afraid I've made another foolish decision in my life.

"I don't like being forced into doing anything but my grandfather left me no choice," Colby says as his laughter dies away. "Charlie, I very much appreciate you helping me, but my pride has taken a bit of a hit. I fought his damn will, but it was either get married or lose the family ranch where thousands of people depend on me."

I learned a little about this as we've chatted in the past week. Colby's grandfather believes a man needs to be settled down. He died six months earlier and left Colby his massive ranch with the caveat that he has to be happily married for twelve months before he inherits it. If Colby doesn't abide by the terms of the will, the land will be divided up, making plenty of investors stand around rubbing their hands together. Therefore, Colby had placed an ad looking for a wife. Stephy had responded to that ad, and now, here we are.

"I'm sorry. I know what a pain in the butt family can be when they think they're helping us," I tell him. It actually helps ease my apprehension to have him remind me of why we're doing this.

"Yes, Gramps was an incredible man. He also had a sense of humor that I think only he appreciated. I'm sure he's laughing from the grave now. I've always been a stubborn son of a bitch, and this is him throwing all of the aces on the table after he's had them hidden up his sleeve all night."

"He sounds like someone I would've gotten along with great." I'm feeling less and less nervous the more we talk. Not all of my anxiety is over as I'll be living at the ranch, and not having any idea what that means.

"I want to see this place that isn't worth losing," Stephy says as we reach the street.

"Well then we should hit the road," Colby says. "What are you driving?"

"We took an Uber from the airport so we're with you," Stephy says. She's not shy at all. She's not worried of getting into the vehicle of a stranger.

"Perfect." He seems a little too pleased.

I'm nervous enough for both Stephy and me. What if this man isn't who he says he is? What if he's some serial killer? Stephy seems to know all about him and she's a genius with the computer, but she can be fooled. It doesn't look like we get much choice now, though.

We're here and we've committed.

Colby leads us to the parking lot and moves up to a huge Ford F350. It looks like a lot of the trucks used on Stephy's ranch. It's the same color as Bentley's old truck. My heart skips a beat and suddenly I'm desperate, wanting to turn back. Can I still run. Why is this man getting to me? It's too soon. I can't spend a year with him.

Colby holds open the front door of his truck open, and I take a breath, then step forward. I'm about to find out what I've done. I'm about to see if my word holds true. I told him a year to save his ranch. Can I do it?

CHAPTER ONE

THERE'S SILENCE IN the courtroom as I look up. I've gone from one marriage to the next in this room full of strangers—well, mostly strangers. There are a few familiar faces, even some friendly ones. I've seen shock, awe, jealousy, and disbelief on their faces. My life has been difficult to follow. I get that. I can barely keep up and I've lived my life. I can't imagine how hard it is for the jury and audience to keep it all straight.

"So, you just come home from Italy after leaving a great man, and you immediately respond to an ad for a *new* husband?" Mr. Hart asks.

"Yes." There's no need to add more.

"Just like that?"

"Yes." We seem to be playing a game of who can say the fewest words. I'm winning with my one-word answers.

"Why?" he asks.

I smile. "Why not?" He won that round of word exchanges.

"You were offered one million dollars for this union," Mr. Hart says.

"Yes."

"Did you take the money?"

"Yes."

"So, you got married for money . . . once again." Mr. Hart looks as if he's finally won a battle with me.

I smile at him. "In your last divorce your spouse paid you ten million dollars. Did you marry her for the money?" I ask sweetly.

There's a gasp in the courtroom and, for the first time, I see Mr. Hart come seriously close to losing it. His face turns red and his hands visibly shake. I know he's wondering how in the hell I've come by this information. He doesn't have a Stephy in his corner.

"My personal life is none of your business nor this court's business," he finally says, spit flying from his mouth. He takes in a breath and forces himself to calm.

"You feel no qualms about invading *my* personal life, so by bringing up a money question, I'm well within my rights to bring up your own."

"That's not how this works, Ms. Diamond."

"I don't think anyone in here knows how *any* of this works, Mr. Hart. I don't think anyone truly knows *why* I'm on trial."

"You've broken the law."

"We've gone over this before. What laws have I broken?" I pause and give him a huge smile that's sure to raise his blood pressure a few more points. "Do your job and prove it if you think I've truly done something wrong."

He turns and walks to his table. He takes a long drink of water. When he turns back to me he's much more composed. There's the opponent I've enjoyed sparring with. I don't like winning unless the person is worth beating.

"You still have a relationship with your last ex-husband. Do you with Mr. Winters?"

"I guess you'll have to hear our story to find that out," I tell him. I see several smiles in the room. They've already learned I'm not easily swayed to tell anything I don't want to tell. I certainly won't tell it on Mr. Hart's timeline. It's mine to tell how I want to tell it and when I want to tell it.

"You really enjoy drawing this out. Are you getting something from it?" Mr. Hart asks.

"Yes."

He waits. I don't add more.

"*What* are you getting from this?"

I lean back. "Healing."

"What have you been so traumatized about that you need this healing?" He knows he has to be careful. There is no measure on internal pain.

I again smile. "I was raised by incredible parents who I'm shocked to know still support me no matter what I do in life. My parents are both very religious but they also believe in freedom and love. They know that I have my own path to walk in life. It might not be the path they wanted for me, but they have learned to love me no matter what. When I lost Bentley, I wasn't sure if I'd live. Through the years I've found a way. Telling this story is reminding me of why I've done what I've done."

None of this matters. I shouldn't need to explain myself, but I have to give more reasons for those who might question my lifestyle to see the benefits in it. I don't want to go to jail. In the beginning I didn't care one way or the other. Now, I have a reason to be free. Now, I have no other choice but freedom. I hope the jurors choose that path for me.

I'm suddenly emotional, my throat tightening, my eyes stinging. I don't normally get upset, but these are unusual times with so many answers left up in the air. I've been edgy for weeks. If it wasn't for Stephy, my parents, and Cash, I don't think I could get through this. They are on my side, and with them I can finish my journey. It's not about my guilt or innocence. It's about my life. I need to tell my story. I need to set myself free. I need to let it all go . . . every . . . single . . . last . . . bit. This means, the good, the bad . . . and the ugly. And yes, there's some ugly. There's some true devastation. There's more good than bad, though. I'm realizing that more and more the longer this trial continues.

Mr. Hart throws me a few more questions before Judge Croesus calls an end to court for the day. For once I'm not ready to leave. I have so much I want to say, so much I *need* to say. My journey with Colby was one that changed me in ways the others never even came close to changing me. This adventure showed me what life would've been like with Bentley. Maybe this is why I'm so sad. No, there's so much more to it. It will take some time to get it all out.

"That was brutal today," Stephy says as we step inside the SUV.

"No, it wasn't. Mr. Hart isn't an awful man, he's just doing his job. He thinks I need to be punished. I just happen to disagree with him."

"Me too," Stephy says with a laugh. "I can pull up more information on him and have him disbarred," she suggests.

I laugh, not realizing how much I need to. "No, don't do that. The poor man would probably make it his life mission to take me down after that. He doesn't like me now, but once this trial is over, I'm sure he'll move on to the next and forget I ever existed. Let's not do something that will give him a lifelong vendetta against us."

"Fine. But if you want to change your mind all you have to do is ask."

"Has anyone ever told you both that you're terrifying?" Cash asks.

"Often," Stephy says. "Yet, people keep coming back for more." She winks at him.

"That's because you're also irresistible," Cash says.

"We get that a lot, too. It's our mesmerizing personalities," Stephy says.

"Or maybe it's the fact that you're witches," he suggests.

"It could be that too. We may never know. We do have a nice big cauldron and alter in our basement." She waggles her eyes at him. I can see the questions in his eyes. Right now he's wondering if she's kidding or not. No, we don't have a wiccan basement, but that would be kind of cool.

We arrive at the hotel and have dinner and drinks downstairs. Cash says he has some work to do, and Stephy offers to help him. They rush off. I'm wondering how much work will actually get done as I make my way to the pool area. I'm finally alone.

I want to go for a walk, but unless I have a specific destination that's logged with the police department I don't get to go anywhere but here and court, or an occasional dinner on the way from court. This trial will only last for so long and then I'll be free to travel the world again. Right now, though, no place sounds greater than home. Maybe I just need a pair of ruby red slippers so I can click them and go back to the farm.

I feel *him* before I see him. How is it that I know he's here? His hand settles on my shoulder and a sigh tries to escape, but I manage to hold it back. I miss him when we're apart. Each day that passes makes me want to be with him more. It's scaring me, but not enough to chase him away. He came back for me. Does that mean something? Is this what Bentley promised me? I don't know.

"Did you have a rough day at court?" he asks in his deep, soothing voice.

"I didn't see you," I say.

"I wasn't there today."

"Are you trying to keep yourself out of the media?"

"I'm doing my own soul searching," he says with a laugh. "The media doesn't scare me."

He climbs onto the back of my lounge then pulls me against him, wrapping his arms around me. I stiffen for only a second before I lean back and let my head rest against his solid chest.

"Why are you still here?"

"I love you," he says.

I feel tears in my eyes. I hate the emotional mess I'm in.

"You might not when *all* of this comes out," I warn.

He caresses my stomach and I feel tingles through my body. He's always been able to turn me on. He always will be able to. The question is will he be around long enough to do it for a lifetime? More importantly, will I allow him to be around that long?

"We both have a past, Charlie. I don't care about that, beyond wanting to know you better. I'm looking forward to our future."

I don't say anything. I turn, and his lips find mine. All of my worries evaporate. I get lost in his arms . . . the rest of the world fades away. I want to stay with him. I want to need him. I want it to last for a lifetime. I just don't know if I can make that happen—I haven't been able to so far.

CHAPTER TWO

B RIGHT MORNING LIGHT warms my face and I try to crack my eyelids only to slam them shut and turn my body away from the open window with a warm breeze blowing inside. I manage to open my eyes again then look around in confusion.

Where am I?

It's only a couple of blinks before I remember the day before. I'm married . . . again. I look at my finger and see a simple gold band on my left hand. Stephy came back with us to the ranch then flew out last night, telling me that I'm fine and I'm now on my own. We didn't see much of this place yesterday, but what I did see was breathtaking.

I lie in bed for several minutes soaking it all in, unsure of what comes next. How am I supposed to act in this fake marriage? What am I supposed to do? I won't find out by lying here all day. At least I know one thing for sure.

I sit up, then climb from the very comfortable bed. The air inside is warm, which I'm used to. I move to the window and look out, loving the view. It isn't all that different from Stephy's ranch in Oregon. No, from *our* ranch in Oregon. It's my home too. I need to get that through my thick skull.

I didn't unpack the night before so I move to my suitcase and gather a fresh set of clothes, then make my way to the bathroom. It's certainly nice, but not as luxurious as the one I had in Italy. I might be getting a little spoiled if a large walk-in shower and separate tub seems small. I laugh as I turn on the water.

I take my time showering, then dress in a pair of my favorite worn jeans, a comfortable cotton T-shirt, and tennis shoes. I didn't bring boots with me, which was stupid. I know what to wear on a ranch. Maybe I didn't want to accept I was coming to a ranch. It's so close to home, filling me with all sorts of emotions I don't want to analyze right now.

I finally make my way out of my bedroom and take the stairs as I search for the kitchen. It isn't difficult to find. I just follow the scent of fresh coffee and bacon. A woman is cooking and looks up as I enter.

"Good morning," I say, unsure if I should pour myself some coffee. I love these adventures, I've been going on for the past five years, but at the same time, it takes me a while to know where I am and if I belong. This part of my journey is never a good feeling at all.

"Good morning. I'm Barb. Colby is long gone, but said to keep the food warm for you. Go ahead and eat; I'm just about to start cleaning," she says with a pleasant smile.

"You didn't have to do that. I know ranch life starts at sunrise. I was more tired than I realized," I say, feeling embarrassed I slept so long. No one should have to wait for a late sleeper.

"It's not a problem at all. We have many shifts here, so someone is always running in and out of the kitchen. I like to have food waiting," Barb tells me. "It makes me feel needed and I love creating new dishes."

"Is there anything I can help with?"

Barb laughs. "I'm very territorial in my kitchen. Just grab some coffee and a plate of food so I'm not offended you don't like my food."

I laugh with her. "I can do that for sure. I'm hungry. Of course, I'm always starving in the morning. My bestie makes fun of me for that all of the time."

"That's good because breakfast is my favorite meal to cook."

I move over to the counter and pour myself a cup of coffee that smells divine. The biscuits and gravy and an egg dish look as if they have half of the kitchen ingredients in them. I take big portions of both and sit down.

Barb turns, sees my plate, and laughs. "I like a woman with a healthy appetite. Too many women these days thinks a meal is lettuce and water." She dishes herself some food and stands on the other side of the counter from me as she nibbles. "I wasn't sure about this arrangement with Colby, but I have a good feeling about you. This just might be fun."

My cheeks heat at these words. Does everyone on the ranch know what is happening between Colby and I? Will they think I'm nothing more than a money-hungry female? They'd have to think that. Who else marries a stranger with the promise of a million dollars at the end of the year?

"I'm lucky I can still get away with eating this much with only a bit of it going to my hips, ass, and boobs and nowhere else. I'm sure that will end sooner rather than later. I need to take advantage of it as long as I can." I decide not to say anything about my marriage to Colby for now. I don't know what I'm supposed to say or how I'm supposed to act. This is all new territory for me.

Barb pats her round stomach. "I gave up on dieting years ago and decided I like the pleasure of food more than nice fitting clothes. I'm not looking for a man, and I think the only reason most single women stay in shape is to attract men."

"There are some real fitness buffs out there," I tell her with a laugh.

"We all have our addictions. I wish I was addicted to yoga, but alas, it's food I love. I remember the day I gave up. I was in the grocery store standing behind this older lady who had a tub of ice-cream, a pie, and a bag of chips in her cart. I'd been dieting for months and had only lost a couple of pounds. I decided right there that I was going to live happy, fat, and grow old." She laughs as she says this.

"I love that attitude. Food is too good to worry about calories. I was in Italy not long ago and gained about twenty pounds without caring at all. I told myself it was okay to gain some weight for the pleasure of such good food. I think I've lost about ten pounds of it, but

I refuse to get back on the scales. Some of my jeans still aren't fitting me."

"Oh, you're giving me a challenge now. Italian cooking is hard to beat. Let's see if I can impress you as much with my cooking."

That would be impossible I think, but I'm too smart to say so. The thought of Italy makes my heart thump. I will miss them, especially Isabella. I still can't believe she's gone. Those months after her death broke my heart. I have no doubt that Nicoli will be good though. He'll find someone new and have a beautiful life. I wasn't supposed to be with him longer than I was. It doesn't make it any easier to keep losing people. I had fun with him and grew to care about him.

I think there are many levels to love. We might all seek the passionate, for time and all eternity kind of love, but I think that sets us up for failure. We need to accept lesser levels of love and appreciate what we have when we have it. All love doesn't have to be forever. It can be for right now.

"I did take a few lessons while living there if you want some tips on Italian cooking. I'm not very good but I learned a few tricks," I offer. If I'm going to be here for a year, it would be nice to have a friend. Everyone knows the staff truly run a home.

"I might take you up on that. I can cook great Mexican, and barbeque like a queen, but I've never mastered Italian," Barb says.

I hold up my hands to let her know I'm far from a master chef. "I haven't mastered it either, but I've learned to make a good sauce and noodles from scratch."

"Well then we're going to have a few cooking days. I suppose I'll share my kitchen with you once in a while," she says with a wink. That was much quicker than expected. I've only been with her a few minutes and have gone from not being allowed in the kitchen to helping prepare a meal. This is good.

"Mr. Winters is a good man. I wasn't happy with his gramps about that stipulation in his will, but I understand why he needed to do it. He loves this place, and he loves the staff who work here. I was afraid of the sort of woman who might show up, but you don't seem too bad."

I laugh. Barb has no problem being blunt. "Barb, I think you and I are going to be great friends. Your loyalty to Colby shows me he's not a bad man. I'm glad to hear it. I was hesitant of a man who'd place such an ad, so I'm sure you have your own suspicions about a woman who will accept one. I can't answer exactly why I did except to say we all have a past, and we all have ways of healing ourselves. This is just another step in my journey. You don't have to worry that I'll hurt him, though. I want nothing from him. I just want to find myself."

She looks at me for several moments as if she's trying to assess if I'm speaking the truth or not. She finally nods as she comes to her conclusion. I don't know what it is but I have a feeling we're going to get along great. I think I'll like being here. It might be difficult at times, but I'm eager to see how it all works out.

"He's a very good man, but he's had bad luck in love. I think that's why his gramps did this. He's afraid he'll be alone forever and the ranch will die out anyway. I just hope this arrangement doesn't hurt him."

The words are a warning from Barb. "We're just helping one another out. I have no intention of doing anything to hurt him," I assure her again. "I think we might be good for each other since neither of us are looking for more than a way to fulfill obligations in our lives. He needs a wife for a year, and I need to do some soul searching."

She nods, then takes both of our plates and begins cleaning. I've been dismissed. I'm okay with this. I want to go outside. I can only be indoors for so long before I grow restless. I refill my coffee and take it with me onto the front porch. I feel as if I've been slapped in the face as soon as I pass through the huge door. That warm breeze that was blowing into my bedroom when I woke up was deceptive. It's only nine in the morning and already the heat is enough to make me want to crawl right back inside. This is definitely hotter than Oregon.

Before I decide what to do, Colby exits a building and moves toward the house. The man looks good, far too good. He's clean, dressed in a dark flannel shirt that has to be killing him in this heat, a black Stetson hat, and a pair of worn jeans that look as if they've been painted on him. His feet are covered with the same pair of worn black boots he had on yesterday, and he looks as if he's made to be on the back of a horse 24/7.

His gaze captures mine, then he looks me up and down from head to toe. He pauses on my footwear choice then slowly travels up my body again, finally meeting my gaze. I feel as if I've just been burned. Does he like what he sees?

"Good morning," I say when I can't stand the silence anymore.

He smiles a bit and I know what he's thinking. It's only nine in the morning, but this is more like afternoon to him. I'm sure he was up by five and has already been out checking the fences or whatever the heck he does before the heat becomes too intense.

"Mornin'." He nods as he moves a little closer. "We need to get you some real footwear if you want to move around the ranch without losing a shoe."

"I know. I left my boots at home. I'll have Stephy send them since they're already broken in." I think leaving them at home was a way of protecting myself. Coming and living at a ranch as a married woman is way too close to home. I know I can get through this, but I don't think it's going to be a cakewalk for me.

"Yeah, it's hard to replace a good pair of boots," he agrees. "Did you eat?"

"Yes, it was delicious. I like Barb. I think we'll get along great."

"I wouldn't trust someone who doesn't like her. She doesn't sugarcoat things like so many people do, and she has good instincts. She's worked here for a very long time."

"People who work on ranches tend to stay. Everyone becomes family," I say. "She says you're a good man."

His expression darkens the slightest bit sending a shiver down my spine. We all have many sides to us, and I want to know what sides this man has. He has a kind side, a loyal side, and it seems a dark side. Which dominates his personality? I know I can't live with a monster for a solid year. I don't think I have to worry about that. Barb wouldn't talk so kindly about him if he was a terrible person.

"I'm not a good man. I'm a man who knows what needs to be done. This marriage is one of those things, just another check on the to-do list." He pauses. "I don't want you getting any ideas about the arrangement. This is a business deal. At the end of a year we will go our separate ways."

There's a flash of something in his eyes that tells me he has his own story just as I have mine. It makes me want to reach out to him, makes me want to help him with his demons. Because I have so many of my own, if I can focus on someone else's, mine won't hurt as much. He's telling me not to fall for him, and this makes me want to draw him in. What is wrong with me? I think I ask this of myself far too often.

I move down the steps and draw closer to him. He's about a solid foot taller than I am, but I'm used to that. Height nor brawn intimidate me. It actually takes a lot to shake me. Maybe that's because of growing up around so many alpha men.

He's not breaking the gaze between us. It almost feels as if he's thrown down a gauntlet and I'm the one picking it up. I should agree with him, reassure him that I feel the same way, and plan to spend my time as far from him as possible. That doesn't seem to be what I'm doing though.

Maybe it's that shadowy look in his eyes that pulls me closer. Maybe it's all in my imagination. People are unpredictable and they're rarely what we expect them to be. If I sense danger or pain, I tend to run toward it while most run away. That's one of my biggest faults. Maybe it's because I was numb or sad for so long. I think I like to feel bolder emotions now that spike my adrenaline.

"We like to say we're bad to keep people away. The love you have from your employees proves you aren't bad at all. You don't have to worry about me falling for you. I'm too broken to fall for anyone. I would like to be friends though if we're going to be sharing the same house for a year."

He doesn't show me what he's thinking, but he doesn't pull away when I reach out and touch his arm. We're already making progress in a very awkward situation. I've made a commitment to stay a full year and I won't go back on that. He could lose everything if I do, and I'm not willing to do that to all of the people who count on him.

"I don't like having a lot of friends," he says.

I laugh. "I can see that in you." His gaze narrows as

I continue. "You're a great looking man who's wealthy and young. Why did you have to do a mail-order bride?" I figure he likes blunt so I might as well be that way.

He gives me the semblance of a smile.

"I didn't want anyone thinking of happily ever afters. It was easier to put out an ad and weed through the crap. You wouldn't believe how many offers of love, babies, and soul mates I got offered. I didn't even have a picture up and I had undying devotion sent my way. I liked your simple reply. It was what I was looking for."

It's my turn to laugh now. "I wasn't the one who initially replied. It was Stephy," I admit.

He looks stunned. "Really?"

"Yep, she thought this would be one more fun adventure in a long line of adventures I've been on for the past few years. She just might be right, though at first I thought she was crazy." I pause for a moment and laugh. "I might be the crazy one though, because I keep going along with it all. To be honest, I like it. I have no regrets so far. Let's see what happens with this newest endeavor."

He's quiet for a moment. "How did she talk you into it? You aren't at all what I was expecting."

"What were you expecting?"

He pauses for a long moment. "Let's take a walk." We begin to move. "I can say the same about you as you said about me. You have money, you're beautiful, young, and seem to hold life by the horns. You don't seem to be the sort of woman to accept a marriage proposal through a random ad."

"Maybe I'm crazy and hiding it well," I offer.

"I think all of us are a little bit crazy."

"That's very true. I was thinking that yesterday as I walked into the courthouse."

"Did you ever worry I was a serial killer?"

"I thought it was a possibility, but what's the fun in life if we aren't living with a bit of fear?"

He looks at me for a second and then he laughs. My steps actually falter at the deep, rich sound of his voice. It's beautiful. He's made it more than clear that he's a man who doesn't allow himself to laugh too often. There's a slight scratch to the sound, and it's striking. Almost everything about this man is gorgeous. I need to be careful. I can't allow myself to fall for him. It would lead to nothing but more heartbreak. I've had enough of that in my life. I want rainbows and puppy dogs now, not sorrow and a broken spirit.

"How much do you know about the property?" he asks as we approach a barn and move inside. It feels good to get out of the direct sun. It's still hot, but not blazing hot.

"I don't know anything. I can tell it's huge, but that's about it."

"Yes, it's huge," he says with a smile. From a man telling me he's not nice, he's warmed up really fast. Maybe he realizes I want nothing from him. I'm not sure what I'm going to get out of this marriage. I don't need the million dollars, though it's foolish to even have that thought. But I also don't know what my next steps in life are yet, so maybe this is exactly where I need to be.

"My family has owned this land for over one hundred and fifty years. We use the land to raise crops, beef cattle, horses, and we have oil wells."

"How big is it? That's a lot of different activities for one ranch."

"We're one of the largest ranches in the United States sitting at just over four hundred thousand acres."

I'm in shock at the number. I thought Stephy's land was huge. It doesn't come even close to comparing. I wasn't aware ranches could be so big. How does a single family maintain so much property?

"The ranch was established in 1852 by my great-great-grandfather. That's why I don't understand why Gramps was willing to risk it all with this marriage crap." His voice grows tense.

"I'm sure he thought he was doing the right thing."

"He was a great man and he was worried the ranch would end with me if I didn't get married, so he figured he had nothing to lose by putting in the stipulation. He knew I'd follow his wishes even if it pissed me off." He pauses. "My brother died ten years ago in an accident. Gramps wasn't the same after. When I didn't talk of marriage, I think he panicked. My parents have been gone a long time and it's down to him and me."

"Will you have kids?" I ask.

He laughs. "I don't know."

"You could always adopt. You have plenty of

room."

He gives me a sad smile. "Yes, there's plenty of room. I don't know what the future holds. I just know my parents divorced when I was young, and I never saw my mother again. My dad died before my brother. I'm beginning to think our family is cursed. Maybe bad things happened on this land. Maybe after me, it's meant to be sold, to be divided up."

I look at him for several minutes. "I don't think you really believe that. You're just at a crossroads right now. Maybe this year will help you work all of that out."

He sighs. "I don't know. The worst word any of us can say is never."

"I agree."

We go silent as we watch the horses playing in the field and the ranch hands working with them. I have a lot to learn about this place. It's not going to be difficult to stay, but I'm not sure how much I'll get to know Colby. We're both lost souls, and I don't know if either of us wants to be found. I do know that we're drawn to one another for some reason. It feels right to be here.

I guess we'll both find out what it all means as we navigate the waters. For now we've established a friendship. This is a very good start. Maybe we need to be together to find ourselves in this big world. Maybe the Fates really are in charge of all of our lives. Only time will reveal the truth. I don't know what my truth is anymore. I don't know if there's a guiding hand out there trying to lead me down a path. I don't know if they are whispering in my ears. If they are, will I accept the answer they are giving me on what path I should take?

I shake my head as I look out at this beautiful land. I've been blessed in life. Yes, I've taken some hard hits, but I've had far more joy than pain. I need to remember that. I need to appreciate who I am and where I am. I need to live in the moment. I think I can do that. I think being here will be great if I allow it to be.

CHAPTER THREE

I SPEND THE rest of the day alone when Colby is called away. When working the land, you never have time off. I wander the enclosures close to the house and am beyond impressed with the horses. It makes me miss the Oregon ranch, makes me miss Bentley.

Being here, I'm living the life I would've lived with Bentley. We were married. We would've run the ranch together alongside Stephy back in Oregon. This place might be bigger, and a long ways from him, but I'm now married to a man who runs the entire operation. My heart breaks a little as I put those pieces together and realize what a foolish girl I am.

Stephy knew this. There's no doubt in my mind that she wanted to give me a glimpse of the life of being a rancher's wife. Why though? Does she think it will heal me, or does she think it will show me something else? This could be a backfire. I don't want to live in fear, but it's creeping inside me anyway.

Night has finally fallen as I walk to the stable. I can look at the horses all day and night. They soothe me when I feel my life is spinning out of control. As soon as my boots arrive I'm going to start riding again. I want to work while I'm here, but I'm not sure what I should be doing. I'll talk to Colby about it after a few days. Right now we're both trying to get our bearings with one another. This isn't an easy situation.

As soon as the sun sets, the unbearable heat calms. I find Colby standing in the barn. Should I turn and walk away? He knows I've come inside. I can see it in the stiffening of his shoulders. Does he want me to go away? Tough. I'm here now and I'm not going to stay out of sight all of the time. I'll be miserable if I do. I stop beside him and climb on the fence, not standing too close, but close enough to feel his body heat.

I click at the horses and one moves over to me, curious. We friended each other earlier in the day. I reach out and scratch her head while looking into her beautiful brown eyes. I always get lost in the eyes of a majestic creature. They are so much easier to bond with than humans.

"This is my favorite part of a ranch," I whisper when I can't take the silence anymore. I finally turn and look at Colby to find his intense gaze burning into me.

I lick my dry lips and his gaze follows, his eyes sparking. I feel an instant response in my stomach. I want to kick him and myself. He can't look at me this way. If this is happening right now, what will it be like in a month? In six months? By the time I have to leave? A shudder runs through me. I can't think too much about that.

Colby leans down, drawing close enough to me that I feel his hot breath on my ear. I want to know what his kiss feels like. I want to know what it will do to my body to have his arms wrapped around me. I'm not shocked to have this desire. He's handsome and virile, and I'm alone with him in one of my favorite places in the world. Can I allow this to happen? Should I allow it to happen? How can I keep wanting different men? They are all unique and different, but it still shames me. I push that thought away.

Should I call him out on what's happening between us? Should I bring up the sexual tension? Or should I pretend it's not there? We haven't talked about what it means to be married to one another. We haven't discussed if he has a woman on the side. We know this is a marriage of convenience. Beyond that, we're both dancing in the dark on this one.

"I'm glad it's you," he tells me, his voice husky. I know he's saying he's glad I'm the one who answered the ad. I'm glad Stephy did, too. I wasn't a couple of days ago, but I am right now.

"I'm glad I'm here too," I admit. I *am* glad. I'm scared. I'm unsure of what's happening, but I don't want to run away.

We gaze at one another for several moments, and then he moves back. I sigh. I'm not sure if I'm disappointed or relieved. If he kisses me I'm afraid the dam will break. What will it let out? Will it flood us both?

"What makes you love this land other than it's been in your family forever?" I need words spoken. I can't take the silence and tension between us and I don't want to walk away. I don't want to go back to my room and be alone.

"It's in my blood," he tells me. He's as good at giving short answers as I am.

"Were you close to your father?" I don't mention his mother since she left and I'm sure that's not something he wants to talk about. If he does, I'm here for a year and he can bring her up.

"I was close to both of my parents. It was a shock when my mother left. My dad moved on quickly and had a string of girlfriends. There were a lot of women willing to do whatever it took to be the next Mrs. Winters." There's bitterness in his voice as he says this.

"Did he find love again?"

Colby laughs a mirthless sound. "No, he didn't. There were a lot of women coming and going, but my mother broke him, and I don't think he ever got the pieces put back together again." It truly is sad how many marriages start with such love and promise and end in despair and bitterness. I've seen it over and over again. I think that's the main reason I've run so quickly at the end of my own marriages. I go into them knowing they won't last forever. I can't ever again think one will last forever—not after the loss of Bentley. That was too hard. That almost killed me.

"Is that why you don't believe in love?"

"I didn't say I don't believe in love. I just said I'm not interested in finding it for myself."

"Even if it means saving this ranch for more generations to come?"

"I won't be here to see it fall apart."

This makes me really sad. "But what about all of the people you care about who have also been here for generations?"

"You sound like Gramps. He told me from the time I was little that this land is about so much more than our family; it affects many lives. He told me to have more pride in the land and in myself."

"But you don't want to take his advice?"

He looks at the horses and thinks about his words. I don't push him. I know it takes time to put thoughts together. I also hate being rushed when I'm searching deep inside for answers.

"I've seen too much bad in the world. I don't want a lifelong marriage of convenience. I don't mind doing it for a year, but I don't want to lose the rest of my life tied to someone I won't be able to stand looking at in a few years. Once kids are involved a person is really trapped. Divorce isn't worth risking a real marriage and a broken home."

"You might be getting a better life if you search for someone you can't live without. There are some amazing marriages. My parents have a great one." I don't add that I had a great marriage that ended far too soon.

He stares at me again and I find myself unable to turn away.

"Are you applying for that job?"

It's my turn to tear our gazes apart.

"No, I'm not, but I can't seem to keep my mouth

shut. When I see someone hurting I want to help fix the problem."

He laughs. "I'm not hurting. I know who I am. I'm not the person Gramps wanted me to be. I don't need a wife and children to be fulfilled. I need my land, hard work, and my scratch itched every so often. Other than that, I'm just fine."

"I've felt that same way with my parents many times. My dad is a preacher and my parents are completely devoted to each other. Their love and lives are completely fulfilled. They want the same for me, but what they have is the rarity. The rest of us settle for fine instead of great."

"What most people have is mediocre. I've never been a man to accept that. If a person is happy to do so, to each their own."

"How old were you when your mother left?"

"You like asking personal questions, don't you?" he asks with a chuckle.

"You don't have to answer," I tell him. "It just doesn't hurt for me to ask."

"Does it go both ways? Do you share personal details of your life with strangers?"

I laugh. "I'm discovering it's nice to share with people who don't know me, it's easier to speak to someone I may never see again, who isn't there to judge. Sometimes it's easier to get it all off of our chests. Sometimes it's not."

"I was eight when my mother left, eighteen when my father died, and twenty-three when I lost my brother."

I reach out again and touch his arm. "That's awful. I'm sorry, Colby."

"I've dealt with it."

"Now you're twenty-nine with this vast empire and you have no one left. It's that way with Stephy. She has it all, but what's the point of having everything if you have no one to share it with?"

"She has you," he points out.

"Yes, she does, for life. She's brilliant and happy. But losing all of your family takes away a piece of your soul. Sometimes we lose people and hate that we're left behind. We just want to be with them."

"Who did you lose?"

"I lost my husband," I say, shocking him and me both. I didn't expect to tell him this. I'm choking up as I tell Colby this personal information I've never shared with any of the other men I've been with. I don't know why I'm sharing with him. Maybe it's because of this place. Or because he's had equally devastating losses in his life. It's so personal. It has to be this ranch that has me wanting, or more accurately, needing to tell my story.

"I didn't realize you were married before," he says. "I'm sorry you went through that."

"It nearly killed me. You wonder why I'm here. That's why. I've been on a journey for the past few years. This is my latest stop. I'm glad to be here. It's hard, though. He was a rancher too and only nineteen when he was taken too soon from this world. We'd just gotten back from our honeymoon. I'll miss him forever, but I promised on his deathbed that I would move on. I've failed on that front. I know what it's like to love and to lose. I also know we can go on even when we don't want to."

"You weren't much more than kids," Colby says. He reaches for me and the connection between us grows. "That must've been horrible."

"It was the worst time of my life. I'm sure it was for you too when you lost the people you loved most. It didn't just happen to you once, though, but over and over again. I can't imagine going through this pain more than once. I don't know how you're still standing."

He gives me a sad smile. "I don't give up easily, and I don't let sadness overwhelm me or control me."

"Even as a child?"

"I was angry with the world for a while when my mother left, and it was harder after my dad died, but we all do what we need to survive, and I forgave his mistakes long before he passed. My brother wasn't as forgiving. I was more prepared when I lost Dad. I wasn't when I lost my brother, but I still had Gramps. I knew his time was coming. It was tough. But maybe that's why he put this stipulation in his will. He knew it would seriously piss me off. It's hard to be sad when you want to kick someone's ass." He chuckles. I love the sound of his laughter.

"Yes, I do have to agree that I'd rather be angry than sad."

"That's why we go through so many emotions when we lose someone. I don't know if I'll ever reach the acceptance part, but I'm over the anger part now . . . well, most of the time." He nods. We stand in silence for a little longer.

"This is your father's land. Have you ever reached out to your mother's side of the family?"

"No. I know where they are, but they stopped coming around after she was gone, and I have no desire to have a relationship with anyone who can leave a kid behind. I've gotten some calls and some emails, but I ignore them all."

"Is your mother still alive?" I wasn't going to ask, but I find myself doing just that. He can stop me at any time if he doesn't want to talk about it.

"No, she isn't." I don't know if he means she's literally dead, or just dead to him. I decide not to push it.

He's looking at the horses and it gives me a chance to study him. We really are two broken individuals. If this were under different circumstances, could we truly like one another? We won't ever know. This is where we are, and this is what we're doing. I could like him though. I could really like him if I was in a place where I was able to do that. I sadly shake my head.

He turns and sees my expression. "What are you thinking about?"

I'm shocked again by my honestly. "I was thinking you could certainly be someone I could like." I see him pull back. I reach for him. "Don't worry, it won't happen. I was also thinking we're both very broken people. I wonder how long we'll allow ourselves to wallow. How long will we punish ourselves? I think Stephy sent me here to figure that out."

"Charlie . . ." He stops himself. I don't ask what he's thinking. I don't want to know. This has all become far too intimate and emotional for me. This place might just be my undoing. I'm coming to realize though I can't be here without having feelings. I can't keep my distance from Colby and keep my sanity. It's not who I am.

"I should head inside." I don't want to, but all of this is a lot. I need to process it.

"Don't go," he whispers. He doesn't look at me. I don't move.

Minutes pass as we gaze at the horses, neither of us speaking. I'm not sure what's happening, but I don't walk away. He reaches out and places his hand over mine as we gaze at the beautiful animals.

We don't speak words, just take a few minutes to absorb this strange connection between us. I close my eyes and breathe. I can almost picture Bentley beside me. The smells are the same in this barn as our barn in Oregon. Colby's hand on mine isn't the same. I connected to Bentley on a spiritual level. I don't know what I'm feeling with Colby.

Even with my connection to Bentley, I have *something* with Colby as well. I don't know what it is, but I don't pull away from him. I want to see this through. I want to figure out exactly what I'm feeling. I'm not sure how much time passes between us with nothing but the sounds of the animals settling down for the night.

"I'm sorry." He finally looks at me as he says this. He slowly pulls his hand from mine and then turns and walks from the barn. I'm breathing heavy. He's certainly sending mixed signals, but I don't know what he wants. I don't know what I want. I stay with the horses a while longer. Finally, I turn and make my way back to the house. He's nowhere to be found.

I go to my room and strip, moving straight for the tub. I sit in it until the water is cold, then I wrap myself in a robe and move to the balcony. I sit there for a long time, looking at the land that hopefully can help me heal.

It will either set me free or place me in a cage for the rest of my life. Only time will tell which direction I'm about to take.

CHAPTER FOUR

I LET OUT a deep sigh as I lean back in my chair and sip on a margarita. Most days at court are good. The time flies by in the blink of an eye. At other times I just need it to end. I can end it at any point I want, but it's not time yet. I have to finish telling my story. It can't end in the middle. I have to make it all the way to the end. If I don't, I'll feel like I'm floating through air with nothing resolved.

"I think it's a requirement at this hotel that all of the workers be hot," Stephy says as she sips on her drink and gazes at the men and women quietly working.

The hotel had a big pool party that ended about an hour earlier and the staff are currently taking down tables and cleaning up garbage. I'm not disappointed to have missed the event. I have my own circus going on daily in the courtroom. All I want in the evening is to enjoy a drink, a cool breeze, and maybe chat with the people I love most in the world.

"You just look for the beautiful men," I tell her. In all honesty they do have a lot of good looking people working at this hotel.

She giggles. "Like you don't. From the list of men

you've married I'd say you have an eye for a six pack and smoldering eyes."

Now, it's my turn to laugh. "I much prefer a man who can make me laugh and looks at me like I hang the moon and the stars. If he's pretty to look at, it's a bonus."

"Most definitely a bonus. We have to be attracted to a person. That's how the world goes around. We find someone attractive, we want to mate with them, have a baby, and a new generation is born. Yes, this can happen without attraction, but even in the animal kingdom, the males strut around trying to impress the females into mating with them."

"Fortunately not everyone has the same definition of attraction."

"I appreciate beauty and I've been turned on many times in my life, but I still haven't found a person I want to stay with forever. Maybe I have a type. Maybe I'm attracted to shallow assholes," Stephy says with a pout.

"That could be a real problem. I don't think that's how it is for me. I purposely look for men I know won't break my heart. I look for anyone who *isn't* Bentley."

"That's because you're afraid to have your heart broken all over again. It's easier to live in the moment, knowing it will end, than risk falling in love and going through that pain again."

"You are probably right. I might have failed on that front, though."

My words stop her. Her drink gurgles as she reaches the bottom and tries to get every last drop. She stares at me for a long moment. I know she's processing my words. I'm surprised I've said them. Maybe I want to talk about this more than I realized.

"Is there something you want to tell me?"

Do I really want to talk to her about this? Am I ready? I feel as if I'm bursting inside, but I also feel if I tell anyone about this it will disappear just as everything good in my life seems to do when I finally try to hold onto it. I'm not sure what to do.

"Come on, Char, what in the hell is going on?" Stephy is sitting up as she gazes at me. "We don't keep secrets from each other and I'm discovering you've kept a lot in the past ten years. Yes, you've told me what you wanted to tell me, but there are gaps I'm learning about in court along with everyone else."

I sigh. "I know I've kept secrets. I know I should tell you all. But I can't yet. I'm doing it this way to hold myself accountable. I'm doing it as I find myself." I stop and look at her, deciding I have to give her something. She *is* my best friend. "There is someone." The words feel as if they're being ripped out of me. She grins.

"Who is it? Are you seeing him now?" She pauses. "I don't see how. You're rarely alone." Again, she pauses. "I guess Cash and I sneak off sometimes in the evening so someone could come in." She glares. "Who is it? Have you slept with him? Is he one of the husbands?" She's practically bouncing in her seat.

"I've seen him since the trial began. He came to me. I was shocked. I thought it was over. I thought I wanted it to be over."

"Who is it?" She asks this so loudly a few of the people working by the pool turn and give us curious looks. My cheeks heat. It's odd that I can feel any embarrassment. I've been laying myself bare before the court and the world, yet I'm embarrassed that strangers look at me and possibly hear a private conversation. What in my life is private anymore? Nothing really.

"I don't want to say who it is right now," I tell her.

"Why not? You know I have ways of finding out." She now has her arms crossed.

"Would you like more drinks?" a man asks, startling me. I didn't seen him come over.

"Yes, two each please, and a basket of fries, a basket of onion rings, and a large tray of sliders with extra pickles."

"Coming right up," the man says before leaving. Stephy faces me again.

"You can find anything but you won't. You'll let me figure this out in my own time. You know I'm going to tell you all when I've worked through it." I easily turn back to our conversation before we were interrupted.

"Ugh. I hate when you sound reasonable. I want to know now. I feel like I'm losing you. It's weird because in the past ten years I haven't felt that way at all. We've grown closer and closer. I've seen you lift yourself from the pits of hell and start to fly. Don't crawl back into a hole. If you need some, I'll give you time, but just know you're killing me."

"I know I am and I'm sorry. I promise I'll tell you everything very soon," I assure her.

"Do you know what your plans are?"

"Right now, I plan on surviving this hearing, hopefully getting set free, and then figuring out the rest of my life after that."

"You're going to be set free. I'll make damn sure of that."

I laugh. "It's insane to think about, but even if I was found guilty you could work your magic and have me set free. Knowing this scares me about our justice system. How many people are free who shouldn't be? How many strings are pulled from higher powers without us realizing it? I've always thought we are the land of the free, but more and more I see that we aren't. We're merely puppets with the people at the top pulling our strings whenever they want."

"Yes, the majority of us are," Stephy tells me. "That's why I love what I do. I see the corruption and I do my part to stop what I can. Unfortunately, there's so much corruption it's impossible to stop it all. So, I protect my own. If they are going to be grotesque, I have zero guilt in countering them even if it so-called 'goes against their laws.'"

"Maybe we all say this. Maybe we say I can break the law because someone else is breaking the law, and then pretty soon we won't recognize the world we live in. Where does it stop?"

"I don't know," Stephy admits. "The bottom line is to ask ourselves if we can look at the person gazing back at us in the mirror."

I stop and think about these words. "I like that. I look at myself a lot and wonder who I am."

"Have you ever looked and not liked the reflection gazing back at you?" she asks.

I have to really think about this question. I finally shake my head. "I don't think I've ever not liked the woman staring back at me. I've had regrets that I tamper down as that does me no good. I've wondered often who I am and where I'm going, but I don't think I've ever not liked myself. A far more difficult question is asking who in the heck am I."

"We all wonder who we are. We all change as we age. We're not the same person at sixteen as we are at twenty-six. So much changes in our lives. We grow, we evolve. We like different foods and different activities. That's the beauty of aging. It's great to see the wrinkles and grey hairs because it shows a life well lived. We can either fight the change or embrace it."

"I agree with that. I am nowhere near the same person I was at sixteen, twenty, twenty-five, and now at age thirty-one. I can't believe I've said that aloud. I hate admitting my age. I've changed year by year."

Stephy laughs. "Yes, you have, especially with each marriage, each new place, and each new life you've lived as a different woman. You've evolved every year and now you're this beautiful creature I love more today than I did yesterday."

"I don't know if anyone should marry young. We change so dang much."

"I agree with you, but I do see some amazing marriages that have passed the test of time even when they married young. Yes, the couples changed, but they did it together."

"What if the couple changes too much and they no longer love one another?"

She reaches out and grabs my hand. "You and Bentley would've changed a lot, but I have no doubt you would've done it together. If he would've lived, you would've stood the test of time."

"Maybe we wouldn't have," I tell her, a tear slipping. "Maybe I've been saved from losing our love of each other."

"That could've happened, but I don't think so. I've seen you change and grow, but look at how much I have changed as well. Bentley is my twin, so all of us would've grown equally. I don't think it's that way for everyone, but it would be that way for us. I love our lives, Char, I love them a lot. We've been on a rollercoaster for a very long time, and I don't want to get off of it."

"I might be ready to get off. I might be ready to live a normal life now."

She laughs. "What's normal?"

"That's a good question. I don't know what's normal anymore. I don't know if I'd even like normal."

"Do you have any regrets?"

I have to think about this. "I always say I have no

regrets, but I don't know, I might have some. I wish people hadn't gotten hurt at my expense. That might be considered a regret. I don't want to go back and change any of it though. I've lived an amazing life adventure and each place I've gone to has helped shape me. I wouldn't be the person I am now without going through the journey I've been on. I think the people I've been with have grown as well. I haven't heard any regrets from them."

"I agree. They love you. They might have wanted to hold you longer, but you impacted their lives as much as they impacted yours. It's been a win, win."

"I don't know if I'd go that far, but I'm happier because of the life I've lived. I fight regrets and I push them away. Regrets don't do us any good."

"What are you the happiest about in your journey?"

I laugh. "What is this tonight? You have a lot of questions."

"They are just as much for me as they are for you. This is a turning point in both of our lives and if you know the answers to these questions, it can help you decide the rest of it, it can help me to know where I'm going next."

"I agree. It's important to know when I've been the happiest, and when I've been the saddest. It's easy to know when I've been at my lowest." There are really two times this has happened, but she doesn't know this yet. She only knows of the first. "That was when I lost Bentley. I didn't think I'd pull out of the despair from losing him. I can't answer when I've been happiest.

There have been so many amazing moments in my life. I've gone to places all around the world and have had adventures most people can't even dream of having. Some of my happiest moments are at home in Oregon, and some are all over the world. I don't know if I can list them all, but it might be something worth diving into."

"Some of my happiest moments have been alone," Stephy says. I raise my brows at her and she laughs. "Most of my happiest moments are with you and my family, but I think it's important to be happy when we're alone. I've had amazing moments riding Shadow at sunset. I've laughed watching a chick flick while gorging on popcorn and M&M's alone on a Friday night. I've skinny dipped at midnight and bungee jumped over a bridge. I've laughed a lot with people. I've also sobbed alone and with you. We can feel many emotions with others and many on our own. We aren't robots. We're individuals with real feelings and it's important for us to always remember that."

"How in the world are you so wise?"

Stephy takes a deep breath. "I like to look at myself and ask if I can be wrong. I don't think enough of us do that. We don't question ourselves. We don't challenge ourselves. If we all did, the world would be a better place and we'd be free to feel *real* emotions without guilt or remorse. I feel so much because I do question myself. I sometimes know I'm making a poor choice, but I do it anyway because the outcome might be worth the bad decision. Sometimes I'm right about that and sometimes I'm wrong."

"We all make decisions knowing we might be making a bad one. We just don't care in the moment we're doing whatever it is that we're doing."

"I think the best thing to ask ourselves after it's all said and done is if we'd change what we've done." She smiles at me.

"Isn't that the same as asking if we have regrets?"

"No, I don't think those are the same at all," Stephy tells me. She thinks for a second. "Okay, consider going bridge jumping. We go out at three in the morning and jump in our jeans. We almost drown because the clothes weigh too much and are too tight, making it hard to swim. We don't regret the bridge jumping. That was amazing and fun and a memory to last a lifetime. We might just wish we'd changed the clothes we wore. Maybe put on a pair of shorts."

I laugh hard at this. I don't know why it hits my funny bone, but it totally does.

"Do you know how much I love you, Stephanie Lawrence?"

"How much?"

I hold my arms out wide. "I love you this much, all around the world and back."

"I love you that much too. It's you and me forever. Other people will come and go, but you and I will be together forever. We might get married to amazing men. We might have children. But at the end of the day, it's you and me against the world no matter who else comes into our lives."

"I know that no matter what I do you'll be there for me, and it's the same for me in regards to you. I also think I'm ready to invite another person into our circle."

"Who is he?" Stephy again demands.

I lean back and smile. "I have a feeling you'll soon find out."

The waiter returns with a bounty of food and our much-needed drinks. Stephy rolls her eyes before glaring at me. I simply laugh as I dive into the food, suddenly having a ravenous appetite. I feel lighter, freer. Being with Stephy does that for me. She makes me realize exactly who I am, where I've been, and where I'm going. Everyone should have a Stephy in their life. I'm sure as heck glad I do.

I'm just about ready to tell her everything. I've held it close to myself for a very long time, but part of gaining my freedom is telling it all. If I want to fully break from my cocoon and fly away, I have to let it all go. I'm almost there.

"You're killing me," Stephy says.

I lean back and laugh. "It's good to have secrets. It's good to let them all out. It's only a matter of time."

She rolls her eyes. I take another drink and one more feather flutters open. I'm about to fly.

CHAPTER FIVE

I'M POUTY. I know I'm pouty. I'm acting like a spoiled child. I need to grow the heck up. I'm twenty-three. If I really think about this, it doesn't feel right. I feel more like I'm thirty. Early twenties seem so young. To most people it might be young. With the life I've lived, though, twenty-three is almost ancient. I've been married five times. When I think about this, it's horrifying. I wonder what's the most times someone has been married. Am I going for a Guinness book of world records?

This thought makes me look at my phone and see who has the most ever marriages. I gasp. Wow, thirty marriages for one man in the United States. Okay, maybe five marriages isn't so bad. I wonder what's the most relationships a person has ever had. I bet it could be in the thousands. If a person has a new relationship that lasts a month ten times a year starting at fifteen years old and ending at eighty, that would be hundreds and hundreds of relationships. Who wants that much drama? Well, then again, it could be fun. I giggle at the thought. One a year is tough enough.

"Let's go for a ride."

I jump as I look up from my phone and see Colby

standing in front of me. He hasn't talked to me since we were at the barn together several days ago and I'm not sure how I'm feeling about the distance. I want to be with him, and then I don't. Obviously I don't know what in the heck I want. My heart is immediately picking up speed, so my body is happy to see him. I'm not sure if my mind is.

"Go for a ride where?"

"It doesn't matter. I want to get out of here."

"You don't need me to go somewhere." He gives me the sexiest smile I've ever seen on him. My heart thumps a few extra beats. Dammit. I don't like this effect he has on me. I also realize I can't stop it.

"Saddle up, lil lady," he tells me with an exaggerated drawl as he pulls off his hat and tips it at me. I instantly giggle. I can't stay frustrated with this man. I like him too much. I like when he flirts with me. Maybe that's just a girl thing. I hope so. I don't want this to be more than it is—a marriage of convenience.

"Where are we going?"

He looks at me, looks at the phone in my hand, then puts his hat back on his head and raises his brow at me.

"Does it really matter?" he asks with a chuckle. "I mean, I see how busy you are right now, but I think some exercise is needed."

I give him a big smile. "Are you saying I'm fat, lazy, and need exercise?"

His smile drops as fast as he holds his hands out in front of him in surrender. "Not even hinting that in any way, shape, or form." He then takes his time as his eyes scan me from head to toe, stopping at my breasts and hips for an extra few seconds. Heat floods me. "I like your body just fine."

Man, this guy has the sexiest, deepest drawl of anyone I've ever met. His voice alone can melt butter on an icy day. I don't understand how he's remained single for so long. There should be a trail of females falling at his feet. Maybe that's why he lives in the middle of so many acres, so he can escape the lusting women of the county. I have him all to myself right now. I'm just not sure what I'm going to do about it.

"Okay, I'll go for a ride. Let me put on my boots." I go inside and quickly change, then set my phone on my side table. I don't need it. We all need to turn off our electronic devices once in a while. It's much easier said than done. We're so connected to the outside world now that it feels as if we're missing a piece of ourselves when we turn it all off. I've discovered my happiest moments are when I don't have a computer, phone, or television anywhere near me. It feels good to see the real world with my own eyes and not through a screen.

I come out and meet Colby in the barn. He has two horses ready. Mine, Pixie, is already saddled. I never trust someone else's saddle job. I inspect all of the straps and catch Colby's eyes.

"I love that you like horses," he tells me. "I love how you care for them too and never trust anyone else to do a job for you."

"I told you my bestie has a ranch. I've been around horses my entire life, and I've always loved riding. There's freedom in climbing on the back of a horse, especially one you love and who loves you."

"There's definitely a bond between a horse and its owner."

"I'm not so sure we own horses. I think they own us. When they want food, we're their servants. We feed them, water them, exercise them, and brush them down. I don't see them doing all of that for us. We're *their* pets."

He throws back his head and laughs. "You have a valid point," he tells me. "The same can be said for cats and dogs."

"Exactly, they all own our lives. We can't make plans without making sure they are taken care of. They get pouty when we leave them whether it's for a few hours or a few days. It doesn't matter if we get them the best care possible. They all think we're their servants and should bend to their will. Cats are also far more needy than dogs."

I'm satisfied with Pixie's saddle, so I easily climb up. It feels good to be in the saddle again. It's somewhere I'm very comfortable. Although it's been a while since I've ridden, so I'm sure I'm going to be sore if we do a long ride.

"I don't know. Cats get a bad reputation," he tells me. "But I like them. They keep the rodents out of the barns and they always come up for a pet."

I laugh as we ride away from the barn. "They come

up for a good scratching and beg for food. You can feed the little buggers and ten minutes later they scream for more food. I don't think they are ever full."

"They know what they want, and they demand it. There's nothing wrong with that," he tells me.

"We all know what we want, but we also know we don't always get it."

"We can all have what we want if we're persistent enough." There's something in his tone that makes me look at him. A hunger in his eyes calls to me. Am I going to keep resisting this hunger or am I going to give in to it? I'll soon find out. We're dancing around each other and we're bound to finish that tango.

We make it out into the open field and I feel the energy in Pixie. She needs to run. I can feel my blood heating, my legs tensing. I need a run just as much.

"I'm about to show you how a real cowboy wins," I say, my only warning before I kick her haunches and she shoots ahead of Colby. I laugh as the wind whips my hair behind me and I lean forward, becoming one with Pixie. It all comes back to me in a flash. I've been off of a horse for months, but riding is in my blood, and I'm comfortable racing as fast as my horse will allow.

I'm in a full out gallop, my hair flying, my competitive juices flowing, sweat drying on my skin. Laughter trails behind me and without a doubt I'm free. There's no better feeling on the planet than this.

I hear Colby on my heels. I might've gotten the jump on him, but he reacted quickly. His horse just might be faster than mine. I lean down a little tighter and push my horse faster. I want to win. He's right on me. I narrow my eyes. He dang well better not be letting me win. I want this victory because I've earned it, not because he lets me take it. I like to win a true victory not a consolation prize.

He's almost on top of me when we reach a tree line and I stop. He passes by before circling back, a huge grin on his face. We ran hard for a solid twenty minutes. I lean in close to Pixie's ear. "Good girl. That was a great run." She neighs at me as she slows. Colby stops beside me, a grin on his face.

"I won," I say with a pant.

"No way. You gave up."

"Nope, that was the finish line."

"Who says it was the finish line?"

"I made it and I say it was." I stick my tongue out at him, and he throws his head back and laughs. I pet Pixie again and she neighs at me. I reach into my pocket and pull out a carrot and hand it over to her. She gives me a thankful look. This is how I get my animals bonded to me. I give them lots and lots of healthy treats.

"She seems to really like you."

"She knows how much I like her. It's really that easy with animals. We love them, give them attention and feed them and they are bound to us."

"Some animals like people more than others, but for the most part animals need fed and cared for and their loyalties are fickle."

I gasp at him. "No way. You are so very wrong. Animals feel love and devotion. Look at soldiers who have been gone a solid year and when they come home their dogs curl up in their laps. They don't forget their owners. They move on when they have to, but they are always sad, missing their family members."

"Then why do adopted dogs bond so quickly to new owners?" he points out. "Because they are loyal to the one who feeds them."

I shake my head. "No. Maybe you don't get animals to bond with you because they know you don't truly love them. Love goes both ways. It's easier for me to love a horse than to love a person. I feel safe loving animals because they need me." I might be revealing too much about myself in this conversation. I feel safe doing so with Colby. I don't know why I do, but there's something about him that tells me I can share anything with him and he won't judge me.

"I like my animals and I respect them. I also know what they need. I'm careful not to fall in love with them. They have a purpose and the reality is they will eventually die, and sometimes outlive their purpose; on top of that, they have a much shorter life span than humans. A horse might live twenty-five years, but that's comparatively short in human years. You will never have an animal from your own birth to your death."

"Since we have them for a shorter time, we need to love them ten times as much. They will forever stay with us in our memories."

"You are very passionate about this," he tells me

with another laugh. "Men are a lot like animals. We are driven by needs . . . many needs. We need the basics at birth—to be fed and bathed—but later in life our needs shift. We're ruled by work, food and . . . sex." He winks at me. I fight a blush climbing my neck. I'm grateful for the heat because it will hide my thoughts and my reaction to him.

"Fixed animals don't need sex."

He again laughs. "Then why does a fixed dog still hump your leg?"

I roll my eyes. "Maybe your pervy dogs do that. I've never had one do that to me. I don't want to be in this world without animals, and I'm going to love the heck out of them while I have them."

"I agree we need them. I agree we care for them and love them to the extent we can. I am shocked at how many people come to work here at the ranch and want nothing to do with animals. Animals are essential for ranch life."

"That's crazy. I guess you do have your oil division, but a ranch and animals go hand in hand. I think of all Texans as animal lovers."

"It was that way in the past, but as more and more cities overtake our land, people forget what it feels like to be one with an animal. More and more people don't have pets and certainly never go out into the country and see how beautiful it is. If they go anywhere, it's to some national park, which is undoubtedly beautiful, but they are in shock thinking those parks are such an anomaly. They are preserved, which is good, but so much country all over the U.S. is just as lovely."

"I can't understand city people. How is it satisfying to live in a high-rise building where you constantly hear traffic and noise and smell pollution? But those same people can't comprehend living out in the country where the nearest Starbucks is over an hour away."

"It's even farther away from here. I do have to admit when I go to town I have to stop and get one of those Carmel Frappuccino's. Those are evil, they're so good."

I laugh again, shocked this manly man would like such a girlie drink. "I can't picture you paying five or six dollars for a single coffee."

"I wouldn't do it on a daily basis, but when it's a treat I have no problem with it."

"I had my first fancy coffee when I was eighteen. My parents took me a few places while I was young, and of course, Stephy, Bentley, and I would go to the city every once in a while, but I refused to even try an expensive coffee. When I did finally have one, I understood what all of the fuss was about. I still wouldn't dream of doing it on a daily basis, but I agree it's a fun treat once in a while."

"Everything in moderation is a good thing. We need to enjoy life and not always think of the consequences or the costs. I'm learning that more and more as I get older."

I look at him for a few seconds. "You seem mellower in the short time I've been here."

He laughs again. "Maybe you're good for me."

"Of course I'm good for you. I'm amazing."

We keep chatting as we ride around his vast property. We aren't going to see it all, it's far too big, but we get to see a lot of it. It's amazing how it changes as we move along. We pass the oil rigs, ugly but doing a great job. We go down paths, see open pastures, and go up and down rolling hills and wooded terrain. We finally go down a trail that ends at a huge pond.

"Oh, I didn't know this was here," I say with delight. "Is it natural?"

"Yes, there's a fresh stream that feeds it. It never dries up."

"Well, my girl is thirsty," I tell him. I trot over to the lake then hop down. I feel a bit of jelly in my legs. I'm going to be incredibly sore tomorrow. It's all been worth it. I need to ride as much as I can this year. There haven't been horses anywhere else I've gone in the past few years.

"This is a good resting place," he says as he climbs down and lets his horse go. I let Pixie go too and they both move to the water and begin lapping it up. I circle Colby who looks at me with a bit of confusion.

"I won, I won, I won, I won, I won," I taunt him while dancing in a circle around him. "I'm the winner," I continue in a sing-song voice.

"*You* are a brat is what you are," he says. I circle him again, and he reaches out and grabs me. He pulls me in tight against his hard, hot body. My smile fades as all thoughts of winning a race disappear. He looks into my eyes and I'm melting. I can tell myself I haven't been waiting for just this moment, but I'd be a liar.

Finally, after what feels like forever, he leans forward and kisses me. It's been worth the wait. I melt against him as his arms tighten. I'm hot, so very, *very* hot. His tongue traces my lips before dipping inside while his hands slide down my back and rest in the dip just above the curve of my butt. I'm panting against him. It's hot. It's intense, and it's making my legs shake.

Almost as quickly as the kiss begins, he pulls back. He holds me for a few more seconds, both of us dazed. He finally lets me go and gives me a crooked smile. My body is on fire.

"What in the heck was that?" he asks.

I find myself giggling. "It was bound to happen. I don't know what is going on, but attraction isn't our problem." I take another step back from him and place my hands in my shirt then pull it off. The lust instantly appearing in his eyes is a good boost for my ego.

"We need to cool off," I say. I turn and quickly kick off my boots and slide off my jeans, leaving me in nothing but my bra and panties. I take one more second to see lust in Colby's eyes. Then I run forward and jump into the cool water. I come back up from the jump and gasp.

"This is cold."

"Feels good," he yells. I see him stripping. Damn, I want to watch the show, but I turn and swim further away in the water. I hear the splash as he jumps in with me.

We're both in the water now with barely any clothes on. Will he kiss me again? Do I want him to kiss me again? Do I want more than kissing? I do. I don't want to admit that, but I really, really want more kissing. I liked the first taste. I'm sure the next will be even better.

I turn as I feel him drawing closer. I'm not sure what to expect, but the splash of water in my face isn't it. I cough, shake my head, then gaze in shock at a grinning Colby as he wades about six feet in front of me.

"Did you really just splash me?" I gasp. He doesn't look at all remorseful. I can't remember the last time I've gotten into a water war. There's no time like the present.

I use my entire body and send a cascade of water over him, wiping the smug look right off his face. I dive beneath the surface, come up, and get another splash right back at me. The war is on. We both splash and dive until we're laughing so hard we're barely able to hold ourselves up in the cool water.

"Mercy," he calls as I splash him again. I let out a relieved breath. I'm not sure how much longer I'll last before throwing up the white flag myself. "I need rest."

He swims over to the edge of the pond, farther away from our horses. I follow him. There's a grouping of river rocks in the water about two feet deep. We both lie back on them, letting the cool water run over us, not having to wade to keep our heads above the surface.

"I'm going to come back here every single day." I love the hot sun on my face while the cool water keeps me comfortable.

"I spend a lot of days out here in the summer when I have the time. I'm sure a lot of my guys do too."

I look around in horror. I don't mind being in front of Colby in my undies, but I don't want the entire ranch to see me this way.

"Don't worry, they are nowhere near here right now," he tells me with a chuckle. "I made sure of it."

"Oh, so you knew we'd be doing some swimming?" I wonder if he was trying to get my clothes off. I realize I'm a little pleased about this.

"I like to take a dip. I wasn't sure if we would today, but . . ." He trails off and shrugs.

"I've never had aspirations of being an underwear model."

"You've missed your calling in life," he says with a wink. "You have one hell of a body."

The compliment travels from my head to my toes. This sexy man with a body that makes me drool, likes my body. I don't hate that at all. I'm also getting hot all over again. If I don't know what I want to do about this sexual connection, I'd better move now.

I push myself from the rocks and swim across the pond. I climb from the water and feel my nipples aching against the wet fabric of my bra. I'm turned on, and with almost no clothes to cover my body I'm not able to hide that fact. I keep my back toward the pond as I slip my shirt over my head. It immediately clings to me. Hopefully the heat will calm down my hard nipples before Colby joins me.

I hear him climb out behind me as I attempt to get my jeans over my wet legs. I start laughing as I hop from foot to foot, jumping up and down trying to get the tight jeans up my wet skin. I jump, lose my step, then inelegantly fall on my butt.

Colby is laughing as he holds out a hand to assist me up.

"That was bound to happen." I accept his hand as he easily pulls me to my feet.

"Need some help?" he asks.

"No, I got this." I leave my pants resting on my thighs as I let the heat dry my upper half. Luckily it's hot enough that I dry quickly and am finally able to get the pants up over my butt and buckled.

When I turn I'm both glad and disappointed to see Colby fully dressed. Both of our shirts are clinging to us, doing nothing to tamper my desire, but at least I'm not looking at his lower regions wondering what he'd look like completely naked. His boxers didn't hide much from my view. I hadn't looked long enough to fully appreciate the beautiful man.

"I guess we'll head back," he says as if he's as disappointed as I am to end this magical afternoon. I could stay at this pond all day and night. There's no doubt in my mind if we did we'd end up naked before the night was out. Would that be so bad? The longer I think about it, the more I think it would be a pretty great idea. We are going to be together for a year. Can we really resist sharing a bed that entire time?

I turn and see his horse . . . and not my own.

"Pixie," I call. Colby looks around. "Will she go far?"

"She never leaves," he says. He then calls for her. Shadow looks up and seems to almost shrug, like saying he can't figure out women. We *are* tough to figure out. Colby and I both call some more but there's no sign of her.

"I'm so sorry," I say. "I should've tied her up."

"I've never had to before," he tells me. "Well, to be honest I haven't ridden Pixie. I always ride Shadow, but I figured she'd hang out at the water."

"What do we do?"

"We're going to have to ride double," he says. He doesn't seem too unhappy about this. I don't think I'm disappointed either. "Maybe all of the whispering you were doing scared her off." He laughs at his own joke.

I glare at him. "Really? I already feel bad enough."

"She'll find her way home. If not, we'll find her," he assures me. "Come on, you're with me."

He jumps into his saddle just like the sexy cowboy he is, then reaches down for me. My heart thumps as I take his hand. He effortlessly throws me up behind him. I immediately wrap my arms around him, my front pressed to his back. Even though it's as hot as hell out, I feel my nipples beading as they press against him. This is going to be a *very* long ride back to the house.

He chats with me as we ride along, but I have a

heck of a time concentrating on our conversation. My breasts press against him and my legs are spread wide. To add to all of this the vibration of the horse hitting my sensitive core, is driving me crazy. I finally stop talking. My voice is getting too husky, too wanton.

I like this a lot. I like this very, *very* much.

It takes forever, and at the same time, just seconds for us to make it back to the house. I'm utterly hot and bothered by the time we arrive. Pixie is inside the barn, munching on some fresh hay with one of the hands telling us she wandered back about fifteen minutes earlier.

I glare at the traitorous horse. I think for only a second about not brushing her down. My love of horses changes my mind fast and I begin grooming the beautiful mare.

"*You* are a traitor," I whisper in her ear. She doesn't seem to care at all as she munches food while I care for her.

My body is aching, and I don't know what to do about it. Colby and I haven't talked about what this marriage means to either of us beyond a contract. We haven't discussed if we want to make some of it traditional or keep it all a business arrangement the entire year. What do I do? Will I have a choice? What does he want to do? Should I make the first move? No. That isn't going to happen.

The only thing I know for sure is our ride home was hot and I'm aching all over. Will our night be just as hot? Will he run from me? Will I run from him?

What do I want to happen? It seems I ask myself these questions a lot. But I never seem to answer them.

I'll either go all-in for the next year or I'll hide away. The one thing I know for sure, it won't take me long to figure it out. We're coming to a wall and we're either going to break through it or smash into it. Which way it goes, I'll soon find out.

CHAPTER SIX

I'VE HAD TWO cups of coffee this morning and I still feel half asleep. I tossed and turned the night before. Now I'm sitting on the witness stand, getting ready to start a new day. I see the wheels turning in Mr. Hart's eyes. He's got something but I have no idea what it might be. It's okay, I can handle whatever is going to come my way.

At least that's what I think until the back doors of the courtroom are flung open and a man walks in. He looks damn good, too good. He looks around while walking down the aisle, then his eyes connect with mine and his lips turn up in the smile that made me fall for him not that long ago.

"Charlie Bloodstone, I love you. I don't care what has happened in your past. I want to marry you. We were cheated and I'm telling you and the entire world right here and now that I'm waiting for you to finish this trial and then I'm going to whisk you away to paradise where I can have you all to myself."

All heads in the room turn to look at the man standing in the middle of the aisle, a huge bouquet of roses in his hand, a big grin on his face, and a nice suit hugging his fine body.

"Order in the courtroom. Bailiff, get this man out," Judge Croesus shouts as he bangs his gavel.

"Charlie, you agreed to marry me once and I almost got you as my wife, but I'm down on bended knee asking you again to be mine. I'll do it right here and right now," William Marks, aka, Willy, the famous NASCAR driver, says as he drops down on bended knee and pulls out a ring box, the shine from the diamond so bright the huge rock can't help but be noticed by the cameras clicking away at this newest scene.

"Willy," I say with a sigh. I begin to stand when Judge Croesus glares at me. I sit back down. I'm fighting hard to keep a smile from my lips. This goofy person kneeling in front of the cameras not caring what the world thinks of him is what drew me to him only a few months ago. We didn't get to finish our vows when our wedding was interrupted with my arrest.

"Order in this courtroom," Judge Croesus says again, his gavel banging forcefully.

The bailiff is heading toward Willy who doesn't seem to care at all. He's not giving up. Of course, that attitude is what took him from driving a souped-up tractor on his father's land to winning the biggest races in the world. He doesn't ever quit and doesn't know the meaning of the word stop.

"They can arrest me, they can lock me away for as long as they want. I don't care," Willy shouts. "As long as I get to be with you when the chains come off, that's all that matters." He jumps back up to his feet and steps forward as if he's going to rush to me. Chatter is going wild in the room, everyone ignoring the judge's orders to quiet down. The cameras are madly clicking on this beautiful man.

This scene is too dang good to miss for the reporters who always seem to find something new in my case. It really is one big circus. Who knows what will come next? I'm in the middle of it now and there's no going back.

"Say yes, Charlie. Make my heart happy," Willy yells as the bailiff reaches him. Willy doesn't try to resist as Phil picks him up from the ground and turns him around. Willy tosses the ring at Stephy who laughs as she catches it. "You give that to my girl and make sure she puts it on. I want everyone in the world to know she's a taken woman."

"I might keep it myself. This is a stunner," Stephy tells him.

Willy throws his head back laughing. "She sure has a great best friend in you, Steph. If I wasn't so in love with her, I might try to chase you." He winks at Stephy. Cash isn't amused with this part of the stunt. He shoots a glare Willy's way. I have to hold back my laughter.

"That's it," Judge Croesus says as he stands. "We will recess for the day while we get this mess straightened out." He turns with a glare at Cash. "If this is a stunt of yours you will be in contempt and locked up right next to Willy for at least a week."

Cash throws his hands up. "I had no idea this was

going to happen, Your Honor. Willy isn't even on our witness list."

Judge Croesus stares Cash down, nods as if he believes him, then turns and walks from the room. He knows he's not going to be able to wrangle this room in now. Phil begins to drag Willy away. I'm free from testifying for now. I jump down from the stand and rush over to Willy.

"You silly, stupid man," I tell him. I want to hug him so much but I might get tackled and handcuffed next if I do.

"Charlie, I love you," he says. He's still wearing a big grin, but I can see the truth in his eyes. What a fool I am not to love him.

"Oh, Willy, I love you too, but I'm not Charlie Bloodstone. That was just one of my characters. I'm Charlie Diamond and I'm not the woman for you." My heart is breaking as I say this.

"I don't believe you, Charlie. We're meant to be together. I don't care who you've been in the past. I just want to grow old with you."

"Willy, you're going to make an amazing husband for somebody someday, but I'm *not* that woman. I wouldn't trade a second of the time we shared, but you have to move on." I turn and look at Stephy who's admiring the diamond that has to be five carats. I take it from her, and she juts out her bottom lip in a pout.

"You take this ring back and give it to a more deserving woman." I tuck the ring into his pocket.

"No way, Charlie, this ring is for you, and only

you. You'll see. I'm not going away. I want you as my wife and I'm going to make it happen. You'll be riding shotgun with me as I win the next race."

I lean forward and kiss his cheek while Phil turns away. "Thank you for loving me, Willy. You'll never understand how much it means to me. You are truly one of the best ones out there in this crazy world."

"I wasn't. I was a bad boy who wanted a new woman at every race. I met you and it all changed. I love you, Charlie, and nothing you say will convince me our love is wrong."

"We have to go, Mr. Marks," Phil says.

"I'll come to you again just as soon as I'm out of jail," Willy promises.

"Don't do it here or the judge is likely to lock you away for a year." He only laughs harder. He's not at all concerned. I must make men go a little crazy. There seems to be no other explanation for why these men are still holding onto me after finding out what all I've done in the past eleven years.

Phil escorts Willy from the room as cameras flash. The reporters look as if they've been handed a million dollars. They are grinning as they write their headlines. One thing for sure, this case isn't boring. There may be days that are less entertaining than others, but part of the fun of the trial is no one knows what might happen next.

"Dang, Charlie, if you weren't already rich, you could simply cash in on all of the wedding rings you've been given in the past decade and live comfortably for the rest of your life," Stephy says as she moves beside me to watch Willy leave the room. "If I wasn't already falling in love with Cash, I might have to chase that man down. He's gorgeous, funny, and has a big, bold life."

"I've given all of the rings back," I tell her. "They were never mine to own, just to borrow. And yes, Willy is worth keeping. I wish I wanted to."

"You're a fool for letting him go." She doesn't say this with malice. She again focuses on the rings, though. "Once those pretty jewels were given to me, I'd consider them mine."

"No, you wouldn't. If you never intend to stay forever, you know they are simply borrowed property. Besides, you know I don't like diamonds."

She waves her hand in the air. "You don't like diamonds because you haven't been given the right one yet."

"Nope, I don't like them because they are cold stones that mean nothing more than a status symbol for the rest of the world to look at. The bigger the ring the more you have." I roll my eyes.

"No way. They represent eternal love. The bigger the diamond the more eternal the love." She's laughing at her own joke.

"I don't even know what eternal love is." I suddenly feel as if I'm going to cry. "I thought I had that with Bentley. I thought I had forever. But I let him go. I moved on. What does that say about me or a forever love?"

"It says that you loved a great man, and you kept your promise to keep living your life. He's looking down on us from heaven and smiling. He's eating some popcorn, probably on the back of a horse, right this minute, and he's so happy to see us laugh. He's happy to know that you just might have found your forever love."

Cash moves up beside us just as Stephy says these words. His head whips around as he looks at me. He seems pleased and confused.

"Are you in love with someone, Charlie?" There's no menace in the words. I think Cash will truly be happy for me if I find and stay with someone.

"I don't know," I whisper. I don't want the reporters to hear this conversation. I don't want anyone to speculate. That's all they will think about if they do. I have a whole story to tell. My life can't be summed up by the ending of my book. Every chapter matters.

"I hope there's a man out there who can lasso you. You really are amazing, Charlie. You inspire love and hope. You make men smile. You charm them, and you give each man a piece of yourself. They give you everything."

"Then doesn't that make me evil? I only give a little and they give their all."

"No, you make an impression, and then they can't let you go. You make the world keep on spinning. You are loved and there's nothing wrong with that. As soon as the last brick around your heart crumbles you'll be free, and you will be loved, and you will love right back. It's really that simple."

I put my arms around Cash and hug him tight. "I want to believe that, Cash. I truly do, but I don't know if fairy tales really do come true."

He winks at me as he pulls back. "Why don't you listen to your own story? You'll learn a lot about yourself. I know I have."

He leans down and kisses Stephy. "I might have gotten a bit jealous there," he admits, which makes her laugh.

"You have nothing to be jealous about," she assures him as she kisses him again. He nods, seeming satisfied with her answer. He then walks away to let us talk.

"You should listen to that man," Stephy says. "He's very wise."

"He's a very good man, that's for sure."

"Are you ready to tell me who the man who holds your heart is? If it's not Willy, who's incredible, I can't imagine who it might be."

"Who says it isn't Willy?" The room is beginning to clear so we start to exit. I'm ready to flee the reporters for the day. I'm very grateful they aren't allowed at the hotel.

"You just told him to move on," she says.

"Maybe that was all for show." I wink at her then walk ahead as I leave her standing there with her mouth hanging open. I find myself smiling.

The world will inevitably find out who my mystery man is, but they won't until I'm ready to tell them. I'm starting to believe that it might just work out. Maybe at the end of this I truly will get a happily-ever-after. Maybe my prince will save me, and in turn, maybe I will save him right back. Soon. I will have all of the answers soon. So will you.

CHAPTER SEVEN

I 'VE BEEN ON the ranch for a month now. We've gotten into a normal routine. It's breaking my heart a little as each day passes. This is the life I would've lived with Bentley. Each day tells me this with certainty. Colby isn't Bentley. I know this. But this ranch life is so similar. I knew this from day one, but the more time that passes, the more it becomes reality. I'm getting a glimpse of what my life would've been. I can't figure out how this makes me feel.

Colby rises at dawn each morning and is out doing chores. I get up a little later and move to the kitchen, and have breakfast with Barb, and help her clean up. I've gotten to help with a few of the dinners. Barb and I get along great. Life is normal. It's routine. Well, it's *almost* normal.

Colby and I have avoided each other a lot, but late at night both of our defenses seem to come down little by little. We've shared a few hot kisses, and have even been caught making out in the barn like a couple of teenagers, causing the staff to laugh at us. Everyone sees this dance we're doing. They all seem to know more than the two of us do. We can't fight this attraction for much longer.

We *are* married I try to reason to myself.

But what does that even mean anymore? Does a piece of paper from a stranger make it okay for us to live as a real man and wife? I'm not in love with him. He's not in love with me. What does love mean, though? We *like* each other. We're certainly attracted to one another. Would it really be so bad to share a bed with my husband?

I fear if I reach the end of this journey and I never feel his touch against my skin, I'll regret it. This is the life I was supposed to live with Bentley. Shouldn't I fully live it to know how I really feel? We have this marriage for a solid year. We have each other. I want to embrace it. I'm also scared to do just that.

I know there's a chance I'll get my heart broken, but I've survived so much in the past few years. Even if I experience heartbreak, I'll survive. I'll still go on. I have Stephy and my parents. No matter what I go through, I'll make it to the end of the road. I made that promise to just that and I can't give up.

Tears sting my eyes. If I somehow don't make it, that won't be so bad either. If I don't grow old, at least I know where I'm going—I'm going to Bentley. Knowing this makes it easier for me to take risks, to give myself to the moment.

I leave my bedroom. I know where Colby is. This isn't the time to think of Bentley. That's not fair to my current husband. It's not fair to me. I don't have to live in the world of either/or. I can live in the *right now*, and I can embrace it and not feel guilty about it.

I walk to the study to find Colby with a glass of bourbon in his hand, his shirt off, and a small fire blazing in the huge stone fireplace. The air conditioner is running as it's been hot, but Colby is like me, he loves the ambiance and the smell of the fire. I can have one every single day even if it's over a hundred degrees outside.

He doesn't see me yet, and I take my time looking at him as he faces the fire, wearing only a pair of pajama bottoms. The man is a rancher and it shows in his physique. He has dark muscled skin that ripples as he moves. His wide shoulders arrow down to a trim waist and a very nice ass. I take a step forward and see him tense. He knows I'm here. We seem to feel each other before we speak. We're connected whether we want to admit to this or not.

Colby turns and I can't help but admire the front of him. I rake my eyes down his solid chest, the sexy spattering of hair that trails down his stomach and disappears into the waist of his pajama bottoms. My mouth goes dry as I continue admiring his body, his arousal obviously coming to life. He can't hide his reaction in the thin pants he's wearing. I want to feel him, taste him, and have him make me think of nothing but him.

He's aroused, and it's turning me on. I tremble as I move forward. If he turns me down, I'll be devastated. I don't think it's going to happen. We've both needed this since the moment we met. I'm surprised we've waited this long. Maybe we've both been afraid to make the first move. Neither of us is afraid now.

I move closer, my body shaking, my core pulsing. I'm hot and achy. My core is saturated, and I feel a hunger I haven't felt in a long time. I open my mouth to speak, and no words come out. I take a breath as I stop a few feet from him. I can't seem to close the final gap. My heart thunders as I look him in the eyes.

"I couldn't sleep." My voice is husky. I see the answering response in his eyes, but he doesn't move closer. Was this a mistake? Does he want this or not? Yes, he's turned on, but that doesn't necessarily mean anything. Should I go? I start to panic and tense as I turn to run away. I'm not good at taking rejection.

Colby finally moves. He closes the gap between us and grabs my arm. He grips me hard as he turns me back to face him. There's such raw hunger in his eyes, but he also seems angry. I don't know if he's angry with me or himself. I don't know what any of this means.

"Stay," he demands. His voice is barely in control and I see the power he's holding back. He's as ready to explode as I am. We might cause an earthquake as we come together. I'm ready for the natural disaster. I'm craving it.

I nod, unable to speak through my tight throat. He's practically shaking as he holds me, neither of us moving. And then he reaches up, winds his hand through my hair, and tugs me to him. I whimper as my body slams against his. Finally, his face descends. He kisses me. This isn't gentle and sweet. This is hungry and passionate, long overdue.

I reach up and cling to him as I open my mouth, our tongues darting and dancing. I press against him, unable to get close enough. I'm crying out for more as we continue this dance and our hands run over each other. We kiss long and hard. Too long. We've taken too long, and now we might consume each other whole. I don't care. I need this. He needs this. I'll have zero regrets.

He pulls back and I cry out, reaching for him. He doesn't slow as he grabs the hem of my shirt and rips it over my head. I barely blink before my bra is torn from me, flung somewhere behind us. He reaches out his hands and holds the weight of my breasts in his palms, squeezing and kneading. I press my thighs together as I burn inside. I need release.

He lowers his head and licks my nipple before biting down on it, causing a sting before soothing it with his tongue. He does this over and over again, caressing, licking, biting, and sucking one nipple then the other. His tongue flicks over me until I nearly collapse on the floor. I don't know how I'm still standing.

"Don't stop," I cry as I hold on to his head, barely managing to keep it together. He reaches down as I begin to crumble and he holds on to my butt while he continues devouring my breasts. I'm pressed against him with my lower half, while my upper body leans back as he worships me.

"Beautiful, so damn beautiful," he growls. He rips his mouth away and steps back. I practically buckle to the floor. He takes another step back. "One second."

His guttural mixture of pain and pleasure gives me confidence. I'm making this strong, confident man shake, making him lose control. I love it. I move forward. I'm not giving him time. I want to taste him. I *need* to taste him.

He sees my intention and I see a change in him. I see the animal come out. He growls as he grabs me, practically tossing my body on the couch as he rips my pants away. I've never experienced such a loss of control—I love it. He's calling to me, and I'm more than willing to answer.

I'm soaked, which he finds as he thrusts a finger inside me. My hips buck up. "More," I demand. I'm so finished with foreplay. I want his beautiful manhood deep inside of me. I see panic in his eyes.

"I don't have a condom," he thunders as if his world has fallen out beneath him. I smile.

"I'm covered. I swear," I tell him. We are barely more than strangers, but he should know me enough by now to trust me. I see the turmoil in his eyes. Then I see the acceptance.

"I can't stop," he says. He leans up and yanks down his pants.

I lose all ability to speak as he springs free. He's been worth the wait. He's worth a lifetime of waiting. He's beautiful as he stands there, all thick and hard, gleaming in the firelight, his pleasure wet on his tip. He's mine, all mine. I get to have all of him—at least on this night. I reach for him. I want to taste him. I *need* to taste him.

Before he can stop me, I sit up and grab the back of his thighs. Not hesitating, I move forward and wrap my lips around his smooth head, sliding him into my mouth and taking him deep. His fingers wind into my hair and pull hard as I suck him, my throat clenching around his head. His thighs shake beneath my fingers as I move back and forth.

He groans as I taste the salty pleasure of him on my tongue. I suck harder, turning my head, licking and sucking his smooth erection. I want all of him, I want him shooting his pleasure down my throat. I take him deeper, and he cries out as I feel him pulse in my mouth. Before he can release though, he pulls hard on my hair, ripping my mouth from his beautiful hardness.

"I want inside of you," he says as he lies over me. He's between my legs, rubbing against the inside of my thighs. I open wider as his tip hits my pleasure point.

"You were inside of my mouth," I tell him, shocked at how raw my voice is.

"That's not enough," he growls. He stops us both from talking as he rushes his mouth to mine again, his tongue dancing with mine as he settles more comfortably between my thighs. I open to him and he slides inside, taking the rest of my limited breath away.

I whimper at how good he feels as his tongue dances with mine while he stretches me. He pushes all of the way in, then rests for a moment so we can adjust to one another. Then I move up, needing movement, needing release. He begins thrusting and I meet him thrust for thrust. The pressure builds and builds. The explosion is coming. It's too fast, but neither of us can stop.

I rip my mouth from his and scream as I clench around him, my body exploding as I shake all over. He cries out my name and heat floods me as he pulses with me, both of us hot and sweaty, both fully sated.

It takes several moments for our hearts to slow. He tries to pull back, but I don't let him. I need him to hold me, I need to hold him. I don't want to let go. I don't want the real world to invade us. A perfect moment with this perfect man, and I never want it to end. I don't want to think. I only want to feel.

No matter how much I want this, though, it's not going to happen. I begin to shake, but this time from pain, not pleasure. He senses the shift in me and pulls back, looking in my eyes with concern.

"What is it, love?"

The words bring tears to my eyes. I reach up and cup his cheek. This is all on me. None on him. This is the life I should've had with another man. This is everything. It's not Colby's fault I fell in love with another man years before. It's not his fault I haven't been able to let that man go. It's all on me. I let the tears fall. I can't stop them.

"I'm sorry. Did I hurt you?" he asks. There's so much compassion in his eyes it makes me feel worse. I need to stop this. I need to pull myself together.

"I'm the one who's sorry, Colby. This isn't on you, this is me."

"I shouldn't have pushed this. It wasn't what we agreed to," he tells me. He tries to pull back but I won't let him. I grab his face.

"No. I'm glad this happened." I pause a long moment. "I'm glad, Colby. I realize though, I need to face some things. I need to go home."

I see a brief moment of panic fill his eyes before he tamps it back down. I see shutters come into place. He believes I'm breaking the agreement. I need to reassure him.

"Will you come back?" I don't like the coldness in his voice. It's so wrong as our bodies are pressed together. He's still inside of me. We're as close as two human beings can be and yet at this moment we're so completely far away from one another.

"I *will* be back. I just need to go home for a couple of days. I promise to be back. I promise to be in your bed again." I try to smile. He's not showing me what he's thinking or feeling. I know he's still turned on. He can't hide that with us pressed together. I want to make this right.

"Will you take me to bed?" I ask. I'm so raw, so vulnerable in this moment that if he turns me down, I might shatter. He looks at me in confusion. I don't know what he'll do. He twitches inside of me but still says nothing. Finally, when I'm ready to scream from the silence, he nods. He pulls from me and the sudden emptiness makes me want to cry more. I push the tears back. I've shed enough for the night.

He doesn't speak as he lifts me up, cradles me to his

chest, and then walks naked through the house. I cuddle against him as he walks into his room, his room I haven't seen before. He lays me down, pulls me against him, and slowly makes love to me again, all without words. He falls asleep when we're done and only then do I let more tears fall. I don't know how long they do.

"I'm coming home," I finally whisper into the night. Then I close my eyes and drift off.

CHAPTER EIGHT

THE SUN IS setting, my favorite time of the day. As the day wraps up, we look to the sky to be reminded we aren't alone. There's a universe out there calling to us. Are there other planets full of people? I don't know, but it's arrogant of us to think we're the only ones in this vast universe. I love the sound of crickets, love to see bats flying, and love the sight of dusk. I even love the clean smells that country life provides. This is something a person can't get in a city.

Tears fall down my cheeks as I lie in the grass and sob. I wipe my face for the hundredth time and begin to count stars. There aren't too many visible yet, but they are there. I've seen them many times before just as I will many times to come.

"Do you remember how many times you told me that just because I can't see heaven doesn't mean it isn't there?"

It's better to believe in something beautiful than to feel blackness. Heaven is real. The ones we love the most are there. We'll be there someday and have an eternity together. Don't ever give up on heaven. If you start to lose faith just look up at the sky and see the magic at work in real time.

This is something Bentley said to me many times before. I feel like he's with me now. I want his arms around me. I want him to be lying next to me. I want it all. Bentley and I had many conversations like this long into the night. If I try hard enough I can feel him with me as I lie on his grave. I've been here for hours and I'm not going anywhere anytime soon.

"Is it real time though? A falling star is one that happened a long time ago and it just takes a while for us to see it," I remind him.

It depends on how many lightyears the stars are away from us. It's something our minds can't comprehend. But instead of thinking of the stars that die, we should focus on the ones that are alive and well, shining down on us, guiding us, giving us a pathway home.

"I miss you so much, Bentley. Why did you leave me?" More tears fall. I'm glad it's just him and me and we're alone.

I never would've left you, my love, never. But God called me home. I know why now, but it's something you can't comprehend yet. You'll understand when you get here. It's beautiful, Char, but I don't want you here yet. I want you living your life. I want you laughing, falling in love, and being free.

"If I do that, we won't be together. I can't fall in love with someone else. I feel guilty even looking at other men, though I have, I have over and over again. I've found pleasure in them, and enjoyed my time with them. I feel bad for what I've done. I know you told me to do it, but I've betrayed our vows."

You would be betraying your promise to me if you weren't living. Nothing brings me more joy than seeing your wings becoming free. You will fall in love, Char, and that's okay. That's more than okay. You have to live for the both of us. Please don't feel guilty. Please know that I love you more than any other person on earth, and to see you hurting kills me all over again.

"But what if that keeps me from you in the end?"

I feel his laughter in my head. I feel his arms around me. Some might say I'm having a mental breakdown. But those who say that don't understand love. There is a veil here on earth. It's a thin veil. If we truly need to be with our loved ones, they are only a thin sheet away from us. We can open ourselves and talk to them. But if we do it every single day we'd never move on. They know this. So, they only come back when it's most needed. Right now, it's needed. Bentley understands this.

Time and love work differently here, Char. I'm okay. You'll find that out long, long into the future. It's okay to fall in love again. It's what I want. More than that, I want you to be free. You have to live your life to the fullest.

"I'm living the life I would've lived with you right now, Bentley. Every day I'm on this ranch in Texas I think about you, and think that It's what it would've been like with you. Colby isn't you. I know he's not, but he's a good man. I'm filled with so much guilt as I live a life with him. I'm also filled with remorse that you and I didn't get more time together, that we didn't get a lifetime of happiness with laughter and kids." I pause and wait. I don't feel Bentley say anything so I go on.

"I needed to do this. I needed to live out this fairy tale. I didn't realize how hard it would be. But at the same time, I'm healing. I've taken several journeys in the last few years but none of them have made me think of you so much. This is a ranch, this is the life we would've shared together. It's so hard. I miss you so much."

I can't talk as I sob. I have to turn on my side and take in deep breaths before I choke. I finally manage to get myself under control again and flip back over to my back. More stars appear in the sky. I'm comforted in the sparkling beauty above me.

Maybe I'm the one who sent you to him.

"What? How could you send me there?" Maybe I *am* losing my mind.

You need this journey, Char. You need to live this life. You need to be set free from me. I'm gone. I can't come back. But you're alive. You're beautiful, kind, loving, and talented. You need to live, you need to soar. You need to move on. Go back to the ranch. Give it your everything, and free yourself from this prison you keep yourself in.

"I'm afraid if I free myself, I'll let you go forever."

You won't let me go forever. I'm always going to be in your heart just as you will always be in mine. But you have a beautiful heart with room for more than one person. Be free, Char. Go live this beautiful life and do it without guilt. I'm leaving now, not because I don't love you, but because I do. Let me go. Please let me go.

"I just want you to hold me." He's leaving me and I'm alone again. I've felt this far too many times already.

I'll always hold you in my heart . . .

Just like that I'm alone again. I know he's gone. I won't hear his voice anymore. I can sink back into the past and hear more of his words of wisdom, but that isn't what I want. I want a real conversation. I want him answering me. I've probably made up this entire conversation, but I refuse to accept that, to believe he hasn't been here with me. I close my eyes and cry until I can't cry anymore. When I open them again the sky is filled with millions of stars. They are twinkling brightly above me and I smile.

"Thank you, Bentley." I have no doubt he's up there looking down at me. I also have no doubt he came down to lie with me for a while, to help me. "I'm going to let you go now. I don't want to, but I need to. It might take a while longer, but I'm going to let you go."

Peace fills my heart as I say these words. I don't talk anymore, but I also don't leave. I lie there for hours looking at the stars, comforted in this place with my first and only love.

Will I love again? I don't know. But at least now I know there's a chance to be set free. There's a chance everything will be okay. Bentley is fine. But will I be okay? I'll see how strong I truly am. I've gotten good at pretending to be someone else. Maybe I'll find myself in one of these images I'm creating. Maybe one of these personas is the person I'm supposed to be. If I don't honestly try, I'll never know. I might find myself in one of the images and then I'll never need to change who I'm looking at in the mirror again.

CHAPTER NINE

I'VE HEARD STORIES of people who can't breathe and feel pressure on their chest as if a huge weight is holding them down. When they finally manage to draw air into their lungs it feels as if a one-ton weight has been lifted off of them. That's how I feel as I arrive back at the ranch in Texas. I was gone for three days, but in those three days a weight lifted from me.

I climb from the Uber and wave the person away. I don't have a bag. It's just me. I didn't pack when I left, and I didn't need to pack to return. It's night and I don't walk to the house. I go straight to the barn. I know where Colby will be. He's here every night at this time. It's why I wanted to arrive now. There's something special about the barn. It's as if all of the worries in the world disappear when I'm with these majestic animals.

Silence greets me as Colby looks over the horses. He knows I'm here. I see the shift in his body. Is he glad I've come back or is he disappointed? I'm a mess, but we've agreed to do this thing together. We both have our reasons, but it's where we're both supposed to be. I approach him.

"I didn't think you'd come back." Colby isn't looking at me as he leans over the fence and gazes at the horses. I smile as I approach, feeling like I'm home.

"I'm going to stay the full year, Colby. I had to go back to Oregon for a few days. I had to say goodbye."

He doesn't turn as I stand behind him and wrap my arms around him. He reaches down and places his hands over mine that are resting on his stomach. I snuggle against his back. This feels right. This is where I'm supposed to be right now. I feel good. I feel free.

"Did you find the answers you were looking for?"

I rub against him, allowing this man to offer me the comfort and peace that will free my mind from the guilt and pain I'm constantly feeling. "I think you and I were meant to come into each other's lives at this moment. Yes, I got some answers. My first husband, Bentley, was the love of my life. He was everything to me. We knew each other from the time we were babies, and we only had a few short years as a couple. When I lost him, I lost myself. I still haven't picked up all of the pieces from my soul getting shattered when he was taken from me."

I'm not crying anymore. I'm simply telling Colby my story. It feels good to share it with someone other than Stephy. Colby turns and pulls me against his chest and holds me. He's not judging me and he's not jealous. He's simply listening.

"How long has it been since you lost him?"

I have to think about it. It's something I've blocked. I don't want to know when he died, I only want to focus on when he lived. "It's been about five years. I didn't move for the first two years. I stayed in my small hometown and was miserable. My best friend was worried about me, *really* worried, and she reminded me that I made a promise to Bentley to live my life, so I agreed with her, and for the past three years I've been on one adventure after another. But no matter what I do or where I go I can't seem to find myself."

Colby is rubbing my back as I speak, and I find comfort in his arms. He picks me up, moves over to the hay, and sits, cradling me on his lap. I bury my head on his shoulder and greedily accept his comfort.

"I can help you find yourself," he tells me.

I smile. I feel so at home right now. I needed to go back to Oregon and talk to Bentley, but there's no doubt in my mind that I also needed to return to Texas to be with Colby. This is where I belong right now. Will one year be enough? I'm thinking it might not be.

"Maybe you and I will help each other. We've both had horrific losses in our lives. Maybe this year will change us both. I didn't think that was possible and in only a month I can't stand the thought of losing you. I don't understand it, but I've stopped trying to fight how I'm feeling."

"Maybe we'll both want more," he says. I feel a pang in my heart. I lean back and look at him. I reach up and cup his cheek. "I've changed a lot, too, Charlie, more than I ever imagined possible."

"Please don't hope for forever, Colby. Please don't fall in love with me. I can't promise you anything beyond this year, beyond this moment. I don't want to lose you, but I haven't been able to hold onto anything important since Bentley. It's not on the other people, it's fully on me. All I know right now is that I didn't like being away from you, and everything in me cried to return, but that most likely will change. I don't want to hurt you in the end, and I don't want you to hurt me."

He looks both sad and determined as he gazes at me. "We never know what will happen, Charlie, we only know we're here right now. I like you being here. I like waking up with you in my arms. I don't know how I'll feel at the end of a year, but I know right now I'm happy." He stops and smiles. "How about we agree to take this thing one day at a time with no pressure on either of us."

"I can agree to that." I'm relieved. I really like the full honesty between us both.

"Good. Now, why don't you tell me about this journey you've been on."

I pause. "I don't think I should do that. Shouldn't we just live in the moment?" I really don't want him to look at me like a floozy.

He laughs. "I normally don't need to get to know people. I prefer to be a lone wolf, but with you all bets are off. Where did you go first when you left Oregon?"

I laugh as I think of my first adventure. "I went to Las Vegas." He's surprised.

"Oh really. What did you do?"

"I was a showgirl, and then I fell and bonked my head, got amnesia, got married, and lived out an alternate life."

His mouth drops open as he gazes at me. It takes him a second to recover. "You were a showgirl in Vegas. I *have* to see a picture of that. Please tell me it was topless." He reaches up and cups my large breasts and squeezes, instantly bringing my desire for him to life.

I laugh. "No, I wasn't topless," I say with a giggle that turns into a sigh as he brushes across a nipple.

"Good, I was only kidding. I don't want the world to see these beautiful curves. For now, they belong solely to me." I love his possessiveness over me. I'm surprised by this, but a warm glow is flowing through me.

Guilt also fills me and I push it down. "I've been with other men," I tell him. I don't want him to be under some misguided illusion that I've been a saint. I haven't in the last few years. There are men out there who wouldn't like me because I've been with a few partners. A few years ago, I might not have liked myself for that same reason, thinking I needed to stay pure. Is that society telling me I'm doing something wrong, or me telling myself? I don't know.

He cups my cheek. "I care about you, Char, and that means I accept your past. I just want to be a part of your present . . . and maybe your future. You don't judge me for what I've done in the past and I certainly won't judge you. I trust you."

He's still caressing me and I'm blessed to have met this man. "I'm so glad Stephy answered your ad."

"I'm pretty damn grateful to your bestie as well," he says with a laugh. "Maybe I'll send her a horse."

I laugh. "I can guarantee she's never gotten a horse in the mail as a gift."

"I'd have it delivered. The post office tends to frown at shipping live animals in boxes."

"Do they have a box big enough for a horse?" I don't know why my mind goes down these paths.

"Well, of course they do, but let's not test the theory. I'm sure we'd get in a bit of trouble."

"Well, you could always send her a Barbie horse," I tell him with a laugh.

"From what I know about Steph already, she just might like that."

"You're right. She's a silly girl. You can't win her with money and diamonds, but a pink Barbie horse might do the trick."

He cups my cheek. "You and your bestie are a lot alike. I wonder what it will take to win you."

A shudder runs through me as I snuggle in a bit closer to him. "I honestly don't know if I'm winnable," I say after a long time.

"I thought the same thing before I met you, Charlie, but now I'm not so sure. I think the key to winning anyone's heart is to find the pathway in. There's a way to win you, and I might just be the one to find the route."

"That would be wonderful." I actually believe this. I want to love again. I also realize I can't force myself to do that.

"Where did you go after Las Vegas?" he asks as he leans down and nuzzles my neck. Tingles are shooting all over my body and I shift on his lap, feeling his arousal. He makes me feel beautiful and desired.

"I went home. I always go home." My voice grows husky.

He laughs before he swipes his tongue up the curve of my neck and then speaks into my ear. "Where did you go after you went home?"

I can barely think now. "I went to . . . um . . . to New Orleans." I gasp as he nips my earlobe. I love how much he's turning me on. I love how excited he's getting from simply holding and touching me.

"Did you get married again?"

His question makes me laugh. What will he think of me? I'm in now, so I don't want to hide my story from him. "Yes, I did . . . in a cemetery at midnight."

This makes him pull back as he looks at me with shock. The wheels turn behind his eyes as he tries to figure out if I'm telling him the truth or not. I shrug my shoulders then pull his head back to my neck. I need more of his kisses. If I keep answering him, will he still want to make love to me? I'll soon find out.

"Really?" he asks before he sucks the skin where my neck meets my shoulders. Goosebumps flow down my arms and my core tightens.

"Yes, I did, with Stephy right there beside me."

"Are you glad you did it?" He isn't asking about the men, just asking me about my adventures. It feels good to let it all out.

"Yes, I am. It's something I can hold in my vault of experiences. No one can ever say I led a boring life when they are speaking at my eulogy."

His hands rub up and down my back and I shift on his lap, wishing we didn't have so many clothes between us. Speaking of my past should dampen my arousal, but it doesn't.

"I bet you've broken some hearts."

I sigh. "I don't know if the men were in love with me or with the experience, but I have felt bad to walk away. In the end it was the right thing to do. That didn't make it easier at the time, and it doesn't make it easier now."

He slips a hand up my shirt and unhooks my bra, then cups my breasts, making me gasp. I'm ready to make love to him right here. This foreplay takes away all of my insecurities and guilt. I want him. He wants me. I love the hunger between us.

"It's hard for any of us to know what real love is. I guess if we can't live without a person that means we're in love." His words make it harder to concentrate as he continues to stroke me.

"Maybe we just need a person who knows how to find us."

There's more of my story to tell, but he doesn't push me. Instead, he pulls his hands away, which make me whimper my disapproval. Then he stands with me in his arms. "I'm going to take you to my room now. I've already moved your stuff in there, which sadly is very limited. We might need to go shopping."

I laugh as he crosses the yard to the house. "I don't need a lot of stuff."

"You are the only woman I've ever heard say that. I have far more shoes than you and that's just wrong."

I'm laughing harder as we walk inside the house. "I have a few extra pairs at home, but I was raised by good, humble parents. I learned early in life that a person doesn't need a lot of things to make them happy. They need family and friends and lots of love. Material items come and go."

"I'm going to spoil you while you're here, Mrs. Winters," he tells me as we step into his room. I smile, liking to be called by this name . . . at least for now.

"How about you spoil me by us being free together with no worries of today or tomorrow." He lays me down on his bed and steps back and begins to strip his clothes away.

"What does free mean?" he asks with a waggle of his brows. "Does it mean free of clothes? Because if that's the case I can guarantee you I'll be more than happy to be free."

"That's a start." My voice grows huskier as he exposes more and more of his beautiful skin. "I can look at your body all day and night."

"The same goes for me," he says.

"I think free is also free of anxiety, free of anger, free of guilt, free of responsibility. Let's be free to run and play and love one another. Let's be free of it all for the next few months."

"I want longer than a few months," he insists as he

crawls on the bed and begins to strip my clothes away.

"I want the full year," I whisper. I'm turned on and losing my train of thought. I love that he can do this to me. I love how much I love being with him. Can it turn into more? I sure hope so. I don't know if I'll let it, but I sure hope so.

"We will laugh. We will love. We will make love every single day. We will swim. We will ride horses. We will look at the stars. We're going to be free in every sense of the word. I'm going to make you never want to leave."

I gaze up at this man as he takes the rest of my clothes off then climbs on top of me. I wrap him in my arms and vow to hold on as long as possible.

"I want to be here right now." It's all I can promise him at this moment. I can't plan for a future I'm still so uncertain of.

He kisses me, then joins our bodies together. I start to fly. I've let go of the past, and I'm living purely in the moment. I might never want to leave . . . I may have found my way back home . . . or at least to a new home. This could last forever. I close my eyes and stop thinking. Right now, it's time to feel.

CHAPTER TEN

CASH, STEPHY, AND I are sitting by the pool having dinner. Mr. Hart didn't have any questions for me today and I'm very glad. I'm too raw. I think he could see that the jury wouldn't have handled him attacking me after talking about Bentley and the pain of letting him go. He's learned that's an area not to attack. He'd much rather hit me on the many husbands I've had. Most people can't comprehend it, and that gives him some poking room. That makes me the scarlet-lettered woman. I should wear that sweater to court someday and see what reaction Mr. Hart has to it.

"It's been a rough week," Stephy says. "I remember when you came home that weekend. You were hurting. I hated that there wasn't much I could do for you."

"No one could do anything for me then. It was something I had to do on my own. You've always been there for me when I've needed you the most. You also know when I need time to myself. I love that we know each other so well that we can hold on tight or let the rope go when we need to be set free."

"Were you able to let Bentley go after that weekend?" Cash asks.

I reach over and pat his hand. He's been so good to me. "Yes, that was the moment I began to release him. It wasn't the end, it still isn't the end, but I've felt much more free after that day. He let me go the day he died in the hospital. He knew he couldn't hold on to me. He loved me enough to set me free. It was me holding on to him that pulled me under. It's like a drowning victim who is so panicked they try to take the lifeguard down with them. Bentley had let me go earlier, but I was clinging to him, not realizing the surface was right there all along and all I had to do was kick my legs to take in some much-needed air."

"Why is it still so hard after all of these years?" Cash asks. He's not being cruel, he's trying to understand me. This isn't something easy to do since I don't understand myself most of the time.

"It's because no matter how much I let him go, he will always own a part of me. I still cry for him, though it's become less and less over the years. He still has a piece of my heart. I've just realized over time that I'm living the life I need to live. When I was on that ranch I was living the life I should've lived with him."

"But was it really the same life?" Cash points out.

I smile. "No. I finally realized that, too. It was ranch life, but Bentley had been gone for five years at that point and, though there were similarities with Colby and Bentley, they weren't the same man. When I was in Colby's arms I wasn't thinking about Bentley. It got easier and easier to let Bentley go the longer I was with Colby."

Cash and Stephy are quiet as we think about our lives for a few seconds. We can easily fall in love, but falling out of love isn't nearly as easy. Yes, marriages fail, and relationships fail, and I don't know why, but to truly fall in and out of love isn't an easy process. It's one that takes time and a lot of effort. If we don't put in the effort, it can kill us.

"Were you happy you went back?"

"Yes, I was glad I went back. For one thing, I made a commitment. I don't like to falter on my promises to someone. For another, it was a part of my journey and I had to see it through. I would've never forgiven myself if I wouldn't have gone back."

"What made you leave if you were so happy there?"

I remember the day I left as if it were yesterday. "My time came to an end." Cash waits. I don't add more.

"Why did it have to come to an end? I understand you had a one-year contract, but it sounds as if he wanted more. It sounds as if he could have been the one."

"I don't know," I admit. "I don't know why I haven't been able to fully commit to someone . . ." I trail off, realizing I almost add until now. Cash seems to pick up on my hesitation. That's what makes him a damn fine attorney. He looks at the whole picture and not just a single piece of a situation.

"Is there something you're keeping from me, Char?" he asks, sitting up in his seat. Stephy giggles as she leans in closer.

"Yes, Char, is there something you want to share with both of us?"

Cash looks between the two of us as understanding lights his eyes. "Have you fallen in love with someone, real love? Is there someone here now? Is this all a game you're trying to get through to have the happy ending?" He's been picking up on this more and more as clues are dropped. It's easy to fool as foolish man, it's impossible to fool a wise one.

Weight lifts off of my chest. "Yes, I've fallen in love."

Cash seems stunned. "Now? Right now, are you in love with someone?" he tries to confirm.

"I believe I am. I've thought I was before, though, so I'm afraid to trust what I'm feeling."

Cash nods as if this is perfectly normal. "Is this someone new or is it someone from the past?"

"She won't say," Stephy says in a huff.

"Char, we're your friends. We all share something special together. You can trust us," Cash says.

"I know I can trust you. It's me I don't trust. I don't trust my heart, my feelings, my ability to discern right from wrong. I don't trust that I'm allowed to be truly happy. Every time I come close it's ripped away from me. I'm trying to figure this all out, and I don't want to do or say anything that will ruin the moment."

"Is it a prior husband?" Cash asks, not letting it go.

"Maybe," I say.

"Well, you've gotten just about as much out of her as I have," Stephy says. She shoots me a glare. I laugh it off. She will never truly be mad at me.

"Is it the cowboy? That makes the most sense from what I've heard so far," Cash says. I see the wheels turning in his head. Stephy could find out so easy. It shows how much she loves me that she hadn't done some snooping. She will spy on the world, but never do it to me. We would die for one another. That's a love I can fully understand. Now, I just need to understand romantic love. It might never happen.

Yes, I believe I'm in love, but I'm not sure what love is. I thought real love was what I shared with Bentley. I *know* we were in love, but we were also very young. We didn't have time to develop that love. We didn't have time to cultivate it and make it grow, to become an old married couple who knew every move the other was going to make before they made it. We were robbed of our time together. Being robbed of that time has shaken what I know and believe.

"I'm not ready to share this relationship yet. I'm sharing everything with the world right now, and I'm afraid if I share what's happening currently I'm going to ruin it. Let me get through my story first, and then I promise to tell you everything."

"You have to promise to tell all even if you decide you don't want to be with this person," Stephy says. "And you have to tell the two of us even if you don't tell the court. I won't be able to stand it if you don't."

"I will," I assure her. "I can't say if I'll be with him forever or not. He tells me that's what he wants, but I'm not sure."

"It's okay to be afraid. You've been through hell and back. No matter what happens today or tomorrow, you always have me," Stephy assures me.

"That is something I've never doubted. I might not trust myself a lot of the time, but I always trust you." Of course, that's gotten me into some trouble too, I think.

"That's because it's easier to trust someone else than ourselves. We are perfectly human, which means we're far from perfect. The mistakes we make are what helps us grow though. I'm so glad for all we've done."

"Me too, Stephy. I'm gladder than words can say. As I've told my story for the past few weeks, I've realized how grateful I really am. I grew with each new experience. I have a lot of growing left to do."

"You better make it quick. We aren't getting any younger," Stephy says with a laugh.

"Age is just a number. We have plenty of good years left," Cash says.

"That I can toast to," Stephy says as she holds up her glass. Cash and I raise ours.

"To friendship and a lot of years to live," I say.

"To winning," Cash adds.

We clink our glasses as we cheer. We have a lot to be grateful for. I'm happy. I'm truly happy. My mood changes from day to day, but I've got great people surrounding me, I've led a wonderful life, and I have a lot more living to do in the years to come. I'm going to do it all and I'm not going to let fear hold me back.

A new day is coming. It's going to be beautiful.

CHAPTER ELEVEN

THE CLOCK IS ticking. It's growing louder and louder as each day passes. My time is running out. I've gone back and forth on whether to extend my time in Texas or not. After nearly a year with Colby, there's no doubt in my mind that if I want to stay longer, he'll be pleased. I don't think either of us are capable of thinking in terms of forever, but we can think in terms of a year, or three years, or maybe even ten years.

Is that what either of us want?

I sadly don't think it's what I want. I'm happy with Colby. Our lives have taken on a beautiful routine. We do ranch chores together, cook together, swim, look at the stars, and make love each night and morning. The lovemaking is phenomenal.

I haven't been with anyone as long as I've been with Colby. Does that mean I want to be with him forever? Does it mean we're supposed to be together? Or am I with him because this is safe, this is comfortable, this is what I know? I can't help but fight myself. I think I might just be my own worst enemy.

I don't know any of the answers because I question everything. Then again, maybe I need to leave because I *am* questioning it. If nothing else, that tells me what

I'm not willing to say out loud or even think about—that I need to leave. I sigh with frustration.

"What has you so lost in your own head?" Colby asks as he moves to me from behind and wraps me in his large arms. I lean back and snuggle against him. I might not know what I want, but when he does hold me I feel as I'm home, I feel I'm right where I belong. That should be my answer. It would be the answer to a normal person. I'm obviously not normal.

"I'm happy." This is the truth. In this moment, I'm very happy and I'm right where I want to be.

He tenses the tiniest bit behind me before he forces himself to relax. "Are you truly happy, Charlie? Your words say you are, but your voice says you aren't."

Tears sting my eyes. I don't want to lie to him. I *am* happy. Stephy has been down a few times to visit me and I've made one more trip home to see my parents, but I've wanted to come back to Texas each time I've left it, I've wanted to be with Colby. For the past week the draw to being here has ebbed for me though. I'm starting to feel the itch to go home—to stay home. I don't know when it happened, but I've stopped thinking of Texas as home. Is it because I've given myself a time limit?

"I've really enjoyed being here, Colby," I whisper.

"I can hear the change in your voice. It's as if your body feels the clock hands spinning as if you've prepared yourself to be here for only a year and you know that year is up." He pauses. I don't say anything as this is what I've been thinking about all day. "You can stay longer than a year. I know we both said to not get too involved, but this relationship is working. We have a routine, we're happy. The people here love you, and . . ." He stops.

I wonder if he's trying to tell me he loves me. Those three words haven't been spoken by either of us. I don't want him to speak them now. I can't say them back. I don't know if I can't because they aren't true, or if I can't say those words to any man but Bentley.

"This land is beautiful. I needed to be here."

He squeezes me. "I notice you're saying *needed* instead of *need*," he points out.

"You are too observant."

"I've grown a lot in my time here with you, Charlie. For the most part it's been wonderful. We took a little while to get into our routine, but we now have it down to a science. I don't want you to go. The thought of never seeing you again breaks my heart."

I turn around in his arms and hug him. "I'm better, Colby. I'm so much better than the day I arrived here. I don't know what it is, but I feel freer. It's as if I'm becoming a new person, maybe even the person I'm supposed to be."

"But you don't feel as if this is where you belong." It's not a question. There's a lot of resignation in his voice.

"We officially have a week left before our one-year mark. I don't want it ruined by wondering what will happen."

"A week isn't long enough," he points out.

"A week can be a lifetime," I counter.

He laughs as he pulls my chin up so he can look in my eyes. "I don't want to let you go, but that's all I'm going to say. The choice is yours. I want you to know that this is your home today, tomorrow, and in ten years. There won't be another woman for me. You're it. Even if you choose to leave, know that I'll be here waiting for you when you're ready to come home."

I feel tears. "Please don't do that. If I go, Colby, you need to let me go. You need to move on with your life and find a worthy wife and have a lot of mini yous. This world needs you to continue, it needs your family to go on. Don't hold out for me to make that happen."

He smiles, though I see pain in his eyes. We swore not to hurt one another, but I know I'm hurting him now. I feel like a monster. I haven't lied to him, but I've shared my body and soul with him, and now I'm pulling away. I'm betraying his trust in me and in all women.

"I don't think you realize who you are. Once a person has a taste of you, it's impossible to find anything or anyone like you. You're not a forgettable woman, Charlie."

"I'm far from perfect, Colby. I'm just a broken person trying to find a new path in life. I keep getting stuck in the blackberry bushes, though."

He laughs. "I will pick out the thorns and rub on the salve to help you heal."

I rub his cheek as I look into his beautiful, soulful, kind eyes. "Yes, I have no doubt that you would do just that. What you forget though, is that sometimes you have to tend to your own needs before you can tend to anyone else's. We can't care for another without making sure we're whole ourselves."

"I disagree. I think we find ourselves by getting lost in those we love."

"If we get too lost we lose who we are."

"We'll just have to agree to disagree. I like myself more now that I care for you. I certainly love my life a lot more."

"Take me for a ride." He nods. He doesn't try to keep the conversation going. We're not in agreement on where we stand, or where we *should* stand. He's aware of that and so am I. I see hurt in his eyes, but he pushes it down, just as he always has. He's too good for me. I'm very aware of that. I regret nothing, though. I have loved this life with him. I still love it.

We take our ride. We let it all go. We laugh and stop at the lake and make love in the water. We act as if we have a lifetime of doing just this. I want a lifetime of this—I amend this—I want to *want* a lifetime of this. I don't want the pull of tomorrow interrupting. I don't want to *want* to leave.

The week flies by much too quickly. We work hard in the morning, swim in the afternoon, cook together, ride the horses, and make love with more urgency than ever before. We both know it's coming to an end. We both know the clock is about to strike midnight.

He doesn't ask me again to stay. He knows the answer. As the days count down, I realize that I have to go. Will I come back? I can't answer that. More of my soul is now on this ranch in Texas than back home. I might be unable to know what love is anymore, but I do know where I belong. Before Texas the only place I could call home was Oregon.

Now I have two places I consider home. I've walked away from Oregon countless times. I guess I'll be able to walk away from Texas as well. It saddens me to realize how easy it is for me. Maybe I'm nothing more than a cold-hearted monster.

I don't want to think that way. Bentley didn't think of me that way, and Colby has told me countless times I'm somebody special. But if I was truly capable of being loved, I'd be able to love just as much.

I wait until the morning when Colby is out riding fences. I've stayed one day past my leaving day. My year is officially up. I cry as I pack my one bag. I look down at it feeling sadder than ever before at how easy it is to pack up my life.

Colby and I stayed up until almost dawn making love. There was desperation in the act as if we couldn't get close enough to one another. He knows I'll be leaving any day, but neither of us say a word about it.

This morning he woke me with a hand on my cheek and a kiss on my lips. I was blurry as he whispered, "I love you." He didn't give me time to respond before he left. I lay there for thirty minutes wondering if that really happened or if I dreamed it.

Now I close up my suitcase. I let a few tears fall before I brush my cheeks. I move to the nightstand and pull out the feather I've had in there for a while. I take out a pen and paper. Another tear falls as I begin writing, smearing the ink on the paper. I leave it.

Colby,

Thank you for this year. Thank you for helping me find myself. Thank you for loving me, caring about me, and protecting me. Thank you for holding me and giving me freedom. I don't know what I'm going to do, I only know I have to go home. Please, please don't come find me. Please don't hold on to me. You have to set me free, and you have to free yourself. Please find your mother's family and forgive them for the past just as we want to be forgiven for all we do wrong. Please find a beautiful woman inside and out and have a dozen children. You're an incredible man, and I'm so very grateful for the past year. I can't imagine not knowing you. This is the hardest it's ever been to walk away. I've spent more time with you as a wife than with Bentley or anyone else. What we've had is real. I don't want that taken away from either of us. I don't know what I'm going to find when I get back home. I only know it's time for me to move on. I believe it's time for you to find yourself as well. Find your mother. Find a family. Don't hold me so tight you can't let go. I've done that. I'm still doing that. I'm still holding onto the past. It's not a good place to be. Please don't do the same. Please, allow yourself to be free.

With love,
Charlie

I fold the note and set it on his pillow with the feather on top. I walk out of the room, and down the stairs. I go into his den and pull out the divorce papers. They have been in there for months. I asked him to have them ready. He wasn't happy, but he had his attorney draw them up. They've sat in the drawer since. I look at them, tears streaming down my cheeks. I sign my name, lay them on the desk, and walk away from them.

I don't turn back as I then move through the house and exit the front door. I climb into the waiting car I called. As I exit the ranch I look back once and swear I see Colby on his horse on top of the hill. I look away. I don't want to think he's watching me leave him. I don't want to think he'll be in pain.

I cry all the way to the airport. Am I making a mistake? I don't know anything anymore. I just know that Oregon is calling me back home and I can't ignore the call. I just know that I have to leave. I wish I knew why. Maybe that would make it easier. I doubt it, but maybe.

CHAPTER TWELVE

"WE CAME TO the end of our year. It was magical. It was perfect. It also had to end. I wasn't in a place I could commit to Colby. I couldn't give him my all, and I knew that was what he was giving me. I had to leave."

Silence greets this final sentence. I feel as if someone is raking my fingers across a cheese grater. It hurts telling this story. I found so much happiness in Texas. I found something I hadn't found until then or since then.

I make eye contact with Mr. Hart who has an evil glint in his eyes. I don't like this look. He most certainly has something up his sleeve. He looks like the cat who just swallowed the canary while no one was looking. I glance over at Cash, who also looks worried. What is going to happen next?

"Thank you, Ms. Diamond. You may step down," Mr. Hart says.

I again look at Cash, confused. He nods at me and I rise from the stand. I slowly walk away, my legs hurting. I was more tense than normal as I shared the ending of my story with Colby. Maybe it's because he's the most like Bentley. Maybe because out of everyone in my life, he had the most impact. He still does.

"We'd like to call Mr. Winters to the stand," Mr. Hart says. I look out at the audience. I haven't seen Colby out there yet. The back doors open and in he comes, striding with confidence down the aisle. He doesn't look at me. I feel my heart lodge in my throat.

Cash reaches over and squeezes my hand as Colby is sworn in. What will he say? I'm not at all sure what's going to happen now. I feel a nervous sweat breaking out on my back. I'm not ready for this. I have so much more to tell Stephy. I look over my shoulder at her and she gives me a sad smile.

"Mr. Winters, thank you for coming," Mr. Hart begins.

Colby looks him directly in the eyes. "I didn't have a lot of choice since you sent a subpoena my way." I can't tell by his voice what he's thinking about this. I didn't want him to have to testify. I figured he wouldn't have to since he hasn't been here.

"I have no idea how this is going to go," Cash whispers.

"Me neither."

"Is there anything you need to tell me?"

"No." Even if there is something, I won't say. I'm opening myself up and sharing my life, but there are absolutely some things I won't share. There are some things that are between me and each of these men who have impacted me so much. I wonder if Colby feels the same. I'm about to find out.

"Were you in love with Ms. Diamond?"

"Very much," Colby replies.

"In the beginning this was an arranged marriage?"

"Yes, it was a mutual agreement for both of us. I told her not to fall in love. I told her this would last for one year and then it would be over. I'm the one who didn't stick to the agreement. With a woman like Charlie, I don't know if that's possible."

"How did it end?"

"In heartbreak. I wasn't sure I'd be able to ever forget her. I still haven't. She kept to the terms of the contract. I was the one who failed," he repeats.

"Did you pay the one million dollars?"

"Yes, I did. She refused to take it, so I had the money wired to an account. I refused to accept it back when she tried to return to sender. There are some out there who will say she did it for the money, that she's done all of this for money. They'd be wrong. She has plenty of her own money, for one. The reason she went on this journey is she was lost. I think she's still lost. She's still on a journey to find herself." He turns and looks at me. "I hope you do. I know I can help you with that like I have in the past."

The pain in his eyes rips me apart. It's been many years since we spent our year together and the way he's looking at me is just as he did back then, just as he did not long ago. This man is far too good for me. I'm a fool to not see that or more accurately to not act on it.

"Have you spoken with her since she left?" Mr. Hart asks. He's clearly upset this questioning isn't going the way he wants it to go.

"Yes."

"Do you care to elaborate?"

"No."

Mr. Hart is clearly irritated with the short replies. I let out a breath. I don't think Colby is going to share anything I don't want this room to hear. I'm not one hundred percent relaxed, but I feel better. Of course, I've been the one to open myself up for these proceedings. Whatever is said will be said. I can't stop it and I can't be upset by it. If I wanted my life kept secret, I wouldn't be right here right now.

"How do you feel about Ms. Diamond as of today?" Mr. Hart seems leery to ask this question. He sees something in Colby's eyes, just as I do, but neither of us can interpret what that something is.

Colby reaches into his pocket and pulls out a velvet box. He sets it on the witness stand. He doesn't open it. I feel tears spring to my eyes. It's more than obvious what type of box that is. It's known worldwide.

"I'd marry her all over again," Colby says. He gives a sad look at the room. "I haven't given up on us. I have faith and hope. I will take any part of her she's willing to give."

"Even after seven years?"

"Five years," he says. I tense.

Mr. Hart looks down at his notes. "I'm showing the timeline that she left seven years ago."

"That's correct."

Mr. Hart realizes what he's saying. "You saw her again after she left?" The attorney again looks like the cat and the canary. I hope the damn bird flies free. I'm not sure what Colby is about to tell this courtroom. I'm praying it isn't what I think it is.

"That isn't any of this court's business," Colby says. "If Charlie wants the world to know she'll tell all of you."

"You *are* under oath, Mr. Winters."

"I understand that, but that doesn't mean you get to intrude into *my* life. There's absolutely nothing you can do to me to break me more than I've already been broken in my life. Charlie came when I needed her the most. I like to think I was there for her when she needed me the most. That's between us. You've gotten too much of our story already. You won't get anything more than I want to give right now."

"You are telling me that with everything you have heard of Ms. Diamond's story, you're still staying loyal to her?" Mr. Hart asks with obvious condemnation.

"I'm telling you with everything I've heard about her, it only makes me love her more. I'd go to the ends of the earth for her. There's nothing I won't do for her. If she'd have me right now, I'd marry her again. I would marry her every year in front of all of our loved ones if that's what she wants."

Mr. Hart rolls his eyes. He's not looking so professional right now. "I thought you didn't have anyone in your life." That was a flat-out snarky comment. I want to stand up and defend Colby.

"I contacted my mother after Charlie left. We've healed our relationship and I've gotten to know my family. Everyone has a story, Mr. Hart. We all have secrets and we all have pain. I realized that because of Charlie. If it hadn't have been for her I would've continued to walk through life a broken man who didn't realize how broken he was."

"You haven't found anyone since Charlie, so how much healing have you actually done?"

Colby laughs. "I didn't say I haven't found anyone." There's a gasp in the room. I smile at him, and nod. He goes on. "I just haven't found anyone like Charlie. But I've healed more from her than you could ever imagine. I now know who I am, and I know the difference between right and wrong. Yes, I still love Charlie, and yes, I still laugh and live my life even when I'm not with her. I'm not some withered man sitting in the corner crying every day and thinking of what could have been. I'm living my life to the fullest. I also hope to have the woman I love back. I will also survive if I don't."

"What a healthy attitude," Mr. Hart says with a lot of snark behind the words.

"Yes, I agree." Colby leans back as he makes himself more comfortable. He looks over at me and winks.

The two of us know something that nobody else in this room knows, not even Stephy. Will I tell them? I'm not sure. Colby is someone I haven't ever been able to let go of, especially after what we've been through.

"Why didn't you fight for Ms. Diamond if you love her so much?"

Colby laughs. "I was the person in her life who

MELODY ANNE

broke the dam wide open. She'd been with other guys after Bentley and before me. I was a reminder of her past. I was the one who showed her the life she could've shared with her first husband. I understood after she was gone how difficult that had to be on her. I figured it out. I figured out how much it was hurting her to live a normal life. I still didn't want to let her go. I was in love with her then and I'm still in love with her now."

"You don't care that she doesn't feel the same?"

"She might feel the same. She has a hard time knowing what real love is. Every time she seems to open herself up, she gets her heart ripped out. I saw it with my own eyes."

"What do you mean you saw it?"

I glare at Mr. Hart. The man knows how to pick up on a scent. He's a dog searching for his bone, and I've royally pissed him off. He will do anything to make me look bad. I don't think I'm going to be able to keep this secret from him—I don't think I'll be able to keep it from the people I love. I have for a long time, but I'm resigned to it all coming out. It doesn't mean Mr. Hart will get it today. It doesn't even mean he'll get it tomorrow. He'll get this secret *if* and *when* I'm ready to tell it.

"Do you think you'll come back together?"

Colby shrugs. "If the stars align, we will." His smile falters as he looks at me again as if we're the only two people in the room. "I'm in love with you and I know you're in love. Maybe it's me." He pauses for a long moment before turning from me. "I don't know if it's

124

me she wants. The heart is a funny thing. If you pull it from the body, it's an ugly organ. It can get clogged. It can, and literally does, kill hundreds of thousands of people each year. But we are nothing without our hearts. We can have them replaced, but I'm not sure if we're the same person when that happens. I think our hearts and our souls are entwined. We don't survive without both pieces intact."

"And you believe that your heart and soul are entwined with Ms. Diamond's."

"I know they are," Colby answers with confidence.

"Do you feel Ms. Diamond is guilty?"

"Of what?" Colby asks.

"Many things," Mr. Hart says.

"No, I think she's being harassed."

Mr. Hart turns back and looks at me with that evil smile he likes to wear. I don't know what this entire interview with Colby has been about, but it's not our relationship. He has something else up his sleeve. He's about to reveal it.

"We can all talk about the virtues of Ms. Diamond, but the bottom line is the bottom line. We are a nation of laws. Without those laws being followed the world would fall into chaos. This country, though relatively young, is an example to other places of how a free society should operate. If we allow people to live lawlessly, we leave the doors wide open for criminal acts."

"I agree with you. I have massive property in Texas. I depend on the law to keep it running smoothly."

"Then you should agree with me that Ms. Diamond has broken some laws."

"I don't agree at all. I think you might not like her lifestyle, and you might not agree with the number of marriages she's had, but you can't say what she's done is illegal."

"You have divorce papers. None of the others do."

"Prove it," Colby says, using the same words I've said to Mr. Hart. That takes away the smug look from the attorney, but only for a few seconds. He plasters the look back on his face. The man realizes that half of the battle is portraying confidence.

I've realized in my life that anyone can be lied to. If you tell a person a lie over and over again with enough confidence in your voice, even if the truth comes out, it's impossible to switch their thinking. What curious creatures we humans are. You can't lie to an animal. You can train them, but you can't lie to them. You can't give them a banana and convinced them it's a steak. You can't hit them and tell them it's affection. Animals are smart. Why are humans so stupid?

I think it's because we operate on pure emotion. We might use logic, we might have brains, but at the end of the day we care more about how we feel than what we see or what we do.

Mr. Hart tries to shake Colby for a little longer. He fails. He dismisses him when Cash doesn't choose to cross examine him. He passes by my table and sets the ring down.

"Colby, no," I say.

"I love you." He then walks away, leaving the ring sitting there. He doesn't stop as he moves down the aisle and exits the back doors. Will he wait out there to talk to me or will he go all the way back to Texas without a goodbye?

I can't chase him down. Judge Croesus hasn't dismissed court yet. I have to sit there for another fifteen minutes before we recess for the day. I don't touch the box as I rise and run to the back doors. I need to know if Colby is out there.

I reach the steps and look around. He's nowhere to be found. My eyes fill with tears as Stephy steps up beside me.

"It's okay," she tells me.

"It's not."

"Is he the one?" she quietly asks.

I don't say anything. She doesn't push me.

She opens the ring box and smiles. I look at it. It sends a pang through my heart. I remember this ring. It's the stars all aligned.

"Are you going to keep it this time?"

I take the ring from the box and love how the sun shines down on it, bringing it to life. "Yes."

She doesn't push me for more as she wraps her arm around me and we descend the steps. This is what I love the most about my best friend. She allows me to process how I'm feeling without pushing me to give her more answers. Everyone needs a Stephy in their life. I will never quit thinking or saying this. I don't know how people go through life completely alone. How depressing would that be?

Tomorrow is a new day. I will reset and reevaluate. Tomorrow it will all be better. Tonight, I will be sad. Tonight, I will cry at the losses in my life. I can still cry over them even if I'm the one who's caused them. That's okay. I'm human, and I'm going to make mistakes. As long as I pick myself up again, I'm going to be fine. I've made it through hell and climbed my way back out. I can do it over and over again if I need to.

CHAPTER THIRTEEN

I'VE BEEN BACK home for six months. Stephy hasn't pushed me this time to start a new adventure. She knows how hard it was for me to leave Texas. She knows I'm having a difficult time holding myself together. I miss Colby. I miss him more than any of the others. I haven't spoken to him since I left. I haven't called, and he hasn't called me. It's over between us. It's what I want. Being this sad over leaving him doesn't exactly prove it's what I want.

"We need to go somewhere," Stephy says as she comes and sits next to me in the den. I have a fire going as I do every night. Maybe I like to torture myself. In this house I should be thinking about Bentley, not Colby.

"I can't seem to make myself go anywhere. I needed to go to Texas. I needed to live that life that mirrored the life I would've had with Bentley, but there's no way I can do anything like that again."

She gives me a smile. "I'm wondering if you're hurting so much because you miss Colby, or if you're hurting because it's made Bentley come to life and you're grieving him all over again."

"It's a little bit of both. I do miss Colby. I was with

him for a solid year, that's longer than any other man I've been with, including your brother. Yes, I was with Bentley growing up, but we were only married a month and that was all honeymoon time. We got cheated. We didn't have a year of living together with our lives completely entwined. Maybe some of my misery is about what I could've done differently with both Bentley and with Colby. Maybe of all of the men I've been with in the last six years."

"Would you give any of it up?"

I shake my head. "No, I wouldn't give a moment of it up."

"Then maybe the best thing we can do for you is to jump back in the saddle and try again. You can't sit here for two years like you did after you lost Bentley. It will kill you. We will be taking a thousand steps backward instead of moving forward. You have to see that."

I nod. "I know, Stephy. I just can't seem to make myself go anywhere."

"Well, that's what you have me for," she says with a laugh. I see her spirit lifting. I haven't been willing to talk about it until now. She knows I'm ready. I don't know exactly what I'm ready for, but I'm ready to quit wallowing in my own self-inflicted misery.

"I love Colby, but it isn't enough. I'm not ready for forever with anybody. I'm afraid I'll never be ready for forever."

"Does that mean you're giving up on *all* men?" Stephy asks, looking worried again.

I finally smile. A real smile. I stand and move over to the bar and make two margaritas. I'm getting a little too good at making them. I turn and see Stephy beaming at me. She's missed me. I need to quit pulling away from her like I have for the past six months.

"I love that you stand by me no matter what. I'm sorry I've been such a downer lately." I move back to the couch and hand her a drink, then sit and take a few large swallows of my own.

"I will always stand by you, no matter what. We can get through anything as long as we do it together." She takes her own drink then looks at me again with hope. "Do I get to plan the next adventure now?"

I nod. "I want to go somewhere far away. I want sunshine and stars. I don't want noise and chaos."

Her smile grows big enough to scare me. "Well then, I guess I'll just have to see what I can do."

"I don't trust that look at all," I tell her.

"Oh, loosen up. Let all of the past six years go and become an entirely new person. I've had your new passport waiting for six months," she says as she jumps up and runs to a drawer. She pulls out the passport and flings it at me. I laugh.

"So, I'm going to be a blonde?"

"Blondes have more fun," she assures me.

"Serpentine?"

"Yep, I love serpentine jewelry."

"It sounds like a snake." I laugh. It feels great to laugh again. Maybe I should've done this months ago. I need to stop fighting Stephy. She seems to have far more answers than I do.

"I want you to make a deal with me," she says.

"What is that?"

"I want you to be done acting like a good girl. I want it absolutely, positively done. It doesn't get you anywhere. You know that saying that good girls go to heaven and bad girls go everywhere? Well, that's going to be our motto from here on out. It's so very, very, *very* true. Good girls are boring. They don't live life. You have been the preacher's daughter for a very long time. You now get to be Charlie Serpentine, and she's a fun blonde who doesn't care about the rules and lives to laugh."

"You're asking for failure if you expect me to live as if there are no consequences. As a matter of fact, I think there is zip, zero, nada chances of me doing that."

"You do realize that zip, zero, nada, and nothing all mean the exact same thing, right?"

"You do realize that I don't care, right?"

We both laugh. She shrugs. "I'm trying to make a point here, Charlie." She throws her hands in the air. "It's a really important point too. I'm done with leading a boring life. I want adventure. I want *you* to have adventure. I want sex with a hot, sweaty man whose only desire is to please me. I want to not be a good girl. I want you to be the same."

I choke on the sip of margarita I just took. "I *have* had sex with a hot sweaty man." I pause and shrug. "I've had sex with a *few* hot, sweaty men."

She rolls her eyes. "I haven't! And you haven't until

you married them . . . prude."

I laugh hard at this. "Really? You really think you can call me a prude?"

"Let's go on vacation. I'll pick an incredible place, and let's just live. Let's go there, have wild flings. I have to lose the V-card. And then we will come back with zero regrets."

"You do realize we can go there together, and *you* can find a hot, sweaty man without *me* finding one," I point out.

"I want us both to have a new adventure."

"We will certainly have an adventure. I don't need a man to do that. I've had enough men in the last five years to last a lifetime."

"You might be having adventures, but you're coming back the same exact person as when you left," she points out.

I start to say something when I realize she's one hundred percent right. I feel as if a light bulb is going off right above my head, or maybe her head, or maybe both of our heads.

"You know what? You're right. I want to be someone new. I want to live like there's no consequences, and live like there's no tomorrow. I might say I'm doing this, but they are just words until I actually do something different."

"That's what I'm talking about," Stephy says.

"Dang straight." I stand up, move over to the desk, and pull out a pair of scissors from the drawers.

"What are you doing?" she asks, looking less confident and a little worried now.

I grab my long brown hair and lop off about five inches in one cut. Stephy's eyes widen. I cut a little more, and the edges are crooked, but it feels so good as it brushes against my shoulders. I've never worn my hair this short. It feels so much lighter. I shake my head.

"Oh, that looks great. I mean, we're going to have to have it fixed, but it looks great. What a good length on you. I can't remember a time I haven't seen your hair hanging down your back."

I move over to the mirror and look at my image. I love it. With it dyed blonde I think I'm going to love it even more. I'm going to like being Charlie Serpentine. Will she think of Bentley? Will she think about Colby or Superman or Warren? Who knows?

"I already feel like a new woman."

"A haircut can do that for a girl. While you're at it why don't you cut up that absolutely hideous blouse you're wearing. I think it was designed for a fifty-year-old woman, not a twenty-five-year-old."

"I like this blouse." I look down at the little pink flowers on it, finding nothing wrong with it.

"You just said you want to be a new woman. Are you lying to me?"

I glare at my best friend, reach for the edge of the blouse, and tug on it. Nothing happens. I tug on it again, and nothing happens. Dang, this material is strong.

"Um, Char, I think the shirt ripping thing only

works in the movies."

"Dammit, I'm trying to be extra dramatic here. If you're going to trash my clothes, I want to destroy them in style." I sigh. I grab the scissors again and run them down the front of my blouse, cringing as I destroy the thing. I have no doubt if I don't destroy it I won't throw it away and then Stephy will make fun of me the next time I wear it. What a jerkface. Maybe I'll cut up one of her shirts for payback.

"Mmm, at least you have a sexy bra on," Stephy says.

"It *is* sexy. I've grown fond of lacy underthings since I've been having sex. Red lace seems to be a favorite for all of the men."

This makes Stephy laugh hard. "This is good to know. It means we need to go shopping. I have the credit card in hand and I'm ready for vacation clothes."

"You're *always* ready to shop. You don't need a vacation as an excuse." I'm standing in front of her with my hair a mess, my shirt cut open, a pair of scissors in one hand, and a margarita in the other. It's just a typical Friday night.

"That's true. I'm always up for shopping. But this time is different. This time we're heading somewhere super-hot and amazing where we're looking for sexy men for wild flings. When we come back from vacation we're going to swear to not revert back to the women we've been. We're in our twenties, not our eighties. We have to start having a real life, enjoying the small and big things, and acting our ages. If we don't we're going to be living together forever with a hundred cats and having the neighborhood kids sneak by to see the crazy cat ladies who yell at them to get off of their front porch."

I laugh at the image of us old and grey, yelling at kids. "That actually sounds like a pretty great life to me."

Stephy shudders. "No way! I refuse to go down like that. We're young, beautiful, talented, smart women and we have the world at our fingertips. There's absolutely zero reason we can't have fun if we do it together."

"You're so right. I'm done pouting, done wallowing in self-pity. I'm going to live from this moment on. I'm not going to have any regrets, and I'm not going to think about what could have been or what I might want to change. I'm going to hold my head high. I'm not going to fight you when you want to go some-where. My life is officially in your hands."

I almost regret the words as soon as they come out when I see the evil glint in Stephy's eyes. This is a woman a person might not want to give unlimited power to. I might've just sealed my own fate. At least she's coming with me again so it can't be all that bad . . . right?

When Stephy grabs her computer, laughs as she looks up at me, and winks, I take another drink. I have to convince myself this is what I want. I might be in real trouble now. That's really saying something, considering what I've already done over the past few years. I've had a wedding in a cemetery, in Las Vegas, at a courthouse, and of course, with my friends and family. What's next, under the water?

No! No more marriages. Just lots and lots of fun with seriously sexy men who will wipe out any thoughts of any of my past husbands. That sends me into a fit of giggles.

"Oh, yes, keep laughing, because our new adventure is officially beginning . . ."

EPILOGUE

CASH AND I are walking into the DA's office. I'm not worried. I should be worried as Cash is stiff beside me. When he came to me this evening he told me he wasn't sure what the DA wanted to talk about.

"Maybe he's dismissing the charges," I tell Cash as he waits outside a door. Cash looks at me with a brow raised. "Yeah, I don't think that's happening either. He hates me and there's no way he's willing to settle for a plea deal."

"Would you settle for a plea?" he asks, seeming shocked.

"Of course not, but it would be nice to have one offered. A girl likes to receive offers."

Cash finally smiles, which is great to see as he hasn't cracked one all day. It's been three days since Colby testified and we haven't been back to court since. Mr. Hart asked for a stay, saying some new evidence has come to light and he's reviewing it. Cash hasn't liked this one little bit. I'm still not worried about it. Poor Cash. This trial might age the man twenty years. I hope not as Stephy plans on marrying him, and I really want to be a bridesmaid for once in my life.

"Mr. Abernathy. Ms. Diamond, Mr. Hart will see

you now," a stern older woman says from her desk, not even bothering to rise.

"Thank you," Cash says as he stands and holds out a hand to help me up. I take it, then let go and walk with him to Mr. Hart's door. It's more than obvious it's his door since his name is up in big, bold letters. The man wants to make sure everyone knows who he is. If I were a DA, I'm not so sure I'd like to have my name splashed like that. He puts away a lot of criminals who might want revenge. He's making it easy for them to find him.

Cash taps on his door, and Mr. Hart calls for us to come inside. We move through the doorway into a very spacious office with a huge mahogany desk and leather chairs. Mr. Hart is sitting behind the desk in a large chair that looks more like a throne. He seems professional and excited at the same time.

"Nice office," I tell him.

My words seem to throw him for a moment, but he recovers quickly. I don't tell him that the office at Stephy's and my house is twice as big. There's no need to get this meeting started off on the wrong foot.

"Thank you for coming down. I wanted to do this here instead of meeting at the courthouse," Mr. Hart says.

"Because you feel more in control here," Cash says. It's not a question, just a simple statement.

Mr. Hart doesn't even try to deny it. "There is something to be said about a nice office."

"Some might like to think of it as intimidation. I've

seen better." I have to fight my laughter at Cash's words. Mr. Hart's eyes narrow for only the briefest of moments before he gathers himself together.

Cash's devil-may-care attitude has shaken many opponents in his career, but the other attorneys have quickly realized he's brilliant and knows how to win cases. They might underestimate him in the beginning, but they soon find out that's a huge mistake. They don't do it again. Mr. Hart certainly doesn't.

"I've brought you here to present this," Mr. Hart says. He passes a folder to Cash and me. I don't bother picking it up. Cash grabs the folder and opens it. I see his shoulders tense all over. I'm still not worried. I have a feeling what's about to come.

"Is this a joke?" Cash finally asks with no emotion in his tone.

"I assure you breaking the law is no laughing matter," Mr. Hart says.

"You're adding more charges?"

"Yes, you are good, Ms. Diamond, very, *very* good. Whoever you have doing your dirty work is a talented professional. We will get them, I assure you, even if it takes time. Everyone messes up eventually. But you, my dear, will not get away with this. You've already admitted to multiple counts of breaking the law."

I still don't say anything.

Cash reads off the new charges. "Identity theft, illegal international travel, lying under oath, false documents." I tune him out as he continues. There are a total of twenty new charges against me. Are some of the charges even real? I guess they have to be if he's listed them. As an attorney I'd think he'd have to know what is technically the law and not the law.

"You are going down, Ms. Diamond. I'm going to make damn sure of it. You might have these men fooled, and you might even have the jury on your side, but you've broken the law. They might like you, but they will still be forced to convict you." Mr. Hart slams his hand down on the desk. I'm sure this has been an effective intimidation tactic for him in the past.

Cash is about to speak but I lay my hand on his arm and smile at him. I'm still not worried. Cash looks confused. I can see *he* is worried. He doesn't understand how good Stephy is at covering our tracks. I can confess to murder and they wouldn't be able to convict me because there'd be no evidence.

"I'd better hurry and finish my story then, Mr. Hart," I say after a solid minute of silence.

I see steam come from the man's ears. He quickly covers up his agitation and I see the cold steel in his eyes as he gives me a dead stare. He thinks he has me, or he wants me to think he has me. I look back at him. I'm not blinking because I'm really not worried.

"Yes, Ms. Diamond, you'd better hurry and finish. You don't have a lot of time left. I've made this personal. It's you against me. And I don't lose."

I chuckle now. "You shouldn't let it get personal, Mr. Hart. I don't, and I'm sharing my entire life. But, I don't mind going up against you. I'm ready. Let the best man win."

With that I stand. Cash stands next to me, looking far more confident than when we walked into the room. He has faith in me, which is smart for him. It's why he's my attorney. The new charges will be read off in court tomorrow. I think this was planned all along. We could fight it, we could even ask for a whole new trial. I'm not worried though. I want to continue just as we are.

Cash is on his computer the entire ride back to the hotel. He's in attorney mode. He barely tells me goodbye as he rushes to his room. I make my way out to the pool. The sun is just starting to set. Mr. Hart made the meeting late. Maybe he wanted to fluster me for the night before court tomorrow.

He didn't do that. I'm sure I flustered him though.

I feel *him* before I hear him. I don't move. I don't turn. My heart does pick up speed. I can stop this whole trial and get on with my life. I won't do that. I'm going to finish it all. I'm going to become whole. Am I worthy of *him*?

"Let's end this trial," he says. He comes up behind me and I let him hold me. It feels good.

"I'm not ready," I say. "I'm going to win. I can't accept anything less."

He sighs, his hot breath in my ear. "Yes, you will. I'm going to win as well."

I laugh. "What are you going to win?"

He nuzzles my neck, sending shivers down my spine. "You. I'm going to win you."

It would be so easy to turn, so easy to fall against

him and forget everything else. I'm not ready yet. It wouldn't be fair to me or to him at this time. Instead, I pull away. I take a few steps before turning and looking up into his beautiful eyes. I smile.

"You just might."

I don't say anything more. I walk away. Walking away is something I'm very good at. Maybe, though, just maybe, I might walk right back into his arms.

PART TWO

Serpentine

Note from Author Melody Anne

This story ripped me up a lot. I cried as I wrote one of the last scenes. I sometimes wonder how this stuff comes to my head and how I write it. But this whole series is so emotional, and it needs to happen. It's a journey that many of us go on. Maybe not too many get married so many times, but we have real trauma, we cry, we get angry, we get scared. I love Charlie and her journey. I love her relationship with her best friend, which is pretty much exactly the relationship I have with mine. I'd die for her. We have ups and downs in life, but most of us focus on the ups. The downs can wipe us out in an instant though.

A side note, Charlie visits Florence Oregon in this book. This is the town I was born in, the town I graduated high school from. This is the town I fled as fast as possible when I was eighteen. It's now, once again, the town I call home. I thought I'd never come back, but then I got married, and I still have family here. I love Florence.

Heceta Head is a very special place for me. It's the place my dad and I went every year. I have so many memories there. It's the place I spread my dad's ashes. I go there every year on his birthday, and sometimes in between. I feel him there. I sometimes cry, and I sometimes laugh. It's our place. I still miss my dad all of the time. I miss my mom, too. We can be surrounded with love and still ache for those we've lost. We can also have happiness guilt free.

Thank you for the love and support in this series. It's soul wrenching. I appreciate and love you. On a side note, my husband loves reading the reviews. His favorite is the one that says the *evil* Melody Anne. He looked at me and asked, "How do they know?" Of course, I cracked up. He's getting a lot of joy in that one. I have told him to be scared of me sometimes with the twisted things that pop into my head. He's still sticking around though, which I'm eternally grateful for. I get lost in my worlds as I write, and I forget to appreciate him as much as I should. He's my rock.

I love you all. I appreciate you all. Now, I'm off to dive back into the crazy life of Charlie . . .

With much love,
Melody Anne

PROLOGUE

HERE I GO again on my own. Walking down a lonely road I've never known. Like a drifter I was born to walk alone.

I seem to always have a song stuck in my head. Now, I don't know why I have *this* particular song stuck since I'm very rarely alone. However, I do cherish some precious moments of seclusion. I'm certainly not alone right now. I'm sitting with Cash waiting for the circus to begin. I'm always waiting on the circus. Now, this makes me want some peanuts and maybe a caramel apple.

You can always stop the show.

I push that voice straight out of my head. I don't want to stop the show. I *can't* stop it. I'm nearly halfway through. If I quit during the intermission, I'll never have closure. I need to close each chapter of my life in the order they occurred. If I don't, I might forever be lost.

"All rise . . ."

I obediently stand. The court is going to get a shock today. I'm prepared for it. I'm still not worried. I don't seem to worry much these days. I might have moments where I want to have a meltdown, but I don't allow myself to obsess over it.

"Good afternoon," Judge Croesus says. He then looks over at Mr. Hart. "Are you sure about this?"

Mr. Hart stands. "Yes, Your Honor."

Judge Croesus stares down at the papers in front of him for several moments as if contemplating whether he wants to proceed or not. Finally, he nods. Then he looks back out at the room and gets a look of resignation on his face.

"Proceed."

Mr. Hart stands, looking far too smug. "Prosecutors generally don't like to alter the initial charges in a court case unless we have strong reasons to believe the police, or the court, got the initial charges wrong. I'm saying this because we are adding to the charges for Ms. Diamond's case."

He pauses as he looks at the jury to see if they are paying attention. They certainly are as they sit up a little straighter in their chairs. They never know what comes next with my case. I know. I know too much.

"New information sometimes surfaces while a case is progressing that either hurts or helps the defendant. A prosecutor is supposed to take all of this information into account when deciding which charges will ultimately be brought against a defendant at trial. In addition to newly discovered evidence, other situations in which a defendant's charges may be enhanced or reduced include a legal error, perjury, fraud, or other extraordinary reasons. Limited resources are often a reason a defendant isn't brought up on too many charges. It takes time and money to investigate a case and present the evidence. We feel strongly that we have enough evidence in this case to bring more charges to Ms. Diamond," he says with flourish.

He then reads the new charges. I don't even blink. Identity Theft. Illegal International Crossing. Lying Under Oath. False Documentation . . . I tune out as he continues. The jury is paying rapt attention.

"We'll be okay," Cash says.

"I know."

I wonder, though, if I will be okay. I'm not sure. I might end up in prison. How do I feel about this? I'm really not sure. I don't think I've ever truly considered it. I guess all I can do at this point is continue on with my story. At the end of the day, what will be will be.

The prosecutor stops speaking and the room erupts as reporters snap pictures and type on their phones as quickly as they can. They all want to be the first to break the story. Hmm, maybe I want to be a journalist in my next adventure . . . *if* I get a next adventure. That's something I haven't gotten to do yet. It might be fun. I've done some writing, and I like it. I think I'm pretty okay at it.

I turn and look behind me at the audience. Phones continue to click as they snap my picture. There are no flashes allowed in the courtroom so the only way I know pictures are being taken is the clicking of the phones facing me. I try to give them my best side. There's nothing else I can do at this moment.

Something catches my eye and I look at *him*. I

smile. He winks. Will he be here until the end? Will he be here after it all ends? Do I want him to be? Can I actually find my happily ever after? I guess I'll just have to wait and find out along with the rest of the people watching. It might be a story worth hearing.

CHAPTER ONE

I WONDER IF a person can crack their cheeks open if they smile too big. If that's the case then I'm in trouble because I can't quit grinning. Here I am walking into a fabulous resort on a Caribbean Island with my best friend beside me. The only sounds are our shoes clicking and the wheels on our bags turning as we draw closer to the check-in counter. I thought I was done going places—I was wrong.

I wish I could take credit for this trip, but once again, Stephy has made the magic happen, and has organized the entire trip. Right now, I have no job, no plans, and no timeline. We are here for a true vacation without a need for marriage and a life remake. I'm okay with this. Actually, I'm *more* than okay with this.

I'm a brand-new woman right now and I'm not going back to the old me. I like this persona. I like *this* woman I am right now. I'm smiling, and that's all it takes to please me these days. I've had too much pain, a lot of it self-inflicted, but I've had enough to last a lifetime. Now, I'm going to be free and I'm going to live as if there's no tomorrow. Whatever happens will happen and I'm going to let it without a fight.

The temperature back in Oregon is freezing, like

low thirties freezing, with wind and snow. Here in the Caribbean, it's warm and sunny without being stifling. I'm going to wear a bikini, not the one that Stephy would like me to wear, but a very sexy, fun, flirty bikini that makes me feel as if I have mile-long legs and a toned stomach. I'm going to refuse to look at my hips. If I do I get a bit too self-conscious, and this trip is for me to be free, not to focus on everything I find wrong with myself.

My heart pounds as we move through people. By now I'd think I wouldn't care what anyone thinks of me. Sadly, I still do. I have to remind myself I'm in a new place with a new name, and no one but my best friend even knows who in the heck I am. I can be anyone I want to be. If I want to be a mousy girl from Prairie Town, then that's who I'm going to be. If I want to be a vixen blonde from anywhere and every-where in the world by the name of Charlie Serpentine, which is a pretty dang cool name, then that's who I get to be. I can act however I want.

Haven't I learned in the last several years that I am whoever I invent—well, whoever Stephy invents, to be honest? Nothing so far has come back and kicked me in the butt. I've lived a lot, have had some incredible adventures, and now I'm in the Caribbean with no responsibilities in front of me. I'm going to take life by the horns and love every second of it. That's the beauty of this situation.

Maybe when I'm back home I'll lose a bit of the vixen I want to be now, but right here I'm Charlie

Serpentine and I dang well need to act like it. I'm a drop-dead, sexy, sassy blonde bombshell. If I can convince myself of this, I'm going to have a blast.

"I should get some major props. This place is phenomenal," Stephy says as she moves with grace and confidence. She always knows exactly who she is. I'd think that would be rubbing off on me by now. I am getting closer. I can give myself props for that.

"You chose well as always," I tell her.

"We've once again lucked out. Some of these resorts list all of these amazing features and activities such as a spa tub and lounges at the poolside, but when you arrive, you find yourself in the middle of the city with a kiddie pool with a hose in it imitating jets and the smell of garbage drifting over you."

I laugh. "I don't think that will ever happen with you, Stephy. You're far too smart to fall for a scam."

"That's right. We're going to love it here and only allow positive vibes to shine through. No thinking of ex-husbands or responsibilities. This is vacation to the extreme," Stephy reminds me.

"I agree. No worries, no timeclock, and no looking back."

Stephy stops and gazes at me. "This new change in attitude is throwing me for a bit of a loop," she says. "I like it a lot more than you fighting me every step of the way."

"We are in our mid-twenties and I realize I have to quit being so dang serious all of the time. I need to embrace my wild child that's been buried for so long."

"I think the past five years have been great for you. The men have come and gone, and I have to admit I'll miss a few of them, but I'm glad you've been living. I love how much you are shining. I love that we're both evolving."

"The guys have really been good for me. I hate to admit it because I know that might motivate you to try and find more partners for me, but I've realized through these journeys how much I love life. I'll always miss Bentley and I'll probably continue to talk to him, but I've now seen how much there is to live for. It was hard leaving Colby, harder than I could've ever imagined, but I knew it had to happen. There's a part of me that still wants to run back to him."

"What if he's the one? What if you're supposed to be with him?"

I think about her words for a few seconds. "I don't feel the pull in my heart. It's more of a pull to the familiarity of our lives. It mirrored my life in Oregon. I think it's the pull to Bentley more than a pull to Colby."

"I don't know. Maybe it's just your conscious trying to convince you of that," she points out.

"Maybe. I could always send him some bikini pics and see if he'll come join us," I tell her with a wink.

She gapes at me before laughing. "Doll, if you send those pics, I think we're going to see them going viral all over the internet. I'm all for it." She holds up her camera as if to take a pic while she wears an evil smile.

"Um, yeah, no. That's never going to happen. I

don't even know why I'm having that thought. I haven't spoken to him since I left. I need to leave the past in the past."

I'm irritated that I'm thinking about Colby right now. It's been six months since we've been together. If we were supposed to be more to each other than we are, then one of us would've called. It hasn't happened. I wish I could figure out how I'm feeling about this. I'm still confused.

"Maybe it's just the sex," Stephy tells me. A woman passes us just as she says this and she stops with a big grin on her polished lips.

"I have no idea what your conversation is all about, but if you're having great sex, don't run from it. I've come here to have my world rocked and to find someone adventurous in the bedroom. Sex has been far too boring lately. If it wasn't for my vibrator, I wouldn't have a damn clue what an orgasm is." She doesn't give us time to respond to her before she walks on by.

Stephy and I stare at her for a few seconds and then we burst out laughing.

"Now, I *know* I'm going to love this place. It's a retreat for sexual healing," Stephy says.

"Oh my gosh, I can't believe that just happened," I tell her. "I can't imagine saying something like that to a stranger."

"Charlie Serpentine will talk like that with no problem. There's nothing wrong with being a sexual woman who knows what she wants and most certainly goes after it."

"Some might call a woman who does that a whore," I tell her.

She rolls her eyes. "Those are stupid people who judge because they aren't getting enough joy in life. Sex is essential to our survival. We might as well like it and demand from our partner what makes us feel the best."

"What if we don't know what feels good?" I ask.

"I don't know," Stephy says with a shrug. "I've been sexually frustrated for so long I might rip a man apart when I find one that turns me on. I just know if someone makes me scream I'm not letting him get away."

"What if he's all dick and no brains?" I ask.

She laughs hard. "As long as he keeps me satisfied in bed, I don't need a conversation."

"Well, this looks like the kind of place you can find that pretty easily." We look around and there are men everywhere. I feel nerves slither down my spine at the thought of approaching one of them and flirting. Yes, I've been married . . . um . . . five times now, but in my defense, I haven't actually approached a man and flirted. It's all just sort of happened.

"Yeah, I hate it when I slip and land on a big fat—"

"Stephy," I gasp before she can finish her sentence as I look around again. She laughs evilly.

"You really are a catch and so beautiful it should be a sin." I roll my eyes.

Stephy tells me all of the time how beautiful I am. Bentley would say the same to me, and of course, the men I've married in the past few years have told me I'm gorgeous and a myriad of other compliments, but I don't see that same woman when I look in the mirror. I think beauty really is in the eye of the beholder.

My hair is platinum in color right now, which is really throwing me off. I have curves, which a lot of the stick thin women walking around in barely any clothes don't have. I'm not sure if the majority of men want thin or curves. I shouldn't care. I know how to highlight my best features with certain clothes, but in a place like this I won't be wearing a lot of fabric. My boobs are a size too big, and my hips very noticeable. I know Nicoli loved my hips. I don't. But, I've told myself I'm not having any negative thoughts, so I push all of these doubts from my brain right this second. No more!

Stephy and I finally move forward to the VIP check in counter. "Do you know any other counter but VIP?"

"Nope," she says, not feeling the least bad about spending money. I need to have her attitude on this as well. I don't know if that will ever happen. I won't even come close to touching the money Colby put in a bank account for me. I have had to dip into the money Bentley left me, especially when Stephy insists on taking me shopping. It's all so frivolous.

Stephy gets us checked in while I people watch. "We hope you enjoy our facilities. If you follow Rico, he'll show you to your cabin," the clerk says with a smile as she hands over our keys.

"Thank you. Have a wonderful day," Stephy says.

"Follow me," Rico says as he moves next to us. He's not bad to look at, if a little too young to be ogling. He grabs our bags as if they weigh nothing, then moves forward, expecting us to follow, which we do.

We move through the back doors of the resort and Stephy and I are both beaming in excitement. The skies are clear and as blue as can be and the air is warm without being humid. We move through a maze of pools that are surrounded with trees and cabanas giving nice little shady areas. There are caves and waterfalls in the pools. Could I be a vixen enough to sneak beneath a waterfall and make out with a stranger? Would I want to do that? Charlie Diamond certainly wouldn't do it, but Charlie Serpentine might.

It sort of turns my stomach to think about it. The kind of guy who'd want to take me beneath a waterfall probably takes a new woman there every day to the exact same place. How many lips would he kiss in a day? Gross. Okay, maybe I don't want to be a vixen. Maybe I just want to appear that way with zero follow through.

Stephy is chatting with Rico as I look around at the seemingly endless grounds of our resort. People are laughing, drinking, and they all seem to be in a great mood. Of course, in paradise it's hard to be in anything other than an incredible mood. If you're grumpy in a place like this then nothing in life is going to make you happy.

A kid launches himself off of a high board, laughing before he splashes into the water. I keep moving forward with my head turned when I slam into the back of Rico who has stopped without me knowing. I wobble on my heels, nearly falling straight on my klutzy butt. I somehow manage to stay on my feet, but just barely.

"Sorry," I mumble.

"No problem," he says with a smile.

"Rico, tennis at two," a male voice calls.

"You got it," Rico replies.

That voice speaking to Rico nearly makes me stumble again. It's deep, and low and sends a few little tingles to my stomach. Maybe this vixen image I'm trying to portray myself as is messing with my brain. I look to the ground afraid to make eye contact with whoever is speaking to our guide.

Just as I decide my shoes are the most fascinating things I've ever seen, I remember I'm not going to be this shy girl from Oregon anymore. I raise my head and look forward. My gaze connects with the man who has to be the one speaking. Holy hell!

My imagination just isn't good enough. The face I was picturing with that voice is even better It's a damn work of art. He's not the type I normally find attractive, as I tend to like cowboys and nerds, but he's absolutely breathtaking. I'm surprised I'm reacting to him on such a visceral level. The man is delicious as he leans against a banister on the deck of a cottage. I hadn't realized we've already reached the cabins that line a huge dock going out into the water.

"Well, hello there," Stephy says. Of course, Stephy

can talk to the man. I find my voice gone. The man nods at Stephy before his eyes come back to me. I rip my gaze away from his probing gaze, but then I'm forced to look at the rest of him. I suppose I can stare at the water, but that's not what I do. Nope. That would be safe and wise. Apparently I don't do safe anymore.

The man has shoulders that look as if they can fill an entire door frame. His shirtless chest is tanned and compliments his deep brown eyes and unruly dark hair. The only clothing on his muscled figure is a pair of surfer shorts that are hanging low on his hips and end just above his knees. Even the man's feet are bare, and sexy as hell. I've never thought of feet as sexy or unsexy, but on this man, every single inch of him is made to perfection. I need to run far and fast from him. I can see that right away. To hell with being a vixen. I want no part of it.

My brain tries to tell me I need to flirt, but I tell that part of my ego to shut the hell up. I've had enough men to last a lifetime. I'm done. My vixen attitude came and went in the blink of an eye. I'm just glad Stephy isn't hearing my internal fight.

"Hello," the man says. It takes me a second to remember Stephy has greeted him. He has to be thinking I'm a deaf mute or something since I'm just gaping at him like a fish out of water. I wouldn't mind diving into the water right now to cool off my suddenly *very* heated body.

Even if I've told myself I want to have a vacation fling, something inside of me is saying this man is danger on a code red alert. My reaction to him is too strong, too powerful, and too scary. If I can't even look at the man without getting burned, I certainly can't talk to him or touch him. I might go up in flames.

"Do you ladies need help?" the man asks when neither of us say anything after his greeting.

"Mmm, you can help us anytime," Stephy tells the man with a wink, not seeming at all affected by him. I know this voice of hers. It's flirty but unaffected. It's how she speaks to all men. I have a feeling if there's a man that really rocks her world, it just might take her voice away. I know that's happening to me a lot these days.

The man laughs as he grips the railing of his cottage and leaps over it, landing right in front of us on the pier. The dock shakes the slightest bit and I think again of diving into the water. It seems like a safer option than standing in front of this man. Stephy seems to like the guy, she can have at him. I'm bowing out right now and stepping from the ring.

"How about you? Do you need help?" the man asks as he steps directly in front of me, only about two feet separating us. I can now smell him, and it's not a disappointment. Heat waves are practically radiating off of his fine shoulders.

"I'm good," I tell him, despising the slight squeak to my voice. "Go ahead and give Steph a hand." I'm the only one who calls her Stephy. The rest of the world refers to her as Steph. She hates when I introduce her as my name for her, not because she doesn't like the name, but because that's ours.

"Hi, Steph," he says, giving her only a brief glance before he looks at me again. "Evan Praise. And you?"

"Praise?" I say, unable to hide my amusement.

"Yes. Does that amuse you?"

I quickly cover my mouth as I find a giggle trying to bust free. I don't know why I'm finding his name so funny. It's horrifyingly rude. I glance at Stephy who's looking at me in confusion. I turn back to Evan.

"I'm so sorry. I don't know what's wrong with me," I tell him between fits of laughter. "It has to be jet lag."

Evan doesn't seem at all offended, but the more I giggle the more irritated I get with myself. What is wrong with me? Why am I acting so inappropriate with this man? First, I find him ridiculously gorgeous and then I laugh in his face. It's like I've never been around an attractive man before. I need to pull it together. I take a step back from him as I try to think of orphaned puppies and tornadoes.

"I've got to go," I finally say. The giggles are down, but the smile isn't. I step around Evan, leaving both Stephy, our guide, and the man who looks confused, behind. I'm not quite sure where I'm going, but I need to move forward. Maybe I'll just reach the end of the pier and jump into the water. I could use a cooling off.

I don't make it far before Evan calls to me. "Charlie." Stephy must've given him my name. Traitor. I'm not surprised. She'll always give in to a sexy man.

I try to pick up my pace. I don't care where I'm going. I just need to escape. My heels are my downfall.

This place is set up for a person to either be barefoot or wear flat sandals. It's not meant for heels. Who in their right mind wears heels to travel all day? I'm an idiot with sore feet, jet lag, and a crazy brain.

My heel catches between the planks and I start to go down. It feels as if it's happening in slow motion. My humiliation of an arrival with a bang is about to be complete. My arms wave in the air as a yell tumbles from my throat. This is going to hurt.

I slam into something hard—really hard. It isn't the pier, though, that catches me. Nope, it's solid arms that are wrapped around my body. I'm thinking the planks below me would be more cushioned than the chest I'm pressed back against. My body is trembling from the adrenaline of the moment and I seem to have forgotten how to breathe. I gasp in a breath of air and damn does it smell good.

"Are you okay?" Evan turns me, but he doesn't let me go. Now, it's not my back pressed against him, but my front. I don't even think to question the fact he's turned me instead of letting me go. Maybe he knows my legs are utter Jello right now and if he let's go I'm going to land on my butt. I can feel his fingers clasped behind my back and my lips are placed right at his neck. I have the urge to swipe my tongue out and have a taste.

Horror at my thoughts stops them faster than a cold shower.

I jerk my head back and make eye contact with this stranger. He's gazing down at me, heat smoldering in his gaze. I feel answering flames igniting in my stomach. That's it, it's official, I'm a total horn dog. I can't seem to be around men anymore without lusting after them. Me! This is *me* having these thoughts. I have always been the bookworm, and now I'm an utter hussy.

"Hmm, seems I've caught you," Evan says in a deep, smooth voice that rolls through my entire body.

I find myself unable to speak as I stupidly stare at this beautiful man who's gazing at me as if he's about to cart me off to his cabin. I wish the thought of that was unpleasant—it isn't.

"Thank you," I finally manage to whisper as I scream at myself to let this man go. He's holding onto me, but I'm not doing anything to pull away. I'm sure I'm sending very mixed signals right now.

"Dang, looks like he's taken," I hear Stephy say. She has to be talking to Rico. Her words effectively pull me from my trance.

"Yep, there's some heat there for sure," Rico replies with a laugh. "I might lose my tennis partner."

"They might be right," Evan says, not tearing his gaze away as he gives me a sexy smile.

Finally, I realize what I'm doing. I tug on him. "I'm fine now. You can let go," I say, my voice far too shaky for my liking.

"Maybe I like you right here," he says, his arms squeezing the tiniest bit more. There's already no space between us. I suddenly realize his lower half is pressing into me. He seems pretty happy to be exactly how we are. Oh my gosh, this is getting messy real fast.

"Let go," I say with more panic than sternness.

He immediately loosens his arms. He looked as if he was about to kiss me until I spoke those two words. I'm shaky as I step back, not sure if my legs are going to keep me standing. I'm shaky and my head feels fuzzy. I might even be worried I've been roofied if I'd had anything to drink in the last hour. Can lust drug a person? Maybe.

Evan smiles at me as he takes another step away. "I look forward to our next encounter, Charlie," he tells me. There's no doubt the words are a promise of what's to come. He's not at all detoured by my rejection. I should be irritated about this—I'm not.

"It's a big place," I say. "I'm sure we can avoid each other." I turn from him and look pointedly at Rico who's grinning.

"This way," Rico says, laughter in his voice. He starts walking again.

"Well, that was a hot way to start vacation. I have to get me one of those," Stephy says as she wraps her arm in mine as we move two cottages down the pier. We're far too close to Evan's cottage. This is bad, this is so bad.

"He's all yours," I tell Stephy.

"Oh, Char, I'd have him in a heartbeat, but that boy is taken. He couldn't keep his eyes off of you."

"He wants an easy girl. I'm already over him. Let's put our things away and then have some fun. I want swimming and margaritas."

"Okay, but I think this vacation is going to be a lot more fun than I originally thought. That boy is hot and I have a feeling we'll be seeing him again really soon. He couldn't take his eyes off of you."

"Men," I say with a growl. Why in the world do we need them so much?

I roll my eyes then go to my room and quickly unpack. It's easy as all I have are swimsuits and flirty little dresses. It's perfectly warm out and we aren't doing much more than lounging at the resort. A lot of clothes aren't necessary.

When we walk from the cottage Evan is nowhere to be found which relieves me . . . I think . . . I hope! Stephy and I settle in by the pool and order drinks. I sit back and people watch, one of my absolute favorite activities.

It's all going to be okay. He's just one man who doesn't mean a thing to me. I'm almost convinced I believe myself. I want to be a vixen who doesn't notice men. Is that a possibility. With my reaction to Evan, I'm thinking the chances are slim to none. I smile as I sip my drink. Well, I want an adventure . . . I might just get one.

CHAPTER TWO

THREE DAYS PASS without a sight of Evan Praise. I'm relieved, or at least that's what I'm telling myself. All of my talk of being a siren has flown right out the window. I've tried flirting with a few men. I'm truly horrible at it. Stephy is amazing. She can make men drop to their knees with her sexy smile and sparkling eyes. I find myself uninterested in talking to anyone and try more for show than anything else. It's obvious to the men I'm talking to. They figure out quickly no fling is going to happen, and they move on.

This vacation isn't what I've been expecting, but it's good, really, *really* good. I need to get men off of the brain and focus on me and what's coming next in my life. Isn't that the question we all ask ourselves? Who am I? Where am I going? What are my plans for the future? What makes me happy? What don't I like? I think if we aren't asking these questions of ourselves then we aren't growing.

"Can I buy you a drink?" I don't even bother looking up from my book until there's an elbow in my side.

"Ouch!" I put my book down and glare at Stephy.

"Someone is talking to you," she says as she nods her head to my other side.

I turn and see a decent looking man grinning down at me. I feel . . . nothing.

"No thanks. I have one." I turn away from him and glare at Stephy again. "I didn't know he was talking to me. My book is good," I tell her.

"Ugh, you are hopeless, absolutely hopeless. You look like a wet dream come to life in your sexy red bikini, and men are falling all over you, but you're too stubborn or blind to even notice them." She pauses and a wicked light comes to her eyes. "Or is it, that you're actually just waiting for one particular man to show up again?"

There's no way I'm telling her that none of the men compare next to Evan. I've only been around the man for about five minutes and that's all it took to make all of the others in the resort pale in comparison. It's not just Evan though, it's . . . Colby. He's still on my mind. How can I think of Colby, and still desire Evan? I think I seriously have something wrong with me.

"I think I'm just not feeling too great today. It has to be one too many margaritas last night," I say. I wonder if she'll allow me to get away with this.

"We haven't stopped drinking since we've got here," she says. I see suspicion in her eyes.

"Yeah, they taste too good."

She stands. "I'm going for a swim. Why don't you lie back, drink some water, and give yourself a pep talk. I want to dance tonight."

I grin. I feel fine. I just don't want to talk about men. She tends to swim for a long time, so I'll come up with a good story to get me out of dancing. It's not that I don't like to do it, it's just that I get sick of the constant grind of men looking for a one-night stand. I was telling myself that's great and it's what I want. I should know myself better than that by now.

Stephy disappears and I finish my drink while I go back to my book, *Searching for Someday* by Jennifer Probst. In my defense, the book is dang great. This author can write. Before I know it I've consumed two more drinks in about thirty minutes and I'm feeling pretty damn great. Stephy still isn't back but I'm not caring all that much. I'm sure she's gotten distracted by some tall, dark and handsome man. She's always been a tease, but I'm wondering if this might just be the place she finds a man interesting enough to spend more than an hour with him.

A pair of legs come into my peripheral vision and I feel a tingle shoot down my spine. I don't even need to look up to know who's standing in front of me—Evan Praise. My entire body comes to full attention as little tingles ripple through me. I haven't seen him in three days and yet I haven't even looked up yet and I feel the connection between us. How in the hell is this possible?

My drink is halfway to my mouth, and I refuse to make eye contact with him. He hasn't moved or said a word. I stop being irritated at my reaction and become fascinated by it. I only spoke to this man for about five minutes and very few words were actually spoken. How is it that I'm so attracted to him?

The lounge next to mine pushes right up to my

chair and then he sits, his leg brushing against mine, sending a shiver all the way through me. Damn, I'm attracted to this man—a deep, core tingling, breast throbbing, bone chilling attracted. I close my eyes and take in a few breaths, only allowing myself to enjoy the sensations for a couple of seconds before I demand my mind and body to reign myself in.

"Hello, beautiful," he finally says. "You look scrumptious." His voice is a low purr that slides over my skin. I feel the rest of the people surrounding us all disappear. Is this what it's like to be in a bubble?

I look up at him and decide in about two seconds how to respond to this man. I can be a prude and fight what I'm feeling, or I can test my vixen ways. I let my gaze trace down his body.

"You don't look so bad yourself, Evan." His mouth almost drops open as if he isn't expecting this reaction from me. Good. I like to surprise people. I seem to surprise myself a ton.

"How is your day going?"

I lick my lips and feel quite satisfied at the spark in his eyes. "Very good . . . now."

His lips turn up in the sexiest smile I've ever witnessed. Dang, I want this man. I came on this vacation determined to be somebody new. If I don't even try it I think I'll have regrets. I'm very aware I'm changing my mind faster than a wildfire spreads. I don't care. I'm going to practice my flirting right now. I ignore the nervous sweat breaking out on the back of my neck.

"I certainly like hearing that," he tells me.

A waiter appears and hands him a drink. It gives me another few seconds to study the man who's wearing a shirt this time with khaki shorts. He looks equally delicious clothed or naked. The shirt does nothing to hide his muscles. I know exactly how those arms feel beneath my fingers.

Sex is on my brain which horrifies me. I push that though away. I'm not cheating I try to convince myself. I haven't ever cheated; I amplify in my brain. I have been with a few men, but it's over when I leave. Knowing this doesn't eliminate the guilt as Colby's smile flashes in my brain. I'm fighting myself until a lightbulb goes off above me.

I can be attracted to this man; I can even have fantasies about him. I can laugh, and flirt, and admire him. I don't have to marry him, and I don't have to sleep with him. I can simply enjoy the normal things any other woman does while on a vacation. It doesn't have to be an either, or, situation.

One thing that I know for sure is that I *really* love the anticipation of the unknown. I don't know what's going to happen in an hour, in a day, or in a week. I don't know what's going to happen in the future. All I know right now is I'm sitting here with an attractive man, and I like how he makes me feel. I can be okay with this.

My nerves relax as Evan turns back to me, his smile absolutely beautiful. He's not having this same internal struggle I'm having. That's more than obvious. He most likely has a new fling wherever he goes without ever looking back. He seems like that kind of man to me. It's okay. The world needs a variety of people to make it an interesting place to live in.

"I had to leave the island for a few days. I couldn't wait to return to see you," he tells me when the waiter leaves.

"Do you live here?"

He shakes his head. "No, but I come back often enough that I feel like a local. It's my favorite little slice of paradise."

"How nice to live close enough to come anytime you want. I think I want to find a paradise of my own, but maybe one that's not so far to travel to," I say.

"The traveling is all a part of the journey," he says. "I enjoy my off time from the moment it starts to the second it ends."

"What called you away?"

He tenses for only a second, but relaxes so fast I wonder if I imagining it. This man is most certainly a player. I don't care. He can play all he wants. Right now, he's here for my ego and to teach me how to flirt . . . even if he doesn't realize that's what he's doing. There's only one exception to this for me . . .

"Are you married, Evan?"

He laughs. "No, I'm not married."

"A lot of people don't wear rings these days," I point out. I wore rings for all of my marriages, but they came off the second I knew it was over. My finger feels empty after the last time I've taken it off. I barely keep myself from rubbing my thumb over the spot as I've done a thousand times in the past six months.

"I never lie," Evan says. The way the words are spoken with a thread of steel in his tone tells me he's speaking the truth. This man might look laid back, but there's power inside of him. I wouldn't want to be his enemy, that's for sure.

"I bet you get your way a lot, too," I say.

He leans back and laughs. "Yes, you'd be correct." He pauses. "Will I get my way with you?" His eyes are smoldering as he says this.

"I haven't decided yet," I tell him. There's no doubt it's the alcohol loosening my tongue. Charlie Diamond would never speak to a stranger this way. Charlie Serpentine will though, I assure myself. Charlie Serpentine is a much more exciting woman.

"I want you so damn desperately you're all I've thought about for the past three days." The low growl accompanying his words go straight to my core. He looks at my nearly empty glass and there's a flare of disappointment in his eyes. "I don't take advantage of drunk women though."

I glare at him as the waitress comes up and places a fresh drink beside me while picking up my old glass. Okay, I *am* drunk, but I'm still not stupid when I drink. If I choose to sleep with the man, it's *my* choice. I don't use alcohol as an excuse to make decisions. I'm not going to sleep with him, but if I want to change my mind that's my prerogative. Right now my brain is so wishy washy I can't even keep up with it. There's no way he can.

"I don't need a lecture or a preacher. You can go away if you're going to be judgy," I say in as haughty a voice as possible.

"You need something. I'm just not sure what that is," he says with a smirk that instantly fires my blood right on up.

"Are you always this much of an ass?" Sober me would be shocked by my words. I'm never rude to people. I assure myself he deserves it though. He did start it after all.

"Most of the time," he says, obviously not offended.

"I don't like mean guys."

"I don't need you to like me." He grins as he reaches out and runs his finger along my thigh. The fire that shoots through me tells me I apparently don't need to like him to be turned on.

"If you don't care what I think then why are you flirting with me?" I ask. Maybe it's my lack of experience in the flirting department, but this conversation seems awfully strange. Where in the heck is Stephy?

"I want to take you to my bed," he says, nearly making me spit out my drink. I shouldn't be surprised by anything Evan says. I can see he knows exactly who he is and he's not afraid to ask or demand anything he wants. I guess I'm just not used to men speaking to me this way.

How can I be attracted to someone like Evan when I was married to Bentley? They are opposite in so many ways. Evan is crass and bold where Bentley was confident and sweet. Can a person change so much in seven years? Have I changed *that* much? I think maybe I have. Maybe I'm attracted to Evan because I know there's no chance I'll fall in love with him. Maybe I'm so much more screwed up than I ever could've imagined I could be. Maybe I just don't know who in the heck I am.

"I've been propositioned before, but I have to say this is the fastest it's ever happened," I tell him, once again acknowledging that the alcohol is loosening my tongue. I might not say quite so much to this man if I was sober. Maybe I need to drink less. Nah, that's just a crazy thought.

"I find I get a lot further in life by being honest. There's no reason to lie. I wanted you from the second I laid eyes on you. When you fell into me the thought solidified. I knew it was only a matter of time."

"If I were to agree to it," I point out.

He leans his head back and laughs as if that's a crazy thought. In his mind us going to bed together is a foregone conclusion.

"Take a walk with me," he demands.

He stands and holds out his hand. I tell myself it's not going to happen, but my body has other ideas as I set down my drink and give him my hand. He helps me to my feet and I'm a little wobbly. I haven't been up for a while. He wraps an arm around me, and I feel much more secure as we begin moving. I like his arm where it is.

"Are you closing out?" the waitress asks.

"Yes," I say as I try to focus on her.

"Put it on my tab," he says. The woman nods and walks away.

"I can pay for my own drinks," I tell him. My head is spinning. This isn't good. I think I've reached beyond the happy buzzed point to the dizzy, falling down point. I don't like this. "I need water."

He moves over to the bar and grabs one, handing it over to me. Then he turns us and moves slowly away from the pool. The sun is setting and the further we move from the noise, the better I feel. I don't even have my purse on me as I left it in the cottage. I realize I've forgotten my book at the chair too. Hopefully I can get it back.

I lay my head against Evan's side as we keep moving. It oddly gives me comfort leaning on this stranger. There's no doubt he's not going to let me faceplant and make a fool of myself. I sort of am doing that anyway. I'm much too old to get this drunk. It's all about control, and I've failed on this day.

I finish my water and Evan takes the empty bottle and tosses it in a garbage can as we pass by. He then pulls a new one from his pocket and hands it over.

"You're prepared," I tell him.

"The night is young. I don't want it to end too soon," he says.

We move down a trail and see soft lights ahead. There's smooth music playing and then I see a few different couples dancing. At least two women appear to be in wedding dresses.

"Is that a wedding?" I ask. I find myself giggling. Of course, I'm seeing a wedding. Evan smiles down at me. He has no idea why this is so funny to me.

"It appears to be a few different couples," he tells me.

"Of course it is," I say, giggling even more. I finish my second bottle of water and I'm feeling much better. I'm still drunk, but the spinning has stopped. Thank goodness for hydration.

"Why is this so amusing?" There's a bar set up on the beach and we move over to it and sit. I drink another water and then order a pina colada before excusing myself to find the bathroom. When I come back I have my pina colada and more water. I think the night is going to be better than the day has been.

"I ordered food," he says as I pick up my drink.

I think for several seconds. "That's good. I don't think I've had anything to eat today."

"The drinks are great, but we need solids too," he says. He pauses for a moment. "Now, back to my earlier question, what is so amusing about weddings?"

I look out at the couples who are dancing. Right as I do, we see another couple step up to the alter and begin their vows as the sun drops below the ocean. It's perfect.

I laugh. Why not be honest? Maybe I'll scare this man away right here and now. It might be the wise thing to do with how he's frying my brain.

"I tend to meet strangers and get married," I say with a shrug. His eyes widen. I don't add more.

"How many times?"

I laugh. "Mmm, five times. No. That's not true. My first marriage was real. Four times, I guess."

Evan's eyes widen as he looks at me. I can see he's trying to decide if I'm telling him the truth or not. I can see the wheels turning. I'm waiting to see if he runs now or tries to get lucky first.

"You are most certainly the most unique woman I've ever met in my life," Evan says after a about a full minute. He then laughs. "I think we were supposed to meet."

"Why is that?"

"Because I don't laugh enough in life." He scoots closer to me. I decide I'm in a dream right now. I'm somewhere between sleep and consciousness and I like it. I like being here with this man in this moment.

I lean against him and he puts an arm around me. I like how it feels. It's both comforting and turns me on. There's something about this man that's pulling me in. I have no desire to go anywhere for the moment.

"You feel very good, Evan," I whisper, moving a little closer as I wrap an arm around him then reach beneath his shirt and feel his hot flesh against my fingertips. His skin trembles beneath my touch. I'm loving how much I'm affecting this big, strong man.

"You are very hard."

I'm not so bold as to run my hands lower, but I assume he's as hard there as he is everywhere else. I think I can stay right like this against him all night. There's nothing wrong with enjoying myself. That little niggling of guilt is trying to creep up, but I quickly push it back down again.

"You are lighting a fire you won't be able to extinguish," he warns, his voice low and sexy, and seeming on the edge of control. It makes me even bolder.

His shirt is open at the neck giving me the perfect opportunity to lean in a little closer and run my tongue along his salty flesh. He groans as his fingers run up my back and tangle in my hair, tugging hard on it. This only turns me on more. I wiggle closer to him, not caring if anyone sees us.

"Charlie," he says in a deep growl that sends fire to my core.

I'm doing this to the man. I'm making him lose control. I don't think it will take much more to send him over the edge. Can I make him come without anyone knowing? Can I bet that vixen? I sort of want to. I want to see this controlled man completely lose it.

I nip at the edge of his neck and his fingers tighten even more in my hair as he pulls me closer. The only reason I'm not in his lap is the arms of our chairs separating us. We're pressed as close as we can be at this secluded table on the beach. His breathing escalates as I run my tongue over his neck again. I might be the one to come from simply touching him. I'm hot all over.

He finally tugs hard on my hair, pulling my head back. There's fire in his eyes as he looks down at me. My thoughts are thrown from me as his head descends and he molds our mouths together sending tingles of awareness all through me. He's not being gentle as he pushes his tongue inside, owning my body in seconds. I'm putty in his hands, his willing slave, willing to do anything he pleases. I don't ever want this kiss to stop.

But it does as we're rudely interrupted.

"Well, well, well, what do we have here?"

He pulls back from me and I whimper in disappointment. The fog is slowly lifting from my fuzzy brain as I recognize the voice. I look up at Stephy.

"I was worried about you when I couldn't find you, but now I see why you ditched me," she says as she pulls up a chair and sits across from Evan and me. "Good to see you again, handsome. Having a good time?"

Evan throws back his head and laughs before smiling at Stephy. "I'm trying to be an honorable man and sober your friend up, but she's hard to resist when she's so persistent," Evan says.

"Oh, is she being a siren?" Stephy asks, seeming quite delighted by this.

"Oh, she's a seductress for sure." He looks back at me and I beam at him.

"I guess I'm seducing him," I say, slowly looking over at Stephy. My best friend bursts out laughing.

The waitress appears and drops off five plates of food, nachos, tacos, shrimp, fries, mini burgers and more. Stephy claps her hands in delights as she picks up a taco.

"I like a man who knows what I want without asking," Stephy says before taking a bite, some sauce dripping down her chin. She wipes it away as she chews, not in the least self-conscious. She doesn't have to be. She's amazing.

"I like to please," Evan says. He hands me a burger and I automatically take a bite. It's good. I take another bite. Maybe the food will help me last a few more hours. I don't want the night to ever end.

"So, what are the plans for the rest of the evening?" Stephy asks.

Evan looks at Stephy, then looks at me, then looks out at the beach. He laughs again as if he's never been more relaxed in his life.

"I have an idea," he says.

"Oh, do tell." Stephy leans in and they begin to talk as I stuff food in my mouth in between drinks. I'm trying to follow, but I give up. I'm free right now, and I like the feeling.

Whatever will be, will be. That's my new motto in life. I hope it treats me well . . .

CHAPTER THREE

O H, MAN DO I have one heck of a headache. More water. I certainly should have drunk more water the night before. I feel the sun coming in shinning on my face. I don't open my eyes as I think back to the night before.

It takes about a full minute, and then I stiffen. No! Are you kidding me? What in the heck was I thinking? I can't blame this on the alcohol. I can't blame it on anything but me living in the moment and laughing and having fun. I got carried away.

I let out a sigh. There's a part of me that wishes I can forget the things I don't want to remember. There's another part of me, a bigger part, that knows it's not okay to run away from my life, even those impulsive things I do in the moment I might want to think twice about when that moment is over.

I don't need to move to know where I am . . . or who I'm with. I finally open my eyes. I turn my head to see Evan soundly sleeping. I'm not panicking. That's a good thing. I do let out another sigh of relief as I see we're both dressed.

Evan let's out a groan as he turns and reaches out to me. I don't move as his arm slides over my stomach. A little sliver of desire flows through me. I push it away. I close my eyes again as I think about the night before. It had all started out well and good. My lids shoot open again as I think about my bestie. She has to die. There's no other choice. It's going to make me sad, but what has to be done, has to be done. I'm going to murder her. I can see her laughing eyes in my mind. Instead of being mad I smile. What else can I do about this? It's happened and I was an active participant in it all.

Evan doesn't appear to be waking anytime soon. I rub my face as I decide it's time to get up. I feel a scratch against my cheek and look down with another smile. On my finger is my favorite ring I've been given.

Last night after Evan, Stephy, and I had an amazing dinner and a bunch of pina coladas, Evan thought it would be fun to join the wedding party that was going on. Couples were getting married, one after the other, so of course Stephy convinces us to do the same. And right there is how I've now found myself married for the sixth time.

As I have this thought I find laughter building inside of me. Six times. I've been married six times. It doesn't matter if it hasn't all been legal. It doesn't matter how it's happened. What matters is I've been married six times. Who does this? Apparently, me with the help of my very sneaky bestie. I don't think I should drink anymore.

I run back to the cottage to find Stephy sleeping. "You are such a traitor," I whisper. I plop myself down hard on her bed making her body jump. She barely even stirs in her sleep. I reach out and smack her right on the thigh. She lets out a yelp as she shoots straight up in bed looking around wildly.

"What in the heck was that?" she yells.

"I can't believe you managed to talk me into getting married again," I say with a glare.

She laughs as she runs her fingers down her face. "I need coffee for this conversation," she tells me. "Holy cow do I have a hangover." She rises and moves into the bathroom. She doesn't immerge for a solid ten minutes. When she does come out, her hair is wrapped in a towel and she looks pretty great in her robe.

"Coffee," she mutters as she moves over to the Keurig and starts a cup brewing. I move to the island and sit. I'm not mad. I'm actually in awe that this best friend of mine can get me to do the things she gets me to do. She should work for the CIA. She'd have all of the criminals doing her bidding in a heartbeat.

"You were determined to get married last night. I made a little suggestion and Evan jumped on it. He then ran out into the grass and picked some and wove you that ring. I fell in love with him in an instant," Stephy says.

I look down at the ring again. This is one I'm not giving back. I really do love it. It's true, the man ran out in the grass and pulled several long, thick pieces then proceeded to weave me a ring. It took him a few tries, but it's absolutely perfect . . . which is the reason I'm still wearing it now.

"Is your goal to get me married once a year?"

Her coffee finishes and she adds sweat cream to it, then leans on the counter and sips it with a sigh before she answers. Her grin is wide when she does.

"I think it just might be. I'm having so much fun with these adventures you're going on that I don't want it ever to end."

"Why don't you start getting married then? It's been six times for me. I think that might be enough."

She laughs. "Why?"

"Why what?" I ask.

"Why does it have to be enough. Six times just makes you seem wishy-washy, but if you are to do it ten or twenty times, you're eccentric. Do you want to be wishy-washy or eccentric?"

I process her words before I start laughing. "I don't think I have to choose either of those options. I think I just need to be smart enough to never speak of this to anyone so they don't lock me up in an asylum."

"You know I'll work my magic and make it all disappear, but it does make a hell of a story."

I think about her words. "You can make it all go away," I say in awe. "It boggles my brain how dang smart you are."

"Yep, I can make every single bit of it disappear. It's all up to you."

"Well, you can't make the men disappear," I point out.

She throws back her head in laughter. "I could make them disappear, too, but I believe in heaven, and I don't need my soul tarnished. Messing with computers is one thing, murder is on a whole other level, the one-way-deep-down-south level."

"Isn't it funny what we're willing to do and not do? I agree with you. "There are some lines I won't ever cross. I'm discovering, though, that the lines are blurrier than I ever thought they'd be. If you would've told me ten years ago that I'd be married six times before officially turning twenty-five I'd have told you to quit doing drugs. But here I am, and here it is."

"I think we either live a boring life, or we live an adventurous one. Some people like normal everyday activities. We obviously don't. We're having fun and I want it to continue. What are your plans with your newest husband?" She stops and winks. "And how was the honeymoon last night?"

"We slept in our clothes. Nothing happened between us. It's odd, Stephy, because I was seriously lusting after the man for days, but when I woke up next to him this morning that desire was fully gone. Well, to be honest, it was there a little, but I think I was enjoying the fantasy of him a lot more than the reality."

She finishes her coffee then brews another cup. She finishes and I brew my own. We then move to the back deck and look out over the water. It's quiet this morning. I love the mornings and the evenings the best. I can take or leave afternoons.

"Any regrets?" she asks.

I think hard on it for a second. "Nope. I don't think I do."

"Do you feel married?"

I laugh. "No, not even a little bit."

"Then why are you still wearing the ring?" she points out.

I look at it. "I like the ring."

"What are you going to say to him when he shows up?"

"I'm not sure yet." We go silent as we drink our coffee and watch people fishing and swimming in the water. I speak again after several minutes. "You know what's strange is I don't want to run away and pretend it didn't happen. I will talk to him and explain that it was fun, but that's it."

"Are you going to spend a few hot nights together first?"

"No. I don't want to."

"You *are* married," she points out.

"I know, but not for long. I can't this time, Stephy. It would be wrong."

"Why is that?"

"I'm still thinking about Colby too often," I admit.

"Do you regret leaving him?"

I don't answer right away as I truly think about this. I finally shake my head. "No, I don't regret leaving him. I'm just unsure where that leaves me now. I don't know what's going to happen next."

"Do you want him to come for you?" she asks.

I shake my head after a minute. "I don't know. I don't know if I want that or not. I don't honestly know what I want."

"I've been there a lot in life. There's nothing wrong

with admitting when we don't have all of the answers."

"Good morning, beautiful."

We turn to see Evan walking up to us, a pair of shorts low on his hips, a tank top reaching the edge of the shorts and showing off his muscled arms, messy hair, and the big grin on his lips.

"Good morning, Evan," I say. A bit of nerves jump in my stomach, but it's not killing me.

Evan hops the railing, then he's standing in front of me. He places his hands on the armrests of my chair, leans down and kisses me. Those tingles come back as he pulls away. They are just a flutter now, though, instead of a whirlpool.

"Got more coffee?"

"Yes, inside," I tell him. He kisses me one more time then goes inside the cottage. He doesn't seem in the least upset over what we did. That's good. I think he'll take all of this well and agree with me that we've had our fun, but it's time to come back to reality.

"Well, looks like that man has no regrets," Stephy whispers.

"That's good. I don't want this to get awkward."

"He's probably a little disappointed he woke up with his clothes on."

I laugh. "Yes, I'm sure he is. I'm also sure he won't have a problem finding someone to fill my place."

"Are you sure you don't want to try him out at least once?"

"I'm a hundred percent sure," I say with a laugh as Evan steps out. He pulls up one more chair and moves it right next to mine.

"How is my wife this morning?" He laughs as he says this. "I never thought those words would be uttered from my lips. I never thought I'd ever marry."

"Well, it *is* a vacation. We have to do crazy things," I tell him.

"Even on the craziest items on my bucket list, marriage wasn't there."

I reach out and pat his leg. "You do know we're getting it annulled," I say. I make sure it isn't a question. He loses his smile for a second, then it pops back into place.

"We're both here a while longer. There's no rush. Isn't the honeymoon the best part of a marriage?" He waggles his brows at me.

"I'm sure it is." I pause a long moment. "The honeymoon isn't going to happen either."

Now he frowns. "I like that we did this. It's the craziest day of my life and we have mass chemistry between us. Why not explore it?"

"I'm not going to lie. I find you hot as hell and you've created some insane sparks in me." I pause a long moment. I need to be brutally honest. "I'm still thinking about my last husband though. I can't have sex with you when another man is on my mind."

He flinches the slightest bit and I see shutters go over his eyes. It might be good for him to hate me a little. It might make it easier. This man won't stay a part of my life. I won't stay a part of his. This will be a story his friends can tease him about when he has a bachelor party before he has a real marriage.

"Well, there's a splash of cold water on what began as a great day," he tells me.

"I'm sorry, Evan. But the sooner we rip off this bandage the better. I don't regret last night. It was impulsive and fun and I'm in love with my ring. I just don't want to lead you on."

"I think you enjoy leading men on," he says. He's growing colder by the second.

This hurts my feelings. I try not to take it personally. I've bruised his ego and he's striking back. It's normal. It might not be okay to intentionally try to hurt me, but if that leads to him moving on, then that's not such a bad thing.

"Maybe you're right because I've hurt some people over the last five years. I haven't done it intentionally, but I'm not free from sin. Let's just do this quick and get it over with."

"I couldn't agree more." He stands. He's gone from flirty and sexy, to cold and hard in the beat of a heart. He doesn't say more as he sets down his coffee cup and leaves.

Stephy and I are silent as we watch his back. He doesn't turn.

"Well, that couldn't have gone worse," Stephy says when he's out of our sight.

"His ego is bruised. I'm sure he'll be fine in a few minutes."

"Do you think he'll talk to us again?"

I shrug. "I realize I don't care." I feel horrible about

this. "What does that say about me?"

Stephy takes my hand. "You don't have to love everybody, woman."

"I should at least *like* a man I marry, even if it is a marriage of twelve hours."

She throws back her head and laughs. "I'm sure a lot of Vegas weddings are with people who can't stand each other when they wake in the morning."

"I woke up with resignation, not anger. It happened. It's just one more chapter in my life."

"I guess I did egg it on," Stephy says with a sheepish grin.

I give her the duh look. She laughs.

"Okay, okay, I *totally* instigated it, but it was fun. You have to at least admit that."

I laugh. "Yes, it was fun."

We have more coffee, not in a hurry to do anything or go anywhere. About an hour passes and then a man in a suit appears who looks completely out of place in this slice of paradise. I raise my brows at him as he stops on the pier looking up at Stephy and me.

"Ms. Serpentine?" he questions.

"Present," I say with a solute. He's formal, so I can't help but mock him.

"I'm here to represent Mr. Praise. I need you to sign some papers," he tells me. "May I come up?"

Wow, who in the hell did I marry? This man is wearing a five-thousand-dollar suit, not the best on the market, and not even close to the worst. He's wearing thousand-dollar loafers, and there's not even a spark of humor in his eyes. He means business.

The fog of the last few days is lifting. Maybe I've been living in a dream, but it's *my* dream and I should get to decide on when I wake and when I dream. Then again, we don't get to choose how long our dreams last. This one is obviously over.

"Maybe I need to quit drinking," I tell Stephy as the man steps up onto our balcony. He has to be burning up in his suit. He doesn't seem to even notice the heat. Maybe he's cold-blooded. I again wonder about the man I've married. I know Stephy can find out quickly about him, but do I care enough to dig? Probably not.

"You do tend to make poor decisions when you drink," Stephy points out. I want to punch her for this statement since *she* eggs on those poor decisions or worse yet, initiates them. We have a witness though, and I don't need to go to a foreign jail for assault. This man looks as if he'll turn me in without a second thought.

"I have papers. Please look over these and sign," the man tells me as he sets them on the table between Stephy and I. There's no way he hasn't heard us speaking, but he doesn't bother acknowledging it. He's here for one thing, and one thing only. He's not going to leave without getting what he wants. Did I marry a man who has a trail of bodies behind him? A shiver rushes through me. I want out of here now. That went from fun to scary in a heartbeat.

I pick up the papers without another word I read

over them. I can't even remember signing a marriage license the night before, but here it is sitting in the pile. Is it really legal, though? Serpentine isn't even my real name. Of course, the ID I have on me says it is. Have any of my marriages been legal? I honestly don't know.

I read for a while. The man, who hasn't told us his name, is waiting. When I take what he deems too long he finally speaks.

"Are you about ready, Ms. Serpentine?"

I shake my head as I look over at the man standing up so straight he can substitute for a board. Maybe, there's a stick where the sun doesn't shine that's propping him up. He isn't sitting, and he isn't even leaning on the rail. He's stiff and so out of place I can't imagine him ever letting down his hair. I find myself wanting to pick up all of these papers and rip them to shreds. The fun, flirty night has turned into a depressing after-thought this morning.

"Who in the hell did you marry last night?" Stephy whispers like she's reading my mind as she peruses the papers over my shoulder.

"I'm not sure," I tell her.

"I'll find out," she says.

"I don't think I want to know."

"I do," she insists. I know there's no stopping her.

The sun has only been up for a few hours. Evan just left our cottage a little over an hour earlier, and yet this man is here with papers. How much power does Evan have? How important is he? Is he some prince from another country? Is he a diplomat? We've shared one evening together, *one*. Sure, that led to a wedding, but still, it was just *one* night. The papers in front of me are ridiculous. I'll sign the annulment, but nothing else.

I finally see the annulment document and read every line on the paper. When I'm sure it is what it's supposed to be, I sign on the dotted line. I can see that Mr. Praise hasn't signed the paper yet. I'm sure he wants it done on my side first. I should be more concerned, but I'm just not. There's nothing he can do that Stephy can't undo, no matter who he is or how powerful of a man.

"I'm not signing anything else."

"Mr. Praise has asked that you do."

"I don't care what Mr. Praise has asked. We were impulsive last night, we got married. I can see that he wants a non-disclosure signed. That's too bad for him. If I do choose to talk about it, I dang well will. You have the annulment papers. I want you to leave now. Take this stuff with you."

The man's shoulders tense for a moment, the only sign he's unhappy. Other than that his expression doesn't change much. He finally nods when he reads the conviction on my face. Short of forcing me to do it by gunpoint he doesn't have any leverage that can make me do what he wants. I wonder if this will be the end of it. I now just want to get out of this place. My head is starting to ache, and this is no longer paradise.

The man leaves.

"Dang, that was intense," Stephy says. "I don't like that man."

"Me either, he gave me the creeps."

"I don't usually get shaken, but he has cold eyes."

"Who in the hell did I marry?"

"I think we're going to be asking ourselves that a lot until we figure it out," Stephy says.

"Maybe it will be a good idea for you to find out."

"Amen to that," she says.

"I think it's time to go home."

I expect Stephy to argue with me, but she doesn't. "Yep, I think you're right," she tells me. "I don't want to go home, though. We'll go somewhere else."

"We should go home," I say.

She shakes her head. "No way. We're still on vacation. I'm just thinking we need to get far away from Mr. Praise and his goon. Maybe Hawaii."

Oh, I like this idea. "Hawaii will be great," I say.

"Yep, I'd rather be on US soil right now, but I still want paradise."

"Hawaii it is," I say.

Stephy and I quickly dress and pack our bags within about thirty minutes. We don't bother checking out. She can do that online from the safety of the airport. She works her magic on the ride over to the airport and gets a private flight that gets us off the ground so much faster than waiting for a commercial last minute. I'm sure the cost is astronautical. For once, I'm not complaining.

Relief floods me as we lift into the air. I don't know who in the heck Evan Praise truly is, and I wasn't in the least afraid of him until this morning. That stunt with his goon really scared me. The look of cold anger in Evan's eyes scared me as well.

"Well, do you have regrets now?" Stephy asks as she hands over a mimosa. It's almost noon and I don't normally drink this early, but I can use something to calm my nerves.

I think about what she's asking and then I throw back my head and laugh.

"What?" she asks. She's calmed down too knowing we're up in the air. We have a quick stop in Mexico for fueling and then we'll be in Hawaii in no time.

"That man scared the crud out of me, but you know what, I still have no regrets."

She's looking a bit stunned for a second. Then she laughs with me. She raises her glass.

"To no regrets," she says with a laugh.

"For yesterday, today and tomorrow," I add. We clink glasses.

We sit back and relax as we move on to our next adventure. I don't know if that's the last I'll ever hear from Evan Praise or not. I guess I'll have to wait and see. At least no one on this planet can ever say my life is boring, that's for dang sure.

I'm going to continue having adventures, and I'm going to continue living with no regrets. When they inevitably pop into my head, I'll push them away. I'm living my life the way I want to live it. I'll mess up at times, but that's all a part of my journey. I want to look back one day and be proud of who I am and I'll I've gotten to do. I'm halfway there.

CHAPTER FOUR

"MS. DIAMOND, WHAT is the point of this story?"

I'm in the courtroom. For a few minutes there I could almost feel the sun on my face from my time in the Caribbean and then in Hawaii. Both places had been heaven. I haven't been back to either since that trip. There's something wrong with that. I need to go again soon. Actually, speaking of these places is making me want to visit all of them. I've never been back to one place after I've left. No, that's not true either. There is one place I've been back to multiple times. I'm not there in my story yet. I'm avoiding that story in this moment—not for long though.

I pull myself out of my thoughts. "Haven't you figured it out yet, Mr. Hart?" I reply with the smile that drives the man nuts. I can see the slight tick in his jaw. I love it. Maybe I'm a bit of a jerk sometimes. Okay, maybe a big jerk a lot of the time. He brings it out in me.

"No, Ms. Diamond, I haven't figured out much at this point. Why don't you explain it to me?"

"The story isn't about you. It's *my* story. *You* have put me on trial. Because you did this, I get to say what

I want to say. If you don't want to hear my story, you can stop it at any time. You can drop the charges and scurry away. If you want the story, then you get the *whole* story, and you hear it the way I want to tell it."

"You've already established that you like to play games, Ms. Diamond. If you think you're winning, you are sadly mistaken. All you're doing is wasting this courts time, wasting the valuable time of the jurors who are serving, and wasting the countries time as they watch. You will pay for your crimes no matter how long you draw this out."

"Wasting the time of the people watching?" I ask.

"Yes, they think they will get more information pertinent to the trial, and instead they hear a bunch of things that doesn't move this case forward."

"Have you ever heard of a remote?"

"What?"

"Mr. Hart, have you ever heard of a remote?"

"I don't understand what a remote has to do with any of this."

"If people don't want to watch this case, they have a lot of options. They can turn the television off or turn the channel. It's really quite easy. It takes less than a second."

That tick is back in his jaw. It's becoming more pronounced the longer this trial progresses. I hope he doesn't have a stroke before it's over.

"Maybe you're right, Mr. Hart. Maybe you're wrong. I guess we'll both find out at the end of the trial."

"Yes, we will." He pauses. "What marriage are we up to now, Ms. Diamond?"

He's sure saying my name a lot. I'm trying to figure out his strategy in doing this, but I'm lost for the moment.

"*I'm* at marriage six," I say, stressing the *I*. The last time I checked, I haven't married Mr. Hart. I'm not saying that's impossible. I *was* pretty drunk a few of the times I said *I do*. I could see a wedding with the surly prosecutor. This almost makes me giggle. I'm smart enough not to do just this.

"Yet, you *still* have no regrets?" He makes sure to stress this as if I have to be crazy to not have regrets for the life I've lived. I think he's the one crazy for living such a boring life. We only have so much time on this planet before we move on to the great unknown. We need to make the most of our time.

"I have no regrets."

"May I remind you that you are under oath, Ms. Diamond? You might not like an answer, but you are required to answer *truthfully* each time."

"You can remind me all day long. I'm very aware I'm under oath. I don't lie. I might not like to tell someone the truth at all times, but I don't lie."

"So, you stand by your word that you have no regrets?"

I can't understand why he's saying this. I don't know where he's going. Normally, I'm very aware of his strategy, but he's changing things up on me right now. Maybe he's reading the way the reporters are speaking about him. He's not coming out looking so good. That's probably why he's switching it all up.

"I've lived my life, Mr. Hart. I've lived my choices, in my world enjoying the life I've created. I've had adventures that I'd never dreamed possible when I was young. When I lost Bentley I thought my world was over. In reality, it *was* over. It took me a long time to learn how to cope, and then, miracle of miracles, I learned how to fly. I don't have regrets because each experience I've lived has helped me grow, has helped me learn, has made me soar high in the sky. I can almost touch the heavens . . . and when I can do that, then I'll finally be home with the ones I love."

He pauses for a second as he analyzes my words. "Are you suicidal, Ms. Diamond?"

"No." I'm not offended by this because it's something that will never happen. "There were times I wasn't sure if I wanted to live or die. Now, I know with a certainty that I don't want to just live, I want to thrive. I want to rise from the ashes of my life before. We all make our own definitions of what our lives are supposed to be like. My choices aren't your choices. We all make different decisions in life that lead us to many places."

"I think that's about the most accurate thing you've said this entire trial, Ms. Diamond."

"That's the most accurate thing I can say in *your* opinion, Mr. Hart. That's your truth, not mine. I won't tell you how to live your life, even though you want to tell me how to live mine. I'm not judging you.

I don't care if you judge me. I'm not saying that with disrespect. I'm saying it because it's *my* truth. Your opinion doesn't matter to me. Your world doesn't intertwine with mine."

"Did the annulment go through with Mr. Praise?"

"I guess since you haven't found the documents you need, I'll do your work for you and give you this one," I say with a somewhat snooty voice. "Yes, my marriage was annulled. It was the shortest one I had."

"Well, congratulations, Ms. Diamond. It appears as if sometimes you know how to follow the law."

"I feel sorry for you, Mr. Hart. You must lead a very unhappy life that you take such joy out of being so rude to people."

"Let me use your own words, Ms. Diamond. I don't care what you think about me. I love my life. I've worked damn hard to put extortionist like you behind bars so that law-abiding citizens can be safe. You *will* go to jail, Ms. Diamond, even if it's the last thing I do."

"First off, I don't take anything from any of the people in my life, so extortionist is the wrong word. Secondly, I hope it's not the last thing you do, Mr. Hart. You're young, and you have a long life to live. When this trial ends, I won't think about you again. I have a feeling you'll think about me for many years to come. No matter what the outcome of this case is, I know who I am. Maybe you need to go on your own journey to find out who you are. You'll think of me for years to come after this all ends because it seems you don't love your own life. Take a piece of advice and seek out some happiness. It's very therapeutic."

That tic jumps as he turns from me. Each time he thinks he gets the upper hand I get irritated and try to slam him down again. Today, he might've bested me. I know I've come across as snotty and entitled. That's not who I am, dang it. I need to reign it in. Maybe he's learned this about me. Maybe that was his plan all along. He will win this case if he can make me seem like nothing more than a spoiled rich girl. I *am* spoiled and I *am* rich, but that doesn't mean I'm a horrible human. I don't own any dogs I carry in five-thousand-dollar purses, and I don't give air kisses to acquaintances.

Well, I might be a bit of a jerk if I'm thinking these type of thoughts. Then again, I can blame it on one too many eighties movies. That's my favorite genre of movies and they always play the snobby girls way up with their stupid purses and stupid pets and rude behavior. I might need some sweatpants and a bonfire, STAT. I nearly giggle at the thought. A bonfire truly does sound like heaven right now.

"I have no further questions . . . for now." Mr. Hart walks back to his table and sits. He doesn't look at me again. I wish for just one day I can be a mind reader.

Cash stands and smiles at me before he takes a slow stroll in front of the jury box. His hands are tucked in his pockets as usual, giving him an air of casual relaxation. He always seems as if he's ready for dinner or the spa, like it doesn't take much to defend me because there's nothing really to defend. I hope this strategy works.

"Ms. Diamond, why did you marry Evan Praise?"

"I've thought about this a lot, back then, and this past week as I reached my story with him. I think all I can say is I was in the moment. It was a beautiful moment, but when I woke up in the morning, I knew our moment had come and gone. It was sad that it came and went so quickly, but in life sometimes that happens. I've learned over the years to embrace each moment, to appreciate every little piece of my story, whether it's for five minutes or five years, and to try and learn something from each of these moments. I don't want to take anything away from any of them."

"Was this the last you saw of Evan Praise?"

I nod. "I never saw him again."

"Was that his real name?"

I laugh. "It would be fitting if it wasn't, wouldn't it?" I say. Several people smile.

"Yes, Ms. Diamond, I'd say that would be fitting," Cash affirms.

"Yes, that was his real name. He was from Brazil. His attorney, or at least, I *think* it was his attorney, scared the crud out of me and Stephy. But we never did hear from him again."

"Was he in a crime family?" Cash asks.

I shrug. "We don't know. But the number of papers his man put down on the table was insane. The non-disclosure one is the thing that scared me the most."

"You obviously didn't sign it as you're sitting here

today talking about the marriage."

"No, I don't live my life in fear. I was scared in the moment, but I refuse to live in fear. I think the fates have more control over our lives than we give them credit for. I think we can live in fear, or we can open our arms and accept what's about to come. For the most part I've done the latter."

"I think your life has been a big adventure, one that many of us envy."

"I wouldn't go so far as to say I've had an enviable life. I would say, it's been exciting, and I've met many wonderful friends along the way. I don't want to take any of it back, the good, the bad, the ugly, the sad, and the wonderful. It's all a part of me now."

"Maybe Mr. Praise will see the trial and want to come and give his side to the story," Cash says.

"I wouldn't mind seeing him again." I stop and give an exaggerated shiver. "Just as long as his goon doesn't come along with him." There are a few chuckles from the audience at my poor acting.

Cash asks a few more questions and then court is dismissed for the day. Now I'm wondering if Evan will come. I wonder what he'd have to say. I haven't thought much about him after we left the island. I don't feel bad about that. I'm sure it's been the same for him. Maybe some of my past should simply stay right there in the past.

With saying that, I'm more than eager to have some of the past resurface. It's a good thing I feel that way, because I can't stop it from happening. The world will soon know that the past is never fully in the past. There's always a chance it comes back up—good or bad.

CHAPTER FIVE

THERE'S NO PLACE like home during the holidays. I was always that girl who couldn't wait for Thanksgiving and Christmas morning. I'd barely be able to get to sleep the entire week before the big holidays. Thanksgiving has always been about love, family, food, and football. Not only do we watch it, but there's always a game before dinner. Mom says we need to work up an appetite to truly appreciate a meal she spends three days working on.

My mom's always been offended if her guests don't come back for seconds or thirds. If people aren't groaning on the floor, the couches, or in their chairs then she hasn't done her job. Christmas is a lot the same. And Easter has been known to send a few people to the hospital thinking they are pregnant their bellies become so round.

Right now, it's Thanksgiving Day, and this year I'm not enthusiastic about it. I've been depressed lately. I know it's stupid and I'm trying to pull myself out of the funk I'm in, but I can't seem to do it.

It's been three months since I was in the Caribbean and then Hawaii. Stephy and I were on vacation for a month straight. We came home tanned and rested. I haven't heard from Evan or his creepy goon since we left.

We got home, and the weather was already turning here in Oregon. Normally, I love the seasons, but not this year. Now, all I see are grey clouds. All I feel is a bite in the air. I want it to end. Even the thought of mom's cooking isn't pulling me out of my winter blues. Stephy is planning another trip for me. I've managed to put her off so far—I don't think I'll be able to do it for much longer. She's telling me she's seeing too many signs of the girl I was after losing Bentley.

I'm careful as I move down the city center of Prairie Town. It's funny to call it a city center. Our town literally consists of a two-block center that holds the majority of the businesses in one line. Sure, we have a post office and some other businesses in surrounding blocks, but if you want to shop, you come to this two-block center. It's always cheered me up on a bad day to walk the blocks looking at all of the Christmas displays. This year it's failing me.

To top off my moodiness, the sidewalks are icy. They've put out the rock salt, but I've always leaned toward the klutzy side, and it's only a matter of time before I land on my behind in the most inelegant way possible. You'd think after twenty-five years I'd be a pro on any surface, ice, snow, sand, rocks. You'd be wrong though.

I rarely drive in Prairie Town since everything is within walking distance. If I do drive, it's normally on a quad. There are more bicycles and recreational vehicles driving about than regular vehicles.

Walking from my parents' house to town only takes about three minutes. Walking from the ranch to town takes about fifteen minutes. The only time I don't appreciate the exercise is when rain is pouring down. I'm almost to the center when a breeze blows through my hood and sends chills straight inside of me. I let out a yelp.

"Suck it up, this is good for me," I whisper as my teeth chatter together. I know I'd normally be laughing over my own misery, but this past week, heck the past several months, I haven't found anything that amusing.

Pushing my face down, I look at the sidewalks as I fight the chilly wind blowing against my exposed nose and cheeks. My lips are most likely bright red without a trace of lipstick on. Every other inch of my body is covered with several layers. There aren't too many people out on the streets as most of them are smart enough to be staying home. They are either cooking, eating, watching the Macy's Thanksgiving Day Parade, or Football.

I'm on my way to moms, but I have to stop in at the store first for the forgotten cranberries. I think Mom leaves them out on purpose. She hates them. But someone most likely showed up and pouted. Now, it's up to me to save the day. Since she hasn't let anyone help her with dinner ever in her life, at least I can contribute in a small way.

I take a step as I near the store, and I begin slipping. Son of a gun. I try to regain my balance as my arms splay out, most likely making me look as if I'm doing some hypnotic dance to the heavens. Maybe I am, maybe I'm praying the icy chill in the air will warm up even five more degrees, just enough not to lose my nose before I make it to Mom's house.

I don't hit the ground, but slam straight into the back of a very bundled, very large man. I grab onto him for dear life, not even feeling bad about it. In Prairie Town we help our neighbors. I suddenly find myself wanting to giggle as I open my mouth. Helping is helping, even it we take someone down with us.

"I'm sorry," I say, sounding more grateful than sorry as laughter spills out. I don't unhand the man as my feet are still trying to slide around. Maybe I should've worn ice-skates instead of tennis shoes. I'd probably be a lot safer.

I try to unhand the gentleman as I step back and immediately start sliding again. Did they forget to rock this part of the sidewalk? I bet there's a camera up somewhere with people laughing as unsuspecting shoppers go down on their asses. That's something Stephy and I would totally do if we could get away with it.

The man who I reach for again is a step too far from me. He whips around, and the only thing that saves my ass is when he grabs me and pulls me close. I've been here before. I slam up against the hardness of his chest. How is he not sliding? Maybe it's the boots he's wearing.

I tense before he speaks. I know *exactly* who he is

without a sound being said. "It seems you are falling for me all over again." I'm afraid to look up.

There isn't a world big enough, or an amount of time long enough for me to forget the feel of this man's arms, or the sound of his deep, rich, southern voice. This voice has haunted my dreams for nearly a year, has woken me in the night with sweats, my body hungry. This voice, these arms, *this* man is someone I haven't been able to let go of.

He isn't letting me go, and I finally tilt my head to look up, seeing his devilish brown eyes sparkling as he holds me tight. His sexy, full lips are turned up in a grin as if it's only been a day since we've parted instead of almost a year. I'm gaping at him, not expecting to see this man in this place. I haven't thought I'd see him ever again.

I open my mouth to speak and can't find words. I try again, and still nothing. Finally, I tug against him and he releases me. I take a cautious step back from him, then another, then another. I stop at about five feet. I don't need to keep stepping and either fall on my butt or fall right back into his arms—literally and figuratively.

Colby looks amazing, truly amazing. His eyes are clear, his face tanned, his lips still turned up. He looks mischievous and happy at the same time. He looks as if he belongs right here. My body is reacting to him the way it did for a full year straight. My heart is thundering, and thoughts of cold have completely evaporated. How can I be cold when heat is warming me from the inside out?

"What are you doing here?" I don't want to ask how he's found me after all of this time. I've told him I'm from Oregon. Though I had a different name with him, I'm not difficult to find with a little information. Besides, people like him with unlimited recourses tend to find what they want to find.

"I came to see you," he says with his smile firmly in place. Of course, he's here for me. It's not as if anyone comes to this town to tour it. We're a flyover town. Those of us who live here, love it immensely. Those of us who escape miss it and come back to visit. But those who pass through barely even notice it. It's on the map, but not a place the fingers point to and says *let me go here.*

"How did you find me?" It's a dumb question, but I can't seem to stop myself from asking.

"It wasn't that difficult," he tells me. "We were together for a solid year and shared just about everything with each other."

"True." I'm not sure how I'm feeling about him being here. I'm in shock, though it seems silly to feel this way. Haven't there been times I've hoped for just this? If I allow myself to be honest with the voice in my own head I'll admit this.

"I miss you," he says with a shrug, no apology in his eyes. He takes a step toward me, and for a strange reason I feel panic. I was just in his arms and I survived it, but I have a feeling if he grabs me again, I'm going to melt against him. He's here. There's nothing I can do about it, and we didn't part on bad terms. I should just enjoy the visit. I backtrack even as I'm thinking this.

"Charlie," he says, his smile fading. "I know I should've called, but I didn't want you to tell me no. I want to spend time with my wife on Thanksgiving."

I gape at him. "I'm not your wife anymore."

"Well . . . about that . . ."

Now, I really am panicked. What in the hell is he talking about? I can't do this. I need to get out of here. I need to clear my head. I turn from him, not quite knowing what I'm going to do. Am I going to run? Am I going to bury my head in the sand? What am I going to do? I'm sure I'll think clearly soon—just not yet.

I start to run and realize right away what a monstrous mistake I'm making. I only make it a few steps before my feet begin sliding out right in front of me while my body is free-falling backward. Oh, crap, this is going to hurt. I'm too far away for Colby to catch me this time. There's no way around this, I'm going down, and I'm going down hard. My head connects with the icy cement and sharp pain shoots through my skull before blessed darkness wipes all thoughts from my brain.

My peaceful darkness is interrupted by the panicked voice of Colby above me. My eyes are still closed, but I hear him loud and clear. "Wake up right this minute, Charlie!" There's such authority in his tone as if there's no doubt I'll do what he wants even when I didn't intentionally knock myself out. It makes my lips twitch as I come back to consciousness.

"How long was I out?" I whisper.

"About thirty seconds," he says, his voice sounding stressed.

I realize I'm in his arms . . . again. His body is just about as hard as the cement, but it's warm and I feel safe. I always liked being right in this place when I was with him. But we aren't together anymore. This is wrong. This shouldn't be happening. I'm not trying to pull away though. I give myself a break as I've just fought with the ground . . . and lost.

Finally, I allow my eyes to flutter open. "Does anyone ever ignore you when you give a command?" I ask.

"What do you mean?" he asks. His face is blurry for a moment and then he comes into focus and I *really* gaze at him. Damn, the man is too beautiful for his own good. He shouldn't be this sexy, it makes the playing field lean way too much in his favor.

"You demanded I open my eyes."

His lips finally twitch. I love this look the most about him. "No, It's very rare in life when people don't do what I say," he admits. "I learned this from the time I was a little boy.

"Oh, it must've been so rough growing up you."

He laughs now. "It was a tough childhood." He might be joking, but I do know he's had some very rough moments. He's pretty much lost everyone who means anything at all to him. I'd rather lose a limb than lose anyone else I love. That hurts far more than any physical injury.

"What happened?" I ask as I try to put the pieces together from the last few minutes.

"You went down hard. You have a bump on your head, and you tried to brace yourself with your hand. We need to go to the hospital, but I don't know where the nearest one is." He stops walking and I realize he's been hauling me over the sidewalks for the past few minutes. He's not even out of breath. Show off.

"No, no, no." I shake my head as I repeat the word. "I don't do hospitals. I hate them. I don't want to go. I'm fine. I remember falling. I just have a little bit of a headache right now," I insist, playing down the throbbing in my head. If I ran to the hospital every time I fall, I'd never be at home. I'm a klutz. Falling comes with the territory.

He gives me a curious look, and I can see the argument in his eyes. I keep shaking my head, even though shaking it is killing me more. I try not to show him this. He's a stubborn man, but I'm about his equal in this department.

"The hospital is over an hour away. My mom's cooking and will kill me if I don't show up with the cranberries . . . or myself," I push.

"Charlie, you have to be looked at. You hit your head hard, and I can see swelling on your wrist. You should probably have a head scan and an X-ray done." He's just standing next to an SUV with me still snuggly in his arms. There are a few people passing us, but nobody does more than say hello and pass on by.

Doesn't anyone find it odd that a stranger is holding me? What if he's a kidnapper? Then again, I've never been a quiet person. If he truly was trying to take me my neighbors know I'd be screaming bloody murder.

Oh my gosh! I realize that at least one person has most likely called my mother by now saying I'm downtown in the arms of a stranger. This town knows everyone who lives in it, and when a man who looks like Colby strolls into town it's known by all of the busybodies within an hour. That's a fact. I groan.

"What? Are you dizzy? I don't care how far the hospital is, we're going."

He puts me into the passenger side of his vehicle and runs around to his side, and quickly starts up the engine. "Where do I go?"

"I wasn't groaning in pain. I was just realizing that my mother has probably already heard that her daughter is being carried around by some sexy stranger," I tell him.

My words stop the panic in his eyes, and he gives me a smile. His worry isn't all the way gone from his expression but at least I've managed to distract him.

"Sexy, huh?" he says.

I roll my eyes. Of course that's what he's picked up on from my misery.

"You already know how sexy you are. That's not big news."

"You can try to distract me all you want, but we *are* going in for you to be checked." He pulls up his phone to get the hospital address. I don't have my phone on me right now. I'm probably going to have a hundred messages or more when I get to it.

I put my hand over his phone. "Fine. But I don't need the hospital. We'll just go to Doc's house. He'll be home," I tell him.

"I don't like it," he says.

"I've been taking care of myself for a very long time, Colby. Don't be one of those guys who treats me as if I'm a dumb girl who needs help figuring things out. You never have before." I give him a stern look and I can see when he caves. Good. I don't even want to go to the doc's but it's better than an hour away to the hospital. My mother is already going to kill me for being as late as I'm going to be.

"I'll take you to doc's, but you need to quit being a pain in the ass," he says, his voice both stern and humorous. I roll my eyes. "Give me the directions."

I lead him to doc's house. It's about a hundred-year-old farmhouse and the front door opens as Colby opens my door and tries to pick me back up. I glare at him as I grab the handle and step down from the vehicle. "I can walk inside on my own," I whisper.

"You will at least hold my arm or it's a no go," he whispers back. The doc is standing on the front porch looking at us with concern and I decide now isn't the time to push Colby. He'll have zero qualms of making a scene. The doc is great at his job and has been in practice here in Prairie Town for fifty years. He's semi-retired now, but as he's birthed a lot of babies here, he's still the number one doc we all like to go to. He gives out great suckers to this day. I don't ever turn one down.

"Hi Doc," I say a bit breathily as his eyes go from me to Colby and back to me.

"Hello, Charlie, what has you visiting me today?" he asks. I love his cheerful smile. I hate hospitals, but I've never complained about going to see Doc.

"I fell and got a little bump on my head," I say with a chuckle. "And my friend, here, is insisting I get it looked at." I can't pretend Colby isn't with me. The doc's eyes zero in him.

"I'm Doc," he says, not giving a name. We all just call him Doc. I honestly don't know what his first name is.

"Colby Winters," Colby says as he holds out a hand.

"Where are you from, Colby?" Doc asks.

"Texas." We're moving inside and straight to the back of Doc's house where he has a medical room set up. He can do just about any small procedure right here at his home. It's great. He worked at the main office in town until about five years ago. Now, he'll drop in there once in a while, but he says he's done his job for many years and now it's time to fish. He can't keep away from medicine for too long though.

"How do you and Charlie know each other."

I'm the one to jump in now. There's nothing Colby can say to Doc that won't get out to the entire town.

"I was working in Texas last year for the bank and met him then," I say. The town and my family still think I work for some international bank that sends me all around the world. It's perfect for all of the places I go. I don't take pride in lying to the ones I love, but it's the only thing that allows me to travel without anyone worrying.

"How did you meet?" Doc asks. He's feeling my hand. He mumbles something, then grabs some bandages and begins to wrap it.

"At the bank," I say. "What's wrong with my wrist?" I need to get this talk off of the personal asap. I don't like lying. It makes me feel dirty.

"You have a slight sprain. It's not a big deal. I'm more concerned about the bump on your head. Do you have a headache?"

"Just a small one," I tell him. "It's actually beginning to ease."

"Okay, I'm going to give you some medicine for today and tomorrow. I want you to eat a good meal and get plenty of sleep. Don't be alone for the next thirty-six hours. If you start to get dizzy or sick, I want you coming right back to me or go to the hospital. I don't care what time of day or night."

"I'll make sure, Doc," Colby says.

"Okay, I will," I say.

Doc hands over the stuff and nods, then shakes hands with Colby and hands me a sucker that makes me beam as I unwrap it. It's not the crappy suckers. It's a cherry Tootsie Roll Pop. I almost always manage to lick it to the center instead of biting into it. I unwrap it and stick it in my mouth as Colby leads me down the steps and helps me back into his vehicle. He starts it up and gives me a look that takes my breath away.

"Are you purposely trying to get me to pull this vehicle off down a deserted road?" The hunger in his voice goes straight to my core. I wasn't trying to do that, but at his words I find myself taking the lollipop from my mouth and licking it a few times. Fire lights in his eyes. I decide I should stop playing right now.

"I'm late to my mom's and I'm sure the doctor has just called her," I say.

"Okay, I'd love to meet your mom."

I turn and stare at him in horror. "How can I explain you?" I gasp. My sucker which has been so dang good now tastes like mold as my mouth goes dry.

He starts his SUV and begins driving from the doc's house. He makes a turn, then another, and then I realize he knows exactly where he's going. I cross my arms and sit next to him pouting. He seems to know everything about me. I do know a lot about him, but I haven't realized until now how much *I've* shared with *him*. He always seemed safe to share with. Now, I'm not so sure. I haven't expected any of the men I've been with to actually follow me back home.

"You've known all along where I'm from," I say. It's a statement. Obviously this is true.

He laughs. "You *are* my wife. Of course, I know where you are."

My head whips around. "Why are you saying I'm your wife. We're divorced." I'm starting to feel panic. I married another man. Sure, it was only for a few hours, but I married another man. I can't be married to Colby still. I'm not that woman. Or am I?

"I never was able to sign the papers. I burned them," he says with a shrug. I sigh as I reach for him.

"Colby, you can't do this," I whisper.

"I'm not easily controlled. You can try to stop me, but it won't do you a lot of good."

I feel my lips twitching. "This isn't going to work, and you can't tell my parents you're my husband. It will give them heart attacks and dinner will turn into a lecture."

"What do we tell them, then?" he asks. He's not seeming too upset at how I'm reacting. Of course he spent a year with me. He knows me pretty dang well. He was probably ready for just this reaction.

"We tell them what we told the doc since he'll share it with the entire town anyway."

He laughs. "So, we're friends from Texas?"

"Yes, friends from Texas."

"Okay, I'm starving. I can't wait to try your mother's cooking since I've heard so much about it."

At these words he jumps from his vehicle and runs around to my side. I feel my stomach sink as he opens my door. I don't want to walk inside. I'm not sure what Stephy will say. I'm not sure how my parents will react. I don't know what's going to happen. I don't like floating unless I'm holding balloons, and right now I feel as if I'm about to be carried into the sky.

I don't have much choice though. I take a deep breath and take his hand. Here goes nothing. Let the games begin.

I get out of the vehicle and look at the driveway in front of my parent's place. There are several cars here already. I feel a clench in my gut. I try to smile and it's coming out all wrong. Colby looks at me and laughs.

"There's a better attitude," he whispers.

I glare at him. Is it wrong to slug a man? I know it's frowned upon, and if my mother sees it, she'll kick my butt and tell me I was raised better than that, but still, it might be worth it. This man is going to drive me crazy in my hometown. It was so much easier when I was on his turf and nobody knew me. Him coming here makes me have to come up with explanations of why he's here.

"I don't want to be here," I tell him. "This is crazy. I think we should go back to my place and talk." I can feel a panic attack starting to come on.

"I thought your mom's expecting you," he says. I can see he's torn. He probably thinks if he gets me back to my place where we're alone, our chemistry will be uncontrollable. He might just be right. It's been a long time since I've had pleasure, longer than I like.

"She is. She'll have a fit if I don't show up. I wouldn't put it past her to come hunt me down. She might be sweet and proper, but she has no problem putting me in my place when I'm a jerk. I love my family. They're amazing. I'm one of the lucky ones who grew up in a loving home with a family many would give anything to have. I met Stephy and Bentley because of my father being a preacher, and my mother loves those who I love. But, I don't like lying to them. I don't like that at all."

"We can tell them the truth," he suggests. I roll my eyes.

"Yeah, I know some family members love doing the shock revelations during the holidays. I'm not one of those people. We aren't telling them a thing," I insist. He laughs again.

"I don't do family events. I haven't had a big holiday dinner in a very long time. I don't want to admit it, but I'm actually excited about this."

His words stop all further argument from me. Who am I to take this experience away from him? He came all of this way to see me and he has no family left. My mom has always taken in orphans making them feel welcome. I'd be an awful person to not give this experience to Colby, especially when he's been so good to me.

"Well, heck, you've made me go from wanting to run away, to wanting to drag you inside. If you're faking this then it's not very nice," I tell him.

He laughs, but I do see a different light in his eyes as if this truly does matter to him. It's actually breaking a few walls in my heart. I'm so used to having a loving family, I've become privileged in the love coming my way. I take advantage of it. Maybe I need to thank my parents more often for the life they've given me.

"I have a thing for turkey," he tells me with a shrug as he tries to make it sound as if this is no big deal.

"Okay, let's go meet the folks," I say with a sigh.

He stops, his smile falling away as he looks at me with a bit of guilt. I then see sympathy in his eyes. What the heck? He can go from joking to cold, to sympathetic, to mad in a heartbeat.

"Am I guilting you into this? That's not okay. If you don't want to do this, we can turn around right this minute. You should probably ask instead of showing up with a random guy. I didn't even think about it."

I laugh. "My mother loves to have orphan holidays. Our door has always been, and will always be, open. We might not have a big home, but it's huge with all of the love in it."

"Now I'm not sure what we should do," he says with a chuckle. "You're making me nervous, and I don't normally get nervous."

"Well, wait until we get inside the house. My mother has been cooking for three days. The entire town might be inside our small abode. Since the place is attached to the church, we sometimes overflow. My dad says it's not a day for preaching, but he always seems to give a heartfelt message to those who seem to need to hear it the most. But it always comes back to mom. She's a nurturer and if she isn't taking care of people, she gets sad. She says it's her calling in life. There will be enough food to feed an army platoon."

"Are the two of you going to stand out here all night or come inside."

The words stop both Colby and me in our tracks. We turn to find my mother standing in the doorway of our house with her hands on her hips, a messy apron over her blouse and slacks, and a big smile on her lips.

"Hi, Mom. How long have you been standing here?" I ask. I can't believe neither of us noticed her until she spoke.

"For long enough to know you're debating on whether to come inside or not. Now, that just won't do at all. I have made enough food to feed an army and my feelings will certainly be hurt if you don't get your behinds in here." She turns and looks at Colby. "It's nice to meet you, Colby. Doc called and said you're here from Texas."

Colby's jaw drops as he gazes at my mother. I start to chuckle. "Told you," I whisper.

"I thought you were exaggerating."

"Nope, the entire town knows you're here by now. They'll be making bets on why you're hear and probably placing a pool on our wedding date."

He laughs. "Should I tell them we're already married?"

"If you want to die," I growl as I nudge him in the ribs.

"Are you going to abuse that man or get your behinds inside. It's freezing out here." My mother is growing impatient.

"Sorry, Mom, but we ran into some trouble. I didn't know Colby was coming to town. I ran into him and then I fell and hit my head and then we went to Doc's, and now, well, now we're here. Colby doesn't have a family so this is all new to him."

I feel a little guilty over throwing Colby under the bus, but I know the family thing will make Mom forgive us both and take him in her arms. I'm right.

"Oh, Darling, you just come on inside and you'll have the best meal of your life and plenty of leftovers," my mom says as she moves down the porch and grabs Colby, pulling him into her arms. "Thank you for taking care of my daughter."

Colby looks in shock as my mother releases him. Mom then grabs my cheeks and looks me over. "I'm very glad he was there for you, Darling. How are you feeling?"

I laugh at how my mother can go so quickly from lecturing me to acting like I'm five again. I sort of want to curl up in her lap and make everything okay, and I'm not talking about my physical injuries. Those will heal fast. I'm not even thinking about them right now. I'm thinking about my heart and the fact I can't seem to get over Colby.

"I'm fine, Mom. I fell down, got a few scratches, and got right back up. It's not a big deal at all."

"Well, I'll always worry about you. That's what a mama does. However, you are my klutzy girl so if you say you're fine I won't fuss too much over you, just as long as you aren't alone. Doc said you have to be with people for at least the next thirty-six hours, and if you get sick and don't tell me I will spank your behind. You're never too old for a good whooping when it's called for."

I laugh hard at this as Colby looks between us.

"My mother hasn't once spanked me. I'm not saying it won't happen someday, but so far I've been safe."

"That's because you're such an incredible daughter. I didn't need to spank you. I'm not against it. Sometimes a firm hand helps shape a strong mind."

"I have to agree," Colby says. "I think this is going to be an incredible day. I'm so happy to be invited."

"Well, let's get inside before a search party comes out for us. I have some eggnog ready to go and an entire table of appetizers while I finish up the main courses."

"Appetizers?" Colby says, his eyes brightening even more.

Mom laughs as she wraps an arm around Colby. He seems quite pleased with the attention from her. He grabs my hand to help me move up the stairs to the house. Then we move inside. I can hear football coming from the den and the house smells incredible. My mouth immediately starts watering.

Colby's stomach growls so loud my mom and I both stop and look at him before we burst out laughing. He gives a sexy, crooked little smile and shrugs.

"It smells really good," he says, not at all sorry. "I haven't eaten since a crappy dinner about six last night."

"Oh, that's no good at all. You grab a plate and fill it with appetizers and sit down and watch football. The team will be here in about half an hour for some live football action. In this house you have to go play hard to earn your dinner. If you don't eat a lot I'm offended, and you don't want me offended."

He laughs. "You won't be at all offended by me. I will eat as much as you'll allow me to," he promises. Then he walks to the table and starts filling a plate. At least he isn't shy.

"Now, you my darling girl, aren't allowed to play football today." I groan. I love playing on Thanksgiving. "Don't give me any sass. You come with me and sit." She leads me to the couch and grabs a blanket. There's a fire blazing in the hearth and the heat and blanket instantly make me sleepy. She pours a cup of warm eggnog and hands it over to me. I take a sip and sigh. It's perfect, just as it is every year.

"Is the preacher's wife supposed to be serving alcohol?" I ask with a laugh.

"Jesus drank wine," she reminds me as she always does. "I'm going to the kitchen. You just holler if you need anything."

"Thanks, Mom." She leans down and kisses my cheek, which fills my eyes with tears. I have to push them away. I don't care how old we get; I think we always want our mom or dad when we aren't feeling our best. She leaves and I settle in nice and cozy.

Colby sits down by my dad and introduces himself and within seconds they are speaking as if they're long-lost friends. I lay back, my eyes half-open. It feels good to be home, warm, and relaxed. It feels good to have Colby in my childhood home. I realize I haven't thought about Bentley for a while. I don't know if this is good or bad.

All I know is that I'm happy right where I am. I was panicked when I first saw Colby, but now that he's here I'm glad about it. I'm glad to see him. I don't know what it means, but it means something. Are we really still married? Or is this a new game I don't know the rules for? I guess I'll find out. What will I do if we're still married? I'm not sure of that either.

"The party can start now that I'm here."

Stephy's voice comes rolling through the house as she makes her way in through the front door. She hasn't turned the corner yet to find Colby here. I wonder what she's going to think about it. I'm sure it's going to please her immensely.

"Hi, Mom," I hear her call. "It smells so good in here I think I gained five pounds from just walking in the front door."

"Well, that's good, because you're too skinny," Mom says.

"You always say that. I think you have to because you like to cook and you need all of us to consume the ridiculous amounts on the table."

"I don't lie. I follow the commandments," my mother says with a laugh.

"Oh my gosh, I think I've just died and gone to heaven," Stephy mumbles through a bite of something she's consumed.

"Don't you fill up on the appetizers. I know you well. You'll grab all of the sweets and not eat your dinner," Mom tells her.

"I would never," Stephy says in her most innocent voice.

"Mmm, hmm. Your best friend is in the den with a few others." Mom chuckles and I hear footsteps.

"Oh, a few others?" Stephy obviously picked up on the innuendo in mom's voice.

It only takes Stephy a couple of seconds to come from the kitchen to the den. I watch as she looks at me with raised brows, then turns and finds Colby. Her eyes go wide. I need to stop her in her tracks. I haven't had time to warn her. I know she won't betray me, but she won't know what story I've given.

"Stephy, you made it," I say as I sit up. I was just about to fall asleep. This chair is far too comfortable. I'm sure the eggnog isn't helping much either.

"Of course I made it. Your mom called and told me to grab the cranberries since you couldn't get them. Now, I can see why." She has a devilish look in her eyes.

"You remember Colby from Texas, my *friend*," I stress.

"Oh, your *friend* from Texas. I didn't know he was coming here." She turns and walks straight to Colby who stands. "It's a pleasure to see you again, Colby. Whatever brings you here?"

"It's great to see you again, too, Steph." He pulls her in and gives her a hug. She pulls back and looks at him, then looks at my dad, then at me. She waits.

"I haven't talked to Charlie in a while and wanted to see what she was up to."

"On Thanksgiving. Very interesting," Stephy says. I clearly see the wheels turning in her head. I hope no one else does.

"What's interesting?" my dad asks. He's into his football game and not paying a lot of attention to us . . . thankfully.

"Nothing, Dad. We're just happy Colby came to see us." I like using the word us, because it takes the focus off of me and Colby. If we're all friends, then it's just friendship. I don't want to give my parents ideas. At least that's what I think.

Then again, I'm not sure what I want, as usual. I love this life that I live, but I keep running away from it. I always come back. But now here is Colby, the man I've stayed with the longest in the past five years. I had a hard time leaving him and I've thought about him a lot in the last nine months.

Now, he's back. What do I do with this? I really don't know.

"Football time," my dad says.

"Oh, yes, I'm going to kick some behind this year," Stephy says as she pretends to be holding a football and does and endzone dance.

"You always try. I think it's quite cute," my dad says as he walks past us and pats Stephy's back.

"Mom won't let me play," I tell her with a pout.

"Oh, good, now I get to interrogate Colby without you interfering," Stephy says with a wink.

"I don't think I like this," I say.

"It will all be okay," Stephy says as she pats my

head and gives me an evil smile.

"Stay relaxed," Colby says. He looks around, seeing that we're alone, then leans down and gently places his lips against mine. He only lingers a couple of seconds, but I'm out of breath as he pulls back. He looks at me as if I hold the world in my hands and then he walks from the room, leaving me alone.

I can hear the game begin outside, hear the laughter and taunts. And I'm soothed by the sound of my mother in the kitchen singing as she stirs and clatters. This is home, it will always be home. Is this how it's supposed to be every day? Is this where I belong? Am I supposed to stay with Colby? Can I have it all?

I wish I knew. I close my eyes and give in to the tiredness I've been feeling since I bonked my head. Maybe a little nap is just what the doctor ordered.

CHAPTER SIX

"**I** THINK I'M going to explode."

Colby laughs as he drives us back to my place. Stephy is in the backseat, not able to drive with the amount of wine she consumed with dinner. I think Colby is the only one sober. He's had an amazing night, eating so much food, my mother has chosen him as favorite guest ever.

"That was the best dinner yet, but I agree, I can't move, and I want to cut my belly open and rip out the massive quantities I've put in it. I tell myself every holiday I'll never do it again, but I don't ever seem to listen."

"She cooks too good. I can't seem to stop," I say.

"I feel great," Colby chirps in. Stephy and I groan together. We're not amused.

"It's so nice that you feel good," Stephy says with a lot of sarcasm before flopping back and closing her eyes.

"I probably should've only had one glass of eggnog," I say. "Especially with the pill the doc gave me."

"Yeah, that was dumb," Stephy says with a giggle.

"I think the food absorbed any of the pill or alcohol's effect though," I add.

"We don't always make the wisest decisions," Stephy says.

"That's very true," I admit.

We pull up to our monstrous sized home. Colby let's out a whistle. His place is huge, but this one is bigger. It's such a waste of space for two people.

"Nice place," Colby says as he gets out of the vehicle. He moves to the passenger side and opens both Stephy's and my door.

"Neither of us can take credit. My parents built it," Stephy says as she stumbles from the vehicle. "I love you both, but I'm going to bed." She starts to wobble away.

"Don't forget to drink lot of water and take two Advil," he calls to her.

She laughs as she waves her hand. "Yes, Sir, right away, Sir," she calls back. She opens the door and walks inside without bothering to shut the door behind her.

"I don't know if I can move," I tell him. We're finally alone again and I'm not sure how I feel about it. I know I'm having all sorts of feelings, but I don't know how to assess any of them.

"You don't have to walk. I've got you," he says with a wink. He then reaches his arms in and pulls me from the vehicle, cradling me close to his chest. I look up, my eyes hooded, my heart racing. I feel both needy and relaxed. It was always this way with Colby. He makes me feel so many different emotions, and many times it's in the space of a few minutes. It's always a wild ride with this man.

Being with him again draws me in more to him. Will I ever get over this man if he keeps popping into my life? I don't think I can. Do I want to get over him? I'm not sure of this either. I haven't believed in love in a very long time, not since losing Bentley. I believe I can love people, just not be in love with them. There's a difference in loving someone and being in love with someone. Is how I feel for him changing me? Am I falling in love with Colby, or have I already fallen in love? I don't know. I don't think I can trust myself on answering these questions. I blame it on the slight concussion.

I sigh as he begins moving into the house, kicking the door shut behind us. I snuggle closer against his chest, smiling when it thumps erratically beneath my ear. I can feel he's turned on, I can tell how it's affecting him with us pressed so closely together. I'm responding to him just as much. It's more than desire, though. I think we both know that. I just don't know how much more.

"You're going to have to give me directions," he says with a laugh as he looks around the huge entryway.

I snuggle a little closer and lead him through the house. It takes about a minute to make it to my bedroom. When we step inside with him holding me, my face goes pale as my blood turns cold.

"What is it?" he asks, quickly moving to the bed and setting me down. "I'm calling the doctor." He reaches for his phone.

My eyes fill with tears and I can't speak, but I reach

out and stop him. Then I hold up a finger letting him know that I need a minute to find my voice. He seems to be in fight or flight mode right now as he tries to determine if he should override me and call the doctor. I hold on to him. I take in some deep breaths. He waits.

"I'm sorry," I finally say. I'm completely sober now. Any fuzziness I was feeling on the ride home has completely vanished.

"What's wrong? Where are you hurting?"

"My heart," I say.

He looks confused. He reaches for my neck and holds his fingers there as he takes my pulse. I give him a semblance of a smile.

"No, I'm not having a heart attack. My head is fine, and I'm not drunk." I let out a sigh. "I don't want to hurt you, Colby."

I see the moment he realizes this isn't about my fall. He looks as if he wants to guard himself, but he wants to be here for me. I reach a hand up and cup his cheek. I don't deserve this man, I don't deserve his affection.

"This is Bentley's home. This is where he grew up. This is where he brought me the night we got married," I say as a tear rolls down my cheeks.

He looks at me as the realization dawns. I don't know how all men would react to this, but I should know how Colby will. His eyes widen the slightest bit and then he reaches for me, pulling me onto his lap and wrapping his arms around me, cradling my head against his neck.

"Oh, Charlie, I didn't even think about that," he says as he rubs his hand up and down my back. "How long has it been now?"

I don't try to stop crying. "He carried me through the house just like you did tonight. I wasn't thinking about him until we stepped into this room. I shouldn't be thinking about him now. It's been seven years. I grew up with him, but we were only a couple for two years and only married for one month. We took a month-long honeymoon, and he died the day we got back. I don't know why I still hold on."

He lets me speak as he continues rubbing my back. He's so kind, so gentle. He's such a rock and yet I still walked away from him. I don't know why. Maybe because of my love for Bentley. Maybe that makes it impossible for me to ever let anyone else inside—even a beautiful man like Colby.

"I've always wondered how people stay in the same home they were with another person in that place. Sometimes it's a necessity, but how are you with another person in the same room you were with someone else? How can you focus on that new person, even if they are the love of your life, when you are in the same place as another? How can you ever be free of that person in a place you built memories with another?"

"I've wondered the same," I tell him.

"I've seen people do it," he says.

"Me, too. I don't think I'm one of those people that can forget."

"I think that's because you love big. I think it's also because you carry Bentley with you always. It's easy to make someone a martyr when they are ripped from us. I'm not saying anything about your first husband, I'm just saying that there are ups and downs in a marriage. You only got to see the ups, so it's been impossible for you to let him go."

"I know. Even Stephy tells me this," I admit.

My tears stop, but I don't want to pull away from Colby. He helps me heal in so many ways that no other has helped me before. I cuddle a little closer to him, needing him to hold me. I don't want to think about Bentley anymore. I don't want to miss him. I don't want to feel guilty. I told him we'd have time and all eternity, and we got one month instead. I need to let him go. I just haven't been able to so far.

"I'm going to hold you tonight, Charlie. I'm not going to do anything else but hold you. You need a friend, and that's what I'm going to be tonight," he says as he lifts me. He then lays me down on the bed and pulls off my shoes. I gaze at him with red eyes and try to give him a smile. He grins back at me. Then he kicks off his boots and takes off his shirt, but leaves his pants on. He moves around the other side of the bed and climbs beneath the covers and pulls me against him.

I don't fight him. I close my eyes and cuddle against him. I feel so cold and the heat from his body is just what I need. I don't want to think about the last time I was in this bed with another man. I don't want Bentley in this room with us. Even thinking this, though, I know I can't make love to Colby in this room, and certainly not in this bed. I don't think I'd ever forgive myself for doing that.

"Tell me what you love most about this ranch," he whispers.

I'm grateful for his words. I start to talk. The more I tell him about the land, and the more he talks about Texas, the more Bentley lifts from my mind. I know my first husband will always be with me. I know I won't ever fully let him go. I just have to figure out how to put him away, how to cherish him from afar, how to have a happy middle ground.

Colby and I talk until I can't keep my eyes open. We talk until my heart settles, and my body relaxes. I fall asleep with him speaking of a favorite camping trip in the mountains, and his hands rubbing my back. I fall asleep with no more tears and no more pain . . . for now.

CHAPTER SEVEN

I WAKE WITH the sun shining in the window just as I do every morning. The only thing different this time is I'm wrapped around Colby. He's on his back sleeping soundly. I lie here for a minute wondering how exactly I'm feeling about this. I'm not sure. I like Colby being here. I've slept alone in this room for the past seven years when I'm not in another location. This is no longer Bentley's and my room, it's just *my* room. It still feels odd to have another man in it. I don't think I'll ever get past this.

I climb from bed and Colby doesn't move. I quickly shower and dress and he's still sleeping. It's odd, because back in Texas he was always up at the crack of dawn with no exceptions. It's an hour past dawn now and he's still soundly sleeping. Maybe I've worn him out. I leave a note saying I'm going for a walk, and then I leave the house.

Stephy and I have a standing date on Friday, the day after Thanksgiving, at our favorite café in town. We aren't big black Friday shoppers, but we like to eat and do some online purchases. I'm running late so she's already left the house. We have a few shops in town she likes to hit up.

I take in some deep breaths as I walk down the surprisingly busy street of Prairie Town. A lot of people are out the day after Thanksgiving. It makes me smile which is nice. My head feels fine which is also great. My wrist hurts far more than my head and it's not bothering me too bad.

It's still cold as heck out, but they've really rocked the roads and sidewalks. I guess enough people have fallen and they don't want any more incidents. At least the cold is keeping me nice and alert. I love the Christmas music playing over the outside speakers. There truly is nothing like a small town to make you feel immersed in the holidays.

It's been a long time since I've woken up with a man next to me. I did wake up next to Evan a few months ago, but I'm not counting that. I don't even remember going to sleep. I'm certainly counting waking up next to Colby again. We spent a year together and most of that time we slept in the same room. I don't regret it. I don't regret leaving either. Of course, I'm determined not to have any regrets.

I can tell myself all day long that my relationship with Colby was all about a contract, but it became more than that. I wouldn't necessarily say love, but I will say it goes deeper than signing on the bottom line. Can we really still be married? I'm not at all sure how I feel about this.

I know if he would've woken with me this morning and turned us, it's very likely I wouldn't have said no to him. I might later regret that, especially in that particular bed. I don't want to have any regrets when it comes to Colby. Would I regret it if we do it in another bed? I'm so confused. I'm a blonde right now. Maybe that's what's frying my brain. This makes me smile.

I reach the café and see Stephy inside at our favorite table. As soon as I move through the doors my cheeks start tingling from the temperature change. Dang, it's below freezing outside. It's a good thing I'm used to both the heat and the cold. I'm starting to get spoiled with my travels around the world. I tend to land in good weather wherever I'm going.

"You're late," Stephy says. She's looking through the paper at all of the black Friday adds. She loves it all.

"I know, I know. You could've woken me," I tell her.

"Mmm, hmm, I didn't want to walk in on two naked bodies," she says.

I feel my cheeks grow hotter as I look down. "We weren't *naked*." I feel such guilt about bringing Colby into our house. Ugh. My brain isn't functioning right. It has to be the knock it took. Then again, this does happen to me a lot even if I haven't slammed my head on a hard sidewalk.

"It's okay, Charlie. I'm sure you've been beating yourself up since you woke, and I'm here to tell you to knock it the hell off. This is *our* home. You can bring men into it. I really like Colby, and I truly love you. All I want is for you to be happy."

"But it's Bentley's room," I say. I look around making sure no one is listening to us.

She grabs my hands and squeezes. "It's your room, Char, your room *only*. We can't hold onto Bentley forever."

"I know, you've told me this a thousand times, but this house . . ." I trail off.

"This house is just a house," she says. "And if you refuse to live in it like it's our place, then I'm going to burn it to the ground and buy us a trailer."

I grin at her. Then I laugh. There's zero doubt in my mind that she's speaking the truth. If I don't relent on this issue, she *will* burn this place down to the ground without a second thought.

"I'll try," I say. "It's all I can offer right now."

"Okay, that's all I'm asking for." She then winks. "So, how did the night go?"

"I told you we slept with our clothes on. Nothing intimate happened."

"Well, that's no fun at all," she tells me with a pout. "I've ordered you a hot chocolate and cinnamon roll by the way. If you want more, you can tell her when it comes."

My stomach rumbles. With how much I ate the night before I shouldn't be hungry, but I always am starving in the morning.

"You are a woman after my own heart," I tell her.

"I know. You couldn't survive without me. But, I can't survive without you. I realized we this morning too that we need to get our Christmas tree. We always get it the weekend after Thanksgiving."

"My arm is pretty sore still. I'm not sure I can carry

a tree." I haven't gotten into the holiday spirit yet this year which is strange for me. Some years I'm really into it, and some I'm not. It was a few years after losing Bentley before I wanted anything to do with Christmas again. My parents love it though. Last year was beautiful.

"You hate tree shopping," she says with a laugh. "You always try to get out of it. At least this time you really went all out by getting a concussion and a wrist sprain."

"Well, you always make me do it anyway," I tell her with a pout. "I think I can be bleeding out and you'd still drag me along to pick out the perfect tree."

"We should just agree that we're always doing this together and then we can quit fighting about it. We will do it together even when we're ninety," she says with finality.

"Maybe we should have a new tradition of getting Nerf guns and shooting out the people's Christmas lights who dare to light them Thanksgiving weekend. I mean, come on, let the turkey day end before we jump into Christmas," I say.

"Okay, Scrooge. Who are you and what have you done with my bestie? You never complain about lights."

"Hmm, this *is* a bit strange. Maybe I'm more stressed than I realize." Colby showing up is more complicated than anyone realizes. That has to be causing me more anxiety than I'm letting myself acknowledge.

"I know! I love the lights. I want them lit for months. It's always odd to have them after Christmas is over, so we have to start earlier and earlier. Maybe we should put them up right after Halloween is over."

"Okay, that might be taking it a little too far," I say. "I do love the pretty colors, though."

"I remember when you used to start playing Christmas music in October, so I think we definitely need to have a happy medium of holiday spirit."

"I haven't been able to stand Christmas music in several years," I say. "I need an immersion stat."

"An immersion into what?" she asks.

"Holiday spirit. I want it back."

"Well, there's a hot guy at our house. Let's wrap him in a Santa suit and say ho, ho, ho." She laughs hard at her own joke.

"You know what, I need to stop feeling sorry for myself. I need to let Bentley go, and I need to celebrate again." I realize as I say this I'm right about it. I like being free, I like loving the holidays, and I like laughing. I can't do any of that unless I let go of the past and live for the moment.

"Yes!" Stephy shouts the word and I glare at her. "Yes, we can be happy. There's nothing wrong with it." She gives me a wicked grin. "Does this mean that Colby has a real chance?"

"That's not what this is about," I insist.

"I say you need to ride that cowboy," she tells me right as the waitress appears with our drinks and rolls. She's smiling so I'm sure she's heard what we're saying.

That seals this, I have to murder my best friend. How many times a year do I decide to do just this? At least a couple on an average year. Maybe I'm not the best friend to keep around.

"I will hurt you," I tell her as I hold my fork over my roll.

"I'm not too worried about it."

"You're hopeless," I say. I take a bite of my roll and moan in pleasure. They make them fresh here and they are huge, gooey, and the best on the planet. "So, how about the new tradition of shooting out people's Christmas lights?"

Stephy laughs. "I'm game. Let's get the Sheriff's place first. He keeps adding more and more every year. His place looks like the North Pole."

"I know, it's amazing. We might not want to shoot at a place where they're likely to shoot back."

"Without risk life isn't an adventure," she says with a shrug.

I suddenly want an adventure. I don't want damage, but I want mischief. I'm not acting my age at the moment. "Okay, we'll wear all black. We don't want to get caught," I say, feeling my heart thud.

"What don't you want to get caught doing?"

I freeze with my fork in the air, my bite of gooey roll near my mouth. My heart then leaps, and my cheeks tingle all over again. Before I even look up I can smell his sweet, woodsy scent slowly drift over me.

Stephy is the one to respond. "I don't think you're cool enough to tell."

"Oh, I'm pretty cool," Colby says with a wink.

"Good morning, Colby," I say, feeling shy. Why? Who knows.

"Good morning, my beautiful wife," he says with a huge grin.

Stephy gasps as my cheeks go scarlet and I look around the café praying no one has heard him. I swear people have fine-tuned hearing in small-town diners just so they can rush out and spread gossip. Life gets boring in a small town if people have nothing to focus on.

"So, it's true, you *are* still married," Stephy says.

"I don't know. That's what he's saying," I tell her. "I'm not sure if he's speaking the truth or not."

"I'll give you my attorney's number. You can call and check with him." He then reaches over and takes a bite out of my cinnamon roll. I look at him in horror.

"No," I say.

He chews on the roll and tilts his head. "What?"

"Nope, I don't share cinnamon rolls."

He looks from me to Stephy, who nods, and then he bursts out laughing. "I lived with you for a solid year. How do I not know this?"

"You should. I'm a beast in the morning," I tell him. I've lost a precious bite.

"Ah, because you always get up after me. I've missed your breakfast ritual until now."

The waitress comes back over. "Can I get you anything more?"

"I need another cinnamon roll and a Farmer's

Breakfast with sausage," I say with a smile. "And a big glass of icy cold milk."

She nods, not surprised at all by my huge order. "I'll take the same and a cup of your strongest coffee," Colby says.

"I just need more coffee," Stephy says. She's barely touched her roll. I finish mine and eye hers.

"Nope, evil woman. I'm sharing it with Colby," Stephy says. She then pushes her plate to him and he smiles at me before taking a big bite and moaning as he chews.

"You're both evil," I say. I don't think they'll really stop me if I reach over and take a bite. Stephy scoots the plate a little further away from me and I glare at her.

"If Colby wants to share then he can," she says. "You have to ask him very nicely." She's evil, she's truly evil.

I give Colby pleading eyes. He leans back and laughs hard. "Will you be nicer to me?" he asks as he holds the plate a little too far away for me to steal from it.

I'm torn as I look from him to Stephy to the plate. I'm getting another roll here in a few minutes, and a full breakfast with it, but the place is unusually busy and it could take a while and he *did* take a bite from my other roll.

"Fine, I'll be a *little* nice," I concede.

He throws his head back laughing as he pushes the plate in between us. I immediately take a bite before he changes his mind.

"I ran into your mother before I came in here," he says.

"She didn't want to come in?" Stephy asks as she looks toward the door.

"No, she had some flyers and looked like she was in a hurry."

"Yes, she always is on Black Friday. She runs the pageant and gets as many volunteers and donations as possible for the raffle."

"Yes, she mentioned the pageant," he says with a shrug. "I somehow ended up volunteering. I'm not quite sure how she did it, but within a minute she was signing my name on her neat little paper on her clipboard."

I gape at him. Before I can say anything the waitress appears and sets all of our plates down. The amount of food on the table should feed three times as many people as us. It will all be gone. He digs into his plate looking far too cheery. I don't know what to think. How long is he planning on staying here? The pageant is a couple of weeks away.

"Wow, this is incredible. I love small town diner food. Nothing beats it," he says in between bites. I haven't even taken a bite yet. It takes a lot to distract me from eating—and I'm being repeatedly distracted.

"How long are you staying?" I finally ask.

"I'm not sure," he says with a shrug. We *are* married, though, and I'm thinking we should probably spend some time together. We don't want the townspeople talking."

"Us staying together *will* make the townspeople talk," I whisper. Stephy isn't helping me out here at all as she sips on her coffee and grins at both of us like she's watching a television show. "Besides, we aren't *really* married, married. We did it for a year and my parents don't know."

"Maybe we should tell them," he offers. He's nearly done with his breakfast.

I start to eat my own. Dang, it's good. I can't stay grumpy when I'm eating a warm cinnamon roll, gravy covered hash browns and runny eggs. Stephy leans over and takes a scoop of hash browns without me growling at her. She can get away with just about anything most people can't.

"We absolutely aren't going to tell my parents we're married. They will kill us both. And you have to be quieter. This town is small, as you've already noticed. If one person overhears this conversation it will spread faster than the damn flu."

"I'm okay with that. I'm not ashamed you're my wife. As a matter of fact, I'm pretty dang proud of it."

I decide I'm not discussing this with him any longer. I look down at my food and continue eating. Stephy chuckles as she finishes her coffee then catches the waitress's eye and holds up a hand. I might put away a linebacker's breakfast but she drinks a trucker's amount of coffee. It's yin and yang.

Colby suddenly jumps up, then leans down, his hands braced on the arms of my chair. I can't move even though I see the intention in his eyes. He closes the space between us and presses his lips to mine. I love food, truly love food, but none of the tastes I've had this morning come even close to comparing to the taste of his mouth against mine. Within a second I forget about my best friend sitting across from me, and the room full of my neighbors. I forget I'm trying to keep distance between me and this man.

For a solid year this man took my breath away from me on a daily basis. It doesn't matter we've been apart for nearly a year since then, because all it takes is his tongue dancing with mine to make me forget anything but him. His fingers weave into my hair and he tugs me to him, deepening the kiss, making me groan against his hot mouth. I find myself pushing from my chair, drawing closer to him, tuning everything out around me.

It isn't until laughter breaks through my lust filled haze that I remember where I am, and that I'm on the brink of losing all control. I pull back, horrified I've participated in this public display. I've never done this before in this town, not even with Bentley. Colby and I might as well take out a full page add announcing we're together. It's going to reach every corner of town within the hour.

"Hot damn, you two, that was hotter than the kiss in Top Gun," Stephy says as she claps her hands together.

"Amen, sister," our waitress, Sadie, says.

I'm horrified. I refuse to look at the rest of the

room which has gone oddly silent. That silence is broken in a few more seconds as whispers begin up and sound like a roar of locusts. I'm sure a few pictures were snapped as well. If we aren't on Instagram already I'm going to be shocked.

In another second someone calls out, *way to go, Colby.* How in the heck do they already know his name? Doc! That's how. As soon as my traitorous neighbor says this, the rest of the café patrons begin clapping. I want to sink into a hole.

Much to my horror Colby stand up, grins at all of the people, then proceeds to take a bow as if he's just performed and is accepting his applause. I'm very, very close to slugging the man.

"Thank you, thank you," Colby says. "I normally maintain myself in public, but I haven't seen my wife in some time, and I've truly missed her."

All color leaves my face as I hear a gasp from the crowd as all of my neighbor's heads whip around to me. The crowd goes silent for about three seconds and then phones come right back out as the clicking starts.

"Colby," I gasp. "You didn't."

"Yep, I did," he tells me, not an ounce of remorse on his face.

"You better get to your parents now," Stephy says, leaning back in her chair with a big grin.

I place my head in my hands. Oh my gosh, my mom is going to kill me. My dad might actually kill Colby. I wonder if I can just find a deep dark cave to spend the rest of my days in. I pull out my phone and hit the power button. Any second it's going to start dinging and I don't want to deal with it.

Stephy is right, it's time to face my parents. The town now knows Colby is my husband. What in the heck am I going to do about it? I think I'm going to begin planning his demise, that's what I'm going to do. Now I've had murderous wishes for two people in my life I care immensely for. If I allowed myself to admit it, I'd have to think I'm the evil one of our group. I can't admit that though. I'm no damage control starting right now . . . and I have no idea where to begin.

CHAPTER EIGHT

I MANAGE TO slip away from the chaos in the cafe by using an excuse of using the restroom. No one argues with that. I don't even feel a little bad at leaving Colby with Stephy. She's a traitor right now. She's loving every second of this and she'll enjoy visiting with the man, getting all of the information she can from him. I just need to get away.

I slip into the kitchen and right out the back door with no one saying a word. I've been coming to this place since I was born. I get several smiles and congrats as I keep my head down and sneak through the back door. I don't say a word to anyone. I don't think this is fixable.

As soon as I step outside I realize I've left my coat on the back of my chair in the diner. Maybe the permanent blush heating my cheeks will keep me warm enough not to notice my coat missing. I don't care. There's nothing that will make me go back inside there. I'd rather freeze to death.

I've always been a private person, and never before have I had a man grab me and kiss me in a room full of people. I stop, horrified. That's not true. I have had that happen before. It happened in New Orleans. I have to again wonder who I am. I think this is freaking me out so much because this is in my hometown. These are all of the people who have known me my entire life, these are the people who were at my wedding to Bentley. What are they thinking of me? It's been seven years since Bentley has been gone. But, still, will this make them think differently of me?

I'm confused. I'm scared of how I'm feeling, and I'm freaking cold. I shiver as I stand on the sidewalk. I need to move. I really will freeze if I don't get going. I need to remember that something else is bound to happen in our town that will take the gossip off of me before too long. This too shall pass.

I finally begin to move, shivering all over. I'm in a daze as I look at the ground. The last thing I need to do is take a new tumble. I make it down the block when I hear a voice call out to me. I freeze. I want to run, pretend I don't hear her, but she will know. There's no doubt she will know.

Charlie," she calls again.

I stop and turn to find my mother moving down the street, a smile on her lips, her cheeks rosy from being outside. I attempt a smile. Does she know? I can't tell from her expression.

"I ran into Colby a little while ago. I was going to come in to say hi, but I've been so busy," she says with a laugh. I don't think she knows yet. Should I tell her? My first instinct is heck no, but it's better to rip off the bandage.

"Yes, he found Stephy and me," I say.

"I've been worried about you, but Colby said you slept really well," she tells me. "How is your head feeling?"

"It's great, mom." Does she know we slept in the same bed together? Why do I feel like a misbehaving child again? Will I still feel this way when I'm thirty? Probably.

"Oh, that's wonderful. It doesn't matter how old you get; you'll always be my daughter and I'll continually worry about you."

"I know, Mom. I love that more than anything else in my life. It makes me feel safe even when everything is falling around me." She doesn't appear to be suspicious of anything. Maybe she doesn't have her phone on her. Maybe none of the shops she's been in for the last few minutes have said a word. I want to let out a relieved breath, but maybe it will just be easier if she already knows. I don't know how to tell her. I do know that there's no possible way of keeping it from her.

"What are you guys doing for the rest of the day?" she asks.

"I'm not sure yet," I say.

"Well, why don't you come back to the house tonight for dinner. I have far too much food leftover."

"I can't believe you didn't send it home with people or deliver it today like you do every year."

"I gave a lot away. I guess I just made way too much this year." I laugh, feeling better. I do love being with my mom.

"You say that every single holiday," I say.

She laughs. "I know. I do love holiday cooking. I have to make all of my favorites, and then try new dishes as well."

"I'm very grateful for that." I pause and take in a deep breath. "Um, Mom, there's something I really should've told you sooner." I shift back and forth on my feet. I haven't been this afraid to tell her something since I stole a piece of gum and got busted. This might just be worse than that.

"What is it, Dear. You look upset." Her laughter instantly dies as she looks at me with that motherly concern that's always been my undoing.

"Um, well, you see, um, well, Colby . . ." I fade away, finding myself unable to tell her.

"What about Colby?"

"Well, we're sort of married." I feel my cheeks heat again. At least it's so dang cold outside that she won't be able to tell the blush from the cold.

"Oh, that, yes I've heard," she says with a laugh and a wave of her hand.

I stare at her in shock. She's acting like I've told her nothing more significant than I've stubbed my toe.

"Did you hear me, Mom? Colby is my *husband*." Maybe she doesn't understand what I'm saying.

"I know, Darling. This town is small. You'll tell me all about it tonight." She doesn't look at all worried. "Don't forget to bring Colby. I guess I need to get to know my son-in-law. He seems to be a really great man."

I can't say a word. I'm in total shock.

"I'll see you tonight at six. I would love to stay and chat but I have a million errands to finish before I get home and turn the leftovers into a wedding celebration dinner. I'll see if I can pick up a cake."

With those words, she walks away with the speed of a hurricane. I stand here staring after her for several moments not sure what to do. How can she not be upset at all? She's just heard I'm married, and she doesn't even blink. Will my father react in the same way? I don't know. This is all too strange.

With a bit of deflation, I turn toward my house and begin jogging. I'm freezing, and I need to get moving to keep ahead of the chill. I don't want to run into anyone else, and if I stand here any longer that's exactly what will happen. Within the hour everyone is going to be talking about Colby and me.

By the time I reach my house, I'm shaking I'm so cold. It takes three tries to get the door open because my fingers don't want to grip the doorknob. The first thing on my agenda is a shower, and then I'm layering up on clothes and my favorite wool socks. Once I get my body temp up to below freezing, then maybe I can clear my head and figure out what to do next.

Neither Stephy nor Colby follow me home. What in the world are they up to? Stephy isn't even texting, and I'm not going to message her. I'm sure she knows I'm home. We both have tracking on our phones so we can rescue each other if we're ever kidnapped. Still, I'd think she'd ask something. Nope. I'm sure the traitor is planning some epic reception for the whole town now that they all know Colby and I are married. How am I going to fix this?

I finally get warm and then I curl up on the couch with a dirty chai, the fireplace roaring, and a horror flick on the television. I start to relax. However, when you want time to slowly tick by, it speeds up. When you want it to go fast, it moves at a snail's pace. I truly consider not going to my parents for dinner. There's no doubt though, that they'll hunt me down if I don't come. Maybe Colby won't show. I think there's a better chance of it snowing in the desert than that happening. I think he's here to stay for now.

It's about five when I hear the door open and the sound of laughter from Stephy and Colby. Have they been together all day? Is that a tad bit of jealousy I'm feeling? No way. For one, I'd never be jealous of my bestie. I trust her with my life. For two, I didn't want to hang with Colby today anyway. I'm glad she kept him out of my hair—at least that's my story and I'm sticking to it.

It doesn't take long for them to enter the den where I'm sitting beneath a blanket. It took me a while, but I'm all warm and cozy now. I don't see a need to go back out in the cold and freeze myself again.

"Hello, Darling. I knew you'd be right here doing this," Stephy says with a laugh as she holds up my coat. "You were so worried about sneaking out you left your coat."

"I know," I mumble. "I was mortified. I can't believe Colby announced to the entire town we're married. What are they saying?"

"There's a lot of congratulations. We went over to Bend and did a little shopping. Colby wanted to get a few gifts. It was great."

"I'm glad you had fun," I say. I finally look at Colby. He's holding a bouquet of flowers.

"Hello, beautiful. You look cozy enough to scrap any and all plans and have me come snuggle beneath that blanket with you," he tells me with a wink.

"Hi, Colby," I reply. I feel a glow on the inside as well as the outside at his words. Why do I keep fighting these emotions with him? It won't do me any good. I like him and I want him to do just that, to snuggle with me beneath a blanket. Why in the world am I hesitating? I think maybe people are right, that all women are crazy. I can have this thought since I am a dang woman who appears to be quite crazy at the moment—well, crazy a little too often for my own health.

He comes over and sits beside me, handing over the flowers. "I've had a good day. It would've been even better with you, but I thought you might need some time to yourself after our busy morning."

"Yes, I did," I tell him. We did live together for a year. He knows me more than most people. I shared a lot with him in our time together. When I get over-stimulated I need a little while to calm down and think. I need to be alone while I do this.

"I'm going to get ready for dinner. I can't wait to see your parents tonight," Stephy says.

"You love drama a little too much," I tell her.

"That I do," she says with a wave before she skips from the room.

"Finally, alone," Colby says. My gut clenches.

Colby cups my cheek and I don't even try to stop him as he pulls me to him and drops his lips to mine. Nothing in me wants to push him away. I've been craving his kiss since we stopped this morning. The second our mouths connect, I'm a goner.

His lips trace mine and I move closer to him, wrapping my arms around his neck as he warms me all over. Instead of freezing earlier, I should've just run back to his arms. I don't want to fight him right now. I don't know what this means, I just know I want to be with him right this minute.

He pulls back and my head is fuzzy. I'm in a daze as I look into his smoldering eyes. He smiles at me as his thumb traces my cheek.

"I can't seem to let you go," he whispers.

"I don't understand what it is," I say.

"Maybe it's love," he says.

"I stopped believing in romantic love a long time ago."

"I don't think you get much of a choice in the matter." His hand moves over my heart. "We can fight feelings all we want, but in the end the heart wants what it wants."

Can it be possible that I'm truly falling for him, or that I already have? I don't know. I hate even thinking these words. I say them in my head and out loud too often. I'm not so arrogant to believe that I know everything, but I do know that sometimes life is out of my hands. Okay, most of the time my life is out of my hands. Maybe I just need to accept this and go with the flow.

"Are you ready to face your parents?"

I smile at him. "I think so."

"Good."

We hear Stephy coming back. I push my cozy blanket away and let Colby help me to my feet. It's time to go and talk to the parents. I guess I'll see what's coming next. No matter what it is, I'll be okay. At least that's something I've learned over the past seven years. I can make it through just about any situation—I already have—and I've survived it all.

Is there something that can finish me? I guess I won't know unless it happens. For now, I'm still standing and I'm still smiling . . . at least most of the time. I like where I'm at in this moment. Can I keep liking it?

CHAPTER NINE

I T'S BEEN TWO weeks since Colby arrived in Oregon. The talk with my parents didn't go nearly as bad as I thought it would. As a matter of fact, it went really well. They like Colby. They aren't shocked we got married. They are a little hurt I didn't tell them, but they made that worse by telling me they understand why I didn't. Sometimes I think it might be easier if they just yell at me and tell me to stop being a brat. Would that help? Would it change what I'm doing? Maybe. I respect them a lot.

I'm glad they aren't. I'm not ready to make changes. Maybe I will be someday, but right now I'm doing whatever I need to do in order to not only survive, but to thrive in this world I'm finding myself immersed in.

Colby had to run back to Texas for a week and I've missed him. He's on his way back now. Tonight, we're having the Christmas pageant. My mother has been running around for days doing last-minute preparations. I'm fussing with my hair, getting nothing right. I'm a hot mess, as usual.

Stephy comes into my room and laughs. "Really, Char, why in the world aren't you even a little bit ready? You do realize we're going to be late . . . again."

Stephy looks phenomenal as usual in a Christmas Red dress that hugs her body and flares at her hips to flirt with her toned legs which look incredible in her silver heels. Her dark hair is cascading down her back, and it makes me feel sorry for the men who will be there tonight dropping at her feet. They are going to be tripping over themselves trying to get her attention. Of course, that's nothing new. Half of the town is in love with her. She doesn't notice for the most part.

"I'm getting there, but I just want you to know that I'm attending this dang event under duress," I say as I look in the mirror again, trying to fix my unfixable hair.

"Yes, you've told me many times you don't want to go. Your mother will kill you if you don't show, and like every year, you love it once you're there. You think you want to be a recluse, but you love a good party. Do you need help getting ready?"

"No, I don't need help," I tell her.

She laughs as she ignores me and grabs a chair. "Sit." I do as she demands with a little pout just so she knows I'm doing this under duress. She begins to work her magic. Stephy knows how to do hair. I think I've actually been waiting for her to get her behind in here and work her magic.

"I really should cut my hair off. I can never do anything with it," I say.

She's using the curling iron and bringing body to my flat hair. She uses the comb and does something on top, then clips it up while leaving strands floating around my face. Within ten minutes she's transformed my boring blonde hair into a halo framing my face.

"I don't know how you do this," I tell her.

"Because I watch a lot of videos," she says.

"I've never been into tutorials." I shrug.

"You've never been into the girlier things in life. I don't get it. You're so beautiful that all you need is a few little touches and you knock socks off."

"I don't want to knock socks off."

"It's long past time you stop being a wallflower."

"I've been on one adventure after another the past few years so you can't call me a wallflower anymore."

"That's true. You haven't fought me too much."

"Yes, now hurry up with your lipstick. I don't want to miss out on the good food," she demands. "I forgot my earrings. Go and get dressed and I'll put my jewelry on."

I stand and she smacks my butt then laughs as she leaves my room. I groan and then laugh as I put on lipstick as commanded, then move into my closet. It's cold and I don't want to wear a dress. I put on a pair of leggings and a pretty red sweater. I look in the mirror and shrug. This is as good as it's going to get.

Stephy comes back and her mouth drops open. "No. No. No. No. You are *not* wearing that," she says, shaking her finger at me.

"It's cold out," I tell her.

"I don't care if it's arctic," she says. "Go back into your closet and grab the green dress I bought you last year that you haven't worn yet." I shake my head. "Do it, or I'm going to terrify you all night. I'll make you miserable."

I glare at her. She looks determined. I cave.

"Fine." I stomp back into my closet. I'm not going to win this battle. I'm going to wear nylons though if I have to wear this dress. I hate nylons, but at least they'll keep some of the chill off of my bare legs. It's far too cold for dresses. We aren't going to be walking tonight, though, and the gym, where the party is, will be nice and heated. I just don't want to wear the dress because it's so form fitting and, well, Colby is coming back. He might read something into it.

I get changed, feeling self-conscious at the snug fit of the dress. I can always put on a sweater or jacket with it. Stephy will try to get it off me, but she can't expect me to go outside, even if it's just to the car, without protection. We could literally freeze to death. I choose a lightweight jacket that I can possibly keep on in the gym.

I come out of my closet and Stephy nods with approval. "Much, *much* better. You're gorgeous," she tells me.

"Well, at least I'm going with you and that will take eyes off of me."

She glares. "I really wish you could see yourself. You are so beautiful, and no matter what's happened to you in life, you always pick yourself back up, even if you're ten stories down. There's an alure in your eyes that draws people in, and, surprisingly, you still have an unbeatable innocence about you, too."

"I'm far from innocent. Now, stop this talk, and let's get out of here right now. I'll try to have a good attitude."

"That's all I can ask for." We walk side by side from the house and I'm glad she has the vehicle running. It's nice and cozy as we climb inside.

I'm nervous as we approach the pageant. Has Colby arrived? He called when he was leaving Texas, but he hasn't let me know if his plane has landed, or if he's back in town. He's been staying with Stephy and I at the ranch while he's been here, but we aren't sleeping in the same room.

Knowing he's in the same house as me is killing me. I haven't ached this much in a long time. I don't know if I want to keep resisting the man. He's been kissing me, but he hasn't pushed it past that. He's letting the decision be in my hands—he's also letting me know he's more than willing to share a bed. I clench my legs together as I think about having him in my arms again. Who am I really fighting? It's certainly not him, it's all on me.

Stephy and I arrive to a packed gym. The silent auction is going strong with people following each other around as they up bids on the best packages such as a weekend trip to Aspen, and a new ATV.

People are laughing as they hold drinks and staff walk around the room with trays of appetizers. Stephy and I grab a glass of wine and a few appetizers as we look around. There's a band playing and several people are dancing. Mom has outdone herself. The kids have a pageant in about an hour, but the rest of the night is all about celebrating the holidays and raising a bunch of money for our school district. This event always makes enough to keep our extra programs that many schools have cut through the years such as cooking class, art, mechanics, and more.

"Wow, Mom has outdone herself this year," Stephy says.

"She's Superwoman. I hope and pray they don't ask her to pass the button to me someday. There's no way I can do even close to as good of a job."

"We can do it together. I love how she gets the best prizes. How does she talk people into donating hotels, vehicles, and jewelry?"

"Because she goes in person and has that dang smile of hers that people just can't resist. She also brings them baked goods, and nobody can say no to Mom's cooking."

"I agree. I'm so lucky I have a good metabolism, or I'd be four hundred pounds," I say as I rub my belly. "I can deal with the hips."

"Don't forget the boobs. You have great boobs."

"Boobs are just globs of fat. That's where all of my food goes to," I say with a laugh.

"Shh, don't tell men this or they might stop playing with them and that would be utterly tragic."

We both crack up. If the majority of men heard how us women talk they'd be horrified. Everyone always makes comments about how crude men can be. They don't even compare to us girls. We just get away with it because of our innocent smiles.

After a few more glasses of wine, I'm feeling a lot better about the night, just as Stephy knew I would. I don't know why I tend to stress out so much about everything. I haven't caught sight of Colby, and it's starting to bug me. I've lost my coat, and I've had several people come up to me congratulating me on my marriage, and now I'm rubbing my empty ring finger self-consciously. What does this mean?

What does any of it mean?

"May I have this dance?"

The butterflies immediately take flight in my stomach as Colby whispers in my ear. Goosebumps appear on my arms and it has nothing to do with me being cold. I'm *very* warm right now.

I turn slowly, and look at Colby. He looks good, way too good in his custom black suit, white shirt, and bright red and silver tie. He points to his pocket where a sprig of mistletoe is resting. His eyes are sparkling, and his lips are turned up.

"You look spectacular, good enough to eat," he says.

"I was just thinking the same about you," I tell him.

"I wonder what we should do about this," he says again and looks down at his mistletoe. I laugh, feeling lighter than I've felt for a very long time. Maybe I need to quit fighting myself and simply go with the moment. What can it hurt in the long run?

I step to him, wrap my arms around his neck and

kiss him. The entire diner saw us kiss a couple of weeks ago. I might as well give the whole town a show right now. In reality, I don't care how many people are looking at us. All I care about is that I've missed him, and I want his lips on mine.

His lips whisper over mine and I sigh against him as he places a hand on my lower back and pulls me in close. The kiss only lasts for a few seconds before he pulls back. I look at him with confusion.

"If we keep doing this, I'm going to embarrass us both. This suit won't hide my reaction to you."

I beam at him. I love that I can affect this man so strongly. I love that he wants me. I'm starting to believe there's nothing wrong with it. I'm starting to believe we might just be able to have a happy ending.

"Let's dance," he tells me.

"Yes, let's dance." I float onto the dance floor with him. I know people are watching. I don't care anymore. I don't know why I don't care, but all I can think about right now is this man. Nothing else seems to matter.

As soon as I'm in Colby's arms I have no doubt at all where tonight is heading. I don't want to fight any of it anymore. Can we actually give this marriage of ours a real go? Can I love him as much as I loved, and still love, Bentley? Can I just accept it's a different love than what I had with my first love? You can love more than one person. Maybe what I need to accept is that one love isn't better or worse. There are many forms of love.

I want this man, I want to keep feeling the way I'm

feeling right now while with him. I get lost in his arms in a sea of people I've grown up around. I'm dancing with Colby in the same place I once danced with Bentley, but for once I'm not berating myself for this act. I'm not trying to replace Bentley, I'm trying to let him go and let myself live.

The music stops as the band tells us they're going to take a ten-minute break. Voices surround us as I stay right where I am in Colby's arms. Now that I've made the decision, all I want to do is keep him close to me.

"I don't want to let you go," he tells me, the beautiful smile on his face making my heart stumble through erratic heartbeats.

"You take my breath away," I tell him. His smile grows.

"That's my line." He cups my cheek, not letting go of my gaze. He has the power to hold me in place and I don't fear it anymore. "I missed you from the moment you left Texas. I missed you this past week when I went back to my empty home. I like being with you, Charlie."

"I missed you, too," I admit. "I try to fight that feeling, but I'm lying to myself."

"I want to give us a real shot. I don't want it to be a contract. I don't want it to be forced. I want to be with you. I want to share our lives between Oregon and Texas. I know how important this place is to you, and you know what Texas means to me. I think we can make it work. I think we can have it all."

I feel hope in my gut. The hope scares the crud out

of me, but I don't shy away from it. "I love your ranch in Texas and the people who work there. I love my home here in Oregon as well. I am scared. I haven't thought in terms of forever in a very long time."

"It's okay to be scared." He pauses. I see conflict in his eyes. He takes a breath and continues. "I'm in love with you, Charlie. I think it happened fast and I fought it as much as you have for the past two years, but I love you. I think of you when you're gone, I think of you when I wake in the morning and when I fall asleep at night. I dream about you. I want more. I'm willing to take it slow, but I'd love to take it fast, too. I'm just letting you know that I'm willing to do whatever it takes for you to trust me. I knew I wanted more when I couldn't sign those papers. You're already my wife, but I want to marry you again in front of our friends and family. I want it to be a real wedding and I want us to be together forever."

I feel equal parts of happiness and fear as he says these words. I open my mouth to respond, then shut it, then try again. I take a deep breath.

"I love you, too, Colby," I whisper. It's hard to get the words out. He smiles. I now cup his cheek. "I do love you, and I do want to try, but I want to be honest. I'm not sure how to do this, I'm not sure I won't hurt you." Tears spring to my eyes as I tell him this. I feel like a monster. I should just be able to tell him I love him with no thoughts of *buts*.

"I know, Charlie, I know," he says as he hugs me with so much love it knocks my knees out from beneath me. I'm shaking. "I'm willing to risk my heart to give us a chance. It doesn't matter anyway, because I'm all in right now. My heart might get more shattered if this goes on a while and ends, but at this point it will be broken anyway."

"Oh, Colby, you're too good of a man for me."

He gives me the most beautiful, unguarded smile I've ever seen. I've run from this man, hid from him, and put him through hell, and yet he still loves me so much more than I deserve.

"We're both broken people, but maybe we can continue to help one another heal. That's what love does."

He stops and drops down on one knee. I hear people around us quieting as all eyes turn to us. My cheeks heat, but I stare at Colby, and ignore everyone else. If there's possibly one person in this audience that doesn't know about me and Colby, that's over now.

Colby pulls out a black box and opens it, showing me the brilliant diamond encrusted band inside. He knows I don't love diamonds, but he also knows I love unique pieces. This band looks like a constellation of stars. It's perfect.

"Marry me again, Charlie, in front of our loved ones. Let's make this a real marriage," he says. His eyes shine with emotion. I nod. How can I do anything else?

"She said yes," he calls as he jumps to his feet and pulls me into his arms. He kisses me and I feel tears on my cheeks. This moment is beautiful. I laugh to think I'm going to get married again for the seventh time. I laugh as Colby kisses me once more as he lift me off of my feet.

Stephy runs to us both and hugs us, tears on her cheeks. "I love you guys."

"Thank you, Steph, this is all because of you," Colby says.

"I've never been so happy I responded to an add," Stephy says.

Several people, including my parents come up to us with smiles and words of encouragement. Everyone is happy. It's exhausting. We don't get a second alone until the pageant begins. I don't need to watch it.

"Colby, take me home," I whisper as we finally find ourselves alone.

His entire body stills as he looks at me. He knows what I'm asking. He grins, then takes my hand and pulls me through the gym, making me laugh. He's not even looking at anyone who tries to stop us. He's on a mission. It's been a *very* long time since we've made love and he's not letting anything get in our way.

I think he makes it back to the ranch in about three minutes. There are a few hair-raising turns in his SUV, and we slide as we come down the drive to the house. I'm laughing, feeling just as excited as he is. I have no more doubts. I won't let myself feel them in the morning either. I spent a year with this man, and I was truly happy. If I would've gotten out of my own way sooner, I think I'd have spent this past year just as happy.

I've looked for flaws in every person I've been with

since Bentley because I wanted to find a reason to let them go. I haven't been able to find faults in Colby because he's a great man. He's not perfect, and neither am I. We're flawed and that makes us more beautiful to one another.

As we rush into the house, I realize I don't ever want to climb from his bed. I want to hold him, and have him hold me. I want to laugh and make love and be close to him with no blocks between us.

He lifts me in his arms just as he did a couple of weeks ago. Instead of it causing a meltdown this time, it excites me even more. He flies through the house. He doesn't take me to my room, he takes me to his. He loves me enough to want no doubts creeping into my thoughts. I lean in and kiss his neck, needing to get our clothes out of the way. This man excites me more than any other person I've been with.

He sets me on my feet inside his bedroom, then pulls me straight into his arms, kissing me the way I've wanted to be kissed from the moment I saw him looking so handsome in his suit. This time we won't be interrupted. This time we're going to finish what we start with no remorse and no regrets.

I want to both take our time and I want to rush. I want to make love all night, but I'm feverish right now. "I want you so badly I'm going to fumble," he tells me. I'm shocked at the vulnerability in his voice. I don't expect him to feel insecure about anything.

"I'm about to explode, Colby. Take me. We have all night." My voice is breathy and needy. I don't care.

I know I can show him everything about me and it still won't scare him away.

He reaches down to the edges of my dress and begins pulling it up. "Damn, whoever made this material needs to get an award. You look so good in it with the way it clings to you. I'm loving it even more as it comes off of you." He pulls it over my head then groans as he rakes his eyes over my black lace bra and the tiny scrap of panties that barely cover anything. I shake as heat flares in his eyes.

"I can barely breathe looking at you."

I can't speak at all. My voice is gone. He's burning but he slows himself down. I can see the restraint in his flexed muscles as he holds himself back. He cups my cheek and looks in my eyes, making me whimper. This is so beautiful, so sweet, and so hot all at the same time.

He kisses me again, this time gently, loving me thoroughly. I sigh against his mouth as his hands caress my back and he moves us toward the bed. We bump into it and he pulls his lips from mine. I can barely gaze at him through my desire.

He lifts me and sets me on the bed, then steps back and tosses off his coat before undoing his pants. I pant as I watch him strip in front of me. My core clenches over and over again. I turn and begin to crawl up onto the mattress before I melt off the side of the bed.

"Stop," he says, his voice barely recognizable it's so deep and needy.

I stop, my ass in the air, my body shaking. He moves up to me and runs his finger along the seam of my panties, making me groan. The material is wet, and I want them ripped from my body. I want him to slam inside me and take me hard and fast and make both of us reach for the heavens.

He pushes my thighs wide and traces his finger up and down the seam of my panties before slipping inside the elastic and running his callused finger across my bare heat. I let out another groan and nearly come from one swipe of his finger against my pulsing core.

He leans forward and runs his tongue along my butt cheek before kissing his way to my panties and licking against my seam before moving to my other cheek. I arch toward him, begging for more as he slips two fingers inside my heat. My head drops to the bed as my body turns to jelly.

He slips my panties aside and runs his tongue along my seam, making my body shake as pleasure builds from deep inside. He holds tight to my hips and laves up and down my hot folds, drinking from me while dipping his fingers in and out, in and out.

He pushes my thighs further apart then grabs the elastic of my panties and rips them away, the delicate lace destroyed. He closes his mouth over my pulsing bundle of nerves and sucks hard while his tongue whips against my flesh. I scream as an orgasm rips through me. He doesn't let up, sucking and licking me until my body slumps to the bed.

I feel Colby pull back and hear a rip as he removes the rest of his clothes. He wants to be naked against me as much as I want him to be. He moves back to the bed and unhooks my bra.

"Turn over," he demands, his voice low and needy.

I turn and he pulls the bra off of me, my breasts spilling free for him. He moves forward and runs his hands over my flesh, stopping on my breasts and squeezing them, making my nipples bead and ache for more. Everywhere he touches is both pleasure and pain.

He finally climbs on top of me, leaning down and kissing me again, this time with more hunger and need than ever before. I grab his head and pull him closer. He leans on one hand trying not to crush me, but I want him to do just that. I want us to be one. I want him inside of me and nothing between us. He grips my hips and slips tighter against me, his arousal pressing against my opening.

I push up to him but he doesn't press inside, instead he rubs his thick head against my slit, arousing me all over again as he moves it across my sensitive folds. I jerk upward and he enters me. I can see playtime is over as his eyes flash with need. He pulls back and then thrusts forward hard, sinking all the way into me.

After nearly a year, I let out a cry of pleasure and pain. It takes a bit to adjust to him. He's filling me everywhere. My breath wooshes from me as I clench around him. I wiggle and I can see the moment he loses the rest of his control. I hold on for the ride, knowing it's going to be the best of my life.

He pulls back, then surges forward again. All teasing has vanished, and I groan as I grip him hard, my nails digging into his shoulders. He moves faster, pushing and pulling in and out of me. We're both covered in a sheen of sweat as we groan and pant and reach for heaven. He hits me, and hits me, and hits me, and I explode in a color of light as my body clenches him. I'm shaking and crying and barely staying conscious.

He yells as he thrusts again and releases with me, pumping in tune with my body, his heat filling me. We're both shaking with the pleasure of the moment, with how tightly we're holding one another, and with the assurance that this is where we belong, where we always should be.

It takes a long while for my body to shop shaking. He turns us and I'm barely awake. I'm depleted in the best way possible. He's still inside of me, right where he belongs, but now he's on his back and I'm on top. I'm very aware he can stay hard all night. I'm very aware he can come multiple times. I've been unable to walk normal after a few of our nights of lovemaking. I'm determined for this to be one of those nights.

"I won't ever have enough of you," he tells me.

I'm exhausted, but I find the strength to sit up, and I move my hips, loving how he feels deep inside of me. It won't take much to bring me back to the brink of pleasure. He lifts his hands and cups my breasts, letting his thumbs rub back and forth over my hard nipples.

We make love again, this time slower, but still just as powerful. Finally, I collapse against him, this time not able to move at all. I chuckle as he rubs my back.

"I don't know why I fight this," I whisper.

"I don't know. Maybe because we're all human and we make very poor decisions."

I laugh. He's right. Leaving him was a poor decision. Hopefully I won't be so foolish as to make it again. I think we are made for each other. I hope I can get that through my thick skull. I hope I can let go of everything else. I love him. I hope it will be enough.

CHAPTER TEN

W E ALL HAVE the best days of our life, and we all have the worst. I didn't think it possible to have a worse day than the day I lost Bentley. I was wrong . . . I was so very, very wrong. My life isn't ordinary. I understand that now. I've accepted it. I'm okay with this.

It's been almost six months since Colby stepped back into my life. We're making it work. We even had a wedding for my family which half of the town showed up for. It was beautiful. I wore a light blue gown that flowed around me, and I was smiling the entire time I moved down the aisle to him, Stephy at my side, my mother and father waiting, their smiles nearly as big as mine.

That day had been perfect. That day I was in love and happy, believing I had a real future. There were to be no more games, no more fear, no more running. There was no need anymore.

There aren't always good days, but there are more positive ones than negative. He's been going back and forth from Oregon to Texas. I've only made the trip back with him a couple of times for short periods. I'm working at home. I've needed to do this. It's giving me stability in a world that too often feels out of my control.

My parents haven't asked about my fictional bank job I'm no longer doing. I'm grateful for that. I don't like lying to them. I don't like lying to Colby either. He's been gone the longest period this time, almost two months. We've spoken often on the phone, but it isn't enough. I find myself pulling from him. I don't know what this means.

He can feel it too. There was an oil explosion back at his ranch keeping him away, but he's coming in today. He doesn't have much time, but he's been trying to get me to come back to Texas with him. He doesn't want our relationship to end. How can it go from magical to this in so short a time? It's on me, it's always on me.

I run my hand over my expanding stomach. I've been able to hide it this long, but I won't be able to much longer. It's April now in Oregon. It's still cold outside with everyone wearing sweaters and coats, but the snow has melted, and the temperatures are climbing. I haven't even told Stephy.

I think I'm not telling anyone because every time something beautiful happens in my life, something else comes along and rips it away. I feel the baby kick and I laugh. "You're active today," I whisper. She kicks me again.

I've been riding a lot. My doctor, which I drive over an hour away to see, says I can maintain my regular life. I was fearful to get on a horse when I first discovered I was pregnant, but now I know it's all fine.

I'm going to be a mother. Awe fills me at this. It didn't feel real until the first time she kicked me. I didn't even realize it was happening at first. I thought it was bubbles in my stomach. But over the week the movements got more consistent, and I knew it was my baby letting me know she's okay inside of me.

I move out to the barn when I hear a vehicle pull up. I step back outside. My stupid emotions are all over the place right now. I can't seem to control them. I go from laughing one second to sobbing in the next. It's crazy.

Colby steps from his truck. He bought one after the first trip back home and here again, and he keeps it at the private strip so he can come and go as he pleases. My heart lurches as he turns and looks at me. I wonder if he can see the change in me. I've only gained ten pounds in five months and my stomach is rounded, but not by much. My sweater covers the bump. If he puts his hand on it, he'll feel the change. How am I going to tell him? How will he respond?

He runs to me and pulls me into his arms, lifting me from the ground. I get a little dizzy as I laugh. He sets me down and kisses me, making all of my worries instantly disappear.

"It's killing me not to be with you," he tells me as he pulls back. He's not angry. I don't get this. To be honest, I'd be angry if he had the power to be with me, but wouldn't do it. How is he this good to me?

"I've missed you," I tell him. I love that it's true.

"Then come back to Texas with me." He doesn't call Texas or Oregon home. They are both our homes.

"I'm working," I say.

"It's important, but we can have a job at both places," he says for the thousandth time.

"We can talk about it later," I say. He looks as if he wants to argue, but he pushes the frustration down. We haven't been together in two months. The last thing either of us wants right now is to fight.

"I'm getting ready to ride. Come out with me."

I know he's tired, but he simply nods as he moves to his favorite horse and saddles him. He tells me about the oil rig that exploded and contaminated a huge are of the ranch. I listen as we move into the hills. I ride so much alone that it's heaven to have him beside me, to hear his comforting baritone.

I'm trying to figure out how to tell him about the baby as we turn a corner. This is when everything goes so very, very wrong. There's a coiled rattlesnake in the path that immediately strikes out spooking my horse. She rears up and I try to gain control of her, but it's too late. I feel myself coming out of my saddle. I desperately try to hold on, but I feel myself flying through the air.

I hear Colby scream out my name, but I can't see him. My stomach is in my throat as the ground grows closer. I slam into it, my head slamming against the hard dirt. I'm dizzy and I immediately feel a burning cramp in my stomach as sharp pain shoots through my arm.

"Charlie," Colby screams as his arms surround me, lifting me from the ground.

I hurt everywhere, my stomach, my arm, my head. I'm crying, I'm dizzy. I don't understand what's just happened.

"It's okay, we're going to be okay," Colby assures me. The tears in his voice contradict his words. I feel a trickle on my face and then taste blood. I realize my head is bleeding.

He brings me to his horse and somehow manages to jump up with me, and then we're flying back down the mountain, all the while he's telling me it will be okay. He's on his phone, calling for an airlift. That's when I look down and see my lap covered in blood. The baby. Oh my gosh, the baby.

"I'm pregnant," I gasp as another cramp rips through my stomach. I don't see his face, but I hear the sob in his voice as he relays the information to whoever he's speaking to on the phone. He keeps telling me it will be okay. For once in my life, I don't believe him. There's so much blood, too much blood.

We make it to the flat part of the land, and I can hear the rotors from a helicopter. I don't know how much time has passed. I'm fading in and out of consciousness. Colby is trying to keep me awake. It's impossible. My head is fuzzy.

He climbs down from the horse and I'm strapped to the gurney.

"She's pregnant. She was bucked from a horse and bitten in the arm by a rattlesnake," Colby cries above the sound of the rotors.

"We're going to take care of her," a man says.

We're moving and then we're in the helicopter. Colby is at my side. He's telling me I'm going to be okay. It will all be okay. Blessed darkness finally takes me away from the pain and fear. I let it pull me under . . .

I'M GROGGY AS sounds fill my head before I open my eyes. It takes a minute for me to remember everything from just before I passed out. My eyes open and I find Colby beside me, his head next to mine on my pillow. He's slumped in a chair, his hand gripping mine. He's crying. I've never seen him cry before.

"Colby," I squeak, my voice raw.

He looks up, his cheeks wet, his eyes red. He doesn't need to say anything. I know. I can't stop more tears from falling. He pushes his forehead against mine and we sob together. I don't want him to say the words, but I need to hear them out loud. It's a solid ten minutes before I say anything.

"Tell me," I finally demand.

He sighs. "We had a little girl," he tells me on a choked sob. She was perfect, absolutely perfect. One pound, ten inches of a perfect human being." He stops as another sob rips from him. "I held her in my hands. She was so tiny. She was already gone when she was taken from you. They had to do an emergency Csection. You were hemorrhaging." He stops.

I go numb. My tears stop. I wish they'd have let me bleed out. I wish I would've gone with my daughter. I won't survive this. I know I've told myself many times that I can survive anything, but this is too much. He doesn't ask why I haven't told him. He doesn't ask me anything. He's not judging me. He's sitting at my side as we both realize the loss we've suffered.

I've known since my second month I was pregnant. He's only known for hours. It doesn't matter. We're both suffering. We've both lost a child today. I don't know how anyone survives this.

It's my fault. I killed my child. Just as I killed Bentley. It's my decisions that lead those I love the most to their deaths. I shouldn't have climbed on that horse. I should've taken Colby inside the house and made love to him and shared the news of our daughter. I should've been with him in Texas. I should've done a lot of things differently.

It doesn't really matter though. None of it matters. It's too late. I can't go back in time and change a thing about this. I can't turn back the clocks. I can't save my daughter. I don't think anything can save me now.

Colby stays by my side all night. The doctor and nurses come in. I barely respond to them. The night passes. I flit in and out of sleep. I never get to hold my daughter. I never get to see her face. I don't want to. I don't think I'll ever get over that. I don't know how I will get over any of this.

On the third day in the hospital they bring Colby

and me our daughter's ashes. I sob again for the first time since hearing the news. This precious life that was inside of me is now in a tiny box. How is this possible? How does such a viable life fit in a container smaller than a soup can. I clutch the box to me and sob and sob. Colby is the one numb now. His eyes are swollen and dark. He's still with me, still supporting me, still holding my hand, but there's a block between us. We both know it.

Stephy has been away in California on business. I've asked Colby not to tell her. I don't want her to know. I don't want anyone to know. He argues with me, and I shut him down. He nods. He won't go against my wishes. I don't know how to keep it from her, but I can't do this again. I can't have people look at me like a victim when I'm the monster.

We leave the hospital and Colby drives me to the Coast. We go to Florence, Oregon. I've visited here before, and there's something about Heceta Head lighthouse that brings me a sense of calm. It's where I want to lay my daughters ashes to rest. I'm slow, my body still healing as we climb the trail to the light-house. It's a clear day, but the wind is blowing. There are people around us, but I ignore them.

Colby and I don't say words as we open the case our daughter's been placed in. I hand it to him, unable to let go. He holds it out to the wind, and we watch as our daughter is carried out to the ocean, the ashes hanging in the air until they finally sink into the sea. I fall against him and shake with my sobs as I say goodbye.

I barely make it back down the trail and he helps me into his vehicle and then we drive to Driftwood Shores where he has a room waiting. He starts a fire in the fireplace and then puts the lounger on the patio and brings me a blanket. I settle in and look at the rapidly swelling waves of the Pacific Ocean. The clouds roll in and rain begins to fall. It's like this a lot on the coast. It can go from sunny and blue skies to a storm blowing in less than a couple of hours. It's something I've always loved. It's fitting to how my heart is feeling right now.

Colby joins me on the patio as lightning flashes across the sky. The ocean looks angry as it picks up force crashing against the shore. The rain pours down hard. Colby sits next to me and holds my hand. A beautiful numbness washes over me.

I realize in this moment that I've completely pulled from him. Everything good in my life leaves me. I lost Bentley, I've lost myself, and now I've lost my daughter. I know there's no way I'll survive if I lose Colby too. The only way to fix this is by letting him go myself. I can't lose him, I need to set him free. I'm aware the logic doesn't make sense. I don't care. I don't care about anything right now.

There's a small part of me that's angry with him, with myself, with God, with life. I push that down. Anger won't help. I need to be numb. I need to not feel. I need to let it all go. If I don't, I'm going to walk out onto this beach and keep moving until the sea swallows me whole. It's what I desperately want to do.

"Please don't push me away, Charlie. I think we need each other now more than we ever have before," he says after silence for nearly an hour.

"I need to grieve," I whisper. My voice is numb, my body is numb. I'm not feeling much at all in this moment.

"You don't need to grieve alone. We can do it together. In time we can heal."

I shake my head. "Time won't fix this."

He looks back out at the ocean. He takes a breath. I can feel the acceptance in him. He knows he can fight me, but he knows it will only hurt us more. He knows this time he can't break through. I don't know if anyone will ever break through again.

"Please," he finally says. I turn and look at him. I truly have never deserved him. He's too good of a man. I knew I'd destroy him. I was right. I just didn't know I'd destroy myself at the same time.

"It's over, Colby. I need it to be over."

He nods. He doesn't have anything left inside of him to fight me. We're both shadows of who we once were. "I will always love you. I will always have hope. I'll be waiting if and when you come back to me." He leans over and softly kisses my lips. I feel nothing—there's no pain, no love, no hate, just a big void. I've turned it all off.

Colby stands. He looks at me one more time and then he walks away. I hear the sliding glass door click shut. I close my eyes. I tell myself I've done the right thing. I might never know if I have. It doesn't matter.

I look back out to the ocean, and it's calling to me. I want so badly to walk to it, to let it embrace me to pour over me and take me to my daughter. I don't know why I don't. The night is still young. I might just do it in a little while . . .

CHAPTER ELEVEN

T HE COURTROOM IS eerily quiet as I stop speaking. One sound comes through loud and clear . . . a sob. I look out and see Stephy. Her eyes are red, her cheeks soaked. She looks at me. I was afraid to look her in the eyes, afraid of what I'd see—judgement, hate, disillusionment. I didn't tell her, the one person I never lie to . . . not ever. All I see though, is pain and . . . love.

"I think that's it for today," Judge Croesus says, his voice subdued. He lightly bangs his gavel. I think we're all done for today. I might be done with it all. I didn't know how much pain bringing this back up would bring me. I now know. It hurts almost as much now as it did when it happened.

Normally when court ends for the day the room erupts with sound. Not today. It's somber. Everyone is moving slow. I stay where I am for a little while as people flow from the courthouse. After a few minutes I finally stand, my knees shaky. I've come to terms with the loss of my baby. It took some time, but I've gone through the gauntlet of emotions and accepted we don't have control over our lives. If it was meant to be, my daughter would be in this world. I'd be holding her hand now, and my life wouldn't have turned out how it has. I wouldn't be sitting in this courtroom.

That's not how my life has gone. Nothing has gone the way I once expected it to go. That doesn't mean it's better or worse, it just means what will be will be. Stephy is waiting at the table, tears cascading down her cheeks as I approach. She throws her arms around me.

"This explains so much," she says on a sob. "You should've told me." Before I can say anything, she keeps talking. "I understand why you didn't. I wish you would have talked to me, and I still love you more than words can say, but you should've told me. I would've helped you through it all."

"I couldn't," I tell her. "I couldn't tell anyone. I'm glad my parents aren't here today. This will be hard on them as well."

"Only because it hurts us all that we weren't there for you. I had no idea how close you came to giving up on everything."

"It was close, but because of you and my parents and even Colby, I didn't give up on anything. I'm very grateful for that now."

She sighs as she pulls back and looks at me. "I never would've pushed you had I known." I know what's she's thinking about. I smile at her.

"That's another reason I'm glad you didn't know. I needed to go there, Stephy. I needed to forget. I needed to heal. If you wouldn't have pushed for that, I wouldn't have gone, and I might've given up. I haven't always made the smartest choices in life, but in the end, it's all working out. That's in big part to you."

"I understand that you didn't want to be babied again like you were with Bentley," she says.

"Exactly. I wouldn't have survived that. I didn't want empathy. I was feeling it was all my fault."

"You don't still think it's your fault?" she says, holding my hands.

"A part of me will always put blame on my own shoulders, but most of me knows I can't change what has been. I'm sure victims of all accident go through the same emotions as I've gone through. If only I would've left five minutes earlier or later, if only I hadn't gotten into that fight, if only . . . We can make up excuses and try to reason all we want, but we can't change what has happened. I've learned that more than anything else in the past decade."

"Do you ever regret pushing Colby away?"

I smile. "I have many times." I haven't told Stephy the next part of my chapter with Colby. The man himself doesn't even know.

"You can change it," she says.

I smile at her again. There's a lot I can change. "No regrets, remember?"

She wipes away the last of her tears. "There's a difference in no regrets, and making smart changes in our lives."

I wrap my arm around her. "I do know that difference. I'm just trying to decide on what changes I want to make."

"Well, maybe we've had enough weddings," she

suggests.

Somehow, I find a piece of laughter in me. "Not even one more?"

Her eyes widen as she looks at me. There are a million questions blazing in her eyes. "Is there going to be one more wedding?"

I wink at her. I don't say anything more. There might be one more wedding. I guess we'll all just have to wait and see.

EPILOGUE

IT'S BEEN A month since I've lost my baby. I'm once again curled up on Bentley's grave, this time alone. It's not his birthday, it's not a special day at all. I just find myself coming here more often lately. I stayed at Driftwood Shores for a week, looking out at the ocean each night trying to decide if the call was great enough to enter the waters. I'm thankful I resisted.

I finally came back home. I once again wear a fake smile. This time, though, people assume it's because Colby is gone. No one knows why. No one is asking me questions. Stephy stares at me with worried eyes. I try to care about this, I try to pull myself together. I can't do much more than rise from bed and move around like a zombie.

"This is worse than when I lost you," I whisper.

I can't imagine what you're feeling.

"It hurts so much I've pushed the hurt down. I'm numb most of the time. I don't cry anymore."

You need to cry. You need to yell. You need to let it all go. If you hold it inside you will explode.

"I don't see a reason to go on. Why should I? I'm not allowed to fall in love. I'm not allowed to find happiness. Why should I keep trying?"

Oh, baby, you will soar someday. Earth is a trial for all of us. Only the strongest get the hardest trials to walk through. I know this hurts, and I don't know the reason for the trials, but you are strong enough to handle it. Please don't give up.

"You're wrong. I'm not strong at all. I feel weak. I feel alone. I can't do this anymore, Bentley."

You can and you will. Let your friends love you. Let them in. Let them help you through this.

"I'm letting you in."

I hear his laughter in my head. *I'm not really here, Char. I'm the voice telling you what you need to hear.*

"I don't believe you. I think you are with me. How can you not be mad at me? I've fallen in love with another man. I've lived a life that was supposed to be ours."

When we truly love someone, we set them free. When we love someone more than ourselves, we want them to be happy, even if they aren't with us.

"I say I'd want you to move on, but I don't know if that's true. The thought of you holding someone else, making a baby with someone else, breaks my heart."

That's because you're still in this world. It would be different if you were in heaven. There's no fear here, no pain, only love and light.

"Then why is it so bad for me to come and be with you?" Anger is now seeping into my voice.

Because it's not your time yet. It will come and it will be beautiful. There's no jealousy here. What's meant to be will be. You're forgetting that you're supposed to live a big life for both of us.

"I am living a big life. I've been married seven times," I say with a humorless laugh.

Well, two of those marriages were to the same man, and one only lasted a few hours. I can still hear laughter in my head.

"You've always made excuses for me."

That's because I believe what I'm saying and because I love you.

"I love you, too."

Don't love me so much you won't love anyone else.

"I'm trying. I really tried with Colby."

You tried your hardest with him, but did you give it your all?

"I was giving it my everything, especially with our child growing inside me, but that was ripped from me. I didn't even get to hold her. I didn't name her."

You can name her now. You can tell Stephy and your parents. You can truly grieve her loss and then you can move on.

I shake my head. "No, I can't do that. They will baby me, they will bring the pain back. I have it somewhat numbed right now."

You don't have anything numbed, you're just masking it. The bandage will eventually be ripped off and then it will be so much worse.

"I don't think so."

I can feel his sad eyes on me. I rise from the grave and make the walk back to the house. I come inside and find Stephy sitting in the den waiting for me. There's a look of worry and fear in her eyes. I hate this look.

"You aren't talking to me, I'm getting really worried now," she tells me.

"I'm fine," I say, just as I always do.

"I don't believe you. Something more happened than Colby leaving. I don't know what it is, but I'm not letting you slip away from me again." She gets up and moves to the table. She grabs something then pushes it at me.

"I don't want to go anywhere," I say.

"I don't care. You either do this or I'm going to have you locked into a hospital. You've lost far too much weight and your eyes are dead. You do this, or your parents will help me have you hospitalized."

She's serious. Do I look that bad? I honestly don't know as I can't remember the last time I've looked in a mirror. I can't even remember the last time I've brushed my hair. Maybe I'm worse off than I realize. I look down at the papers in my hand.

"Where is Catalina Island? I've never heard of it."

"It's off the coast of California. It's a little piece of heaven and I have it all arranged for you."

"What's arranged?"

"You're going down there and fishing. I've gotten you a boat."

"I know nothing about fishing. I've done it here and there, but I don't know enough to actually drive a boat. I don't know bait or tackle. I don't want to learn it either."

"I know you don't. I also know how your mind

works. You will have no choice other than to learn it because you won't stand being less than the best at it."

I sigh. I don't want to do this. I know she's deadly serious about locking me up in a mental health hospital though.

"Are you coming?"

"No, not this time. You need to go on your own. You need to heal from whatever is breaking you. You need to meet Mona. She's going to make it all better. I promise you."

"Who is Mona?"

"You'll see." She finally smiles.

There's something in her eyes that tells me she's speaking the truth. There's something in my soul that is crying out for me to go to this place. I think she's right. I think I do need to get away. I think I do need to speak to this stranger named Mona. I nod at her as I look at my new name. I guess I'm going to Catalina Island as Charlie Emerald. I'll see what comes next in this crazy life I'm living. I'm not ready quite yet, but I know I'll be going there . . . soon.

Read where it all began

Note From Melody Anne
The Anderson World Read Order

The Andersons originally began as a three-book series when I started my writing career. But I fell in love with Joseph and the Anderson dynamic. I went on to write other series, but I found I was bringing Joseph along, wanting to take him with me to all of the worlds I was creating. So, in came his twin brother George, who just happens to be one of my favorite uncles. He lived in Cordova, AK, where I spent a summer when I was sixteen, which is why I sent my couple there in *Blackmailing the Billionaire*. I loved that town. He moved to Anchorage, and I can't wait to go there again and do some fishing which I've become addicted to.

Well, at the end of book seven of the Andersons, I thought it was all finished once again, and then a fan wrote me an email and said they'd had a dream that Joseph and George were staring at a newspaper, and they saw a man who looked just like them. And I was in love with the idea of a stolen baby plot. So, in came Richard, who is another favorite uncle of mine. Richard was stolen at birth as their triplet. Back when Joseph's mother had her babies, fathers weren't often in the

303

delivery room, and the doctor just figured she already had two babies and wouldn't miss a third. So, in came five more kids for Joseph and George to play cupid with.

At the end of that story, Joseph would go on to meddle in the lives of his friends' children, and so his legacy has continued to grow. I left openings in many of my books because I can never truly say those magical words of "*the end*" and so a new branch of Andersons were found in my Montlake series, *Anderson Billion-aires*.

Then I, with friends, were storyboarding about possible ideas, and that's how this newest spin-off happened with *Anderson Special Ops*. This series has been so much fun, because I'm co-writing it. I have a friend who knows the world of special ops, so he's been giving strong outlines, and chapters for these new men we've created in this fun new world. We have a lot of ideas of where this will all lead.

Now, I'm getting a lot of emails, asking about the order to read. I've created so many stories at this point, that even I'm a little lost on the order, but I'm going to list it as best I can with staying in the right timeframe. The newest, of course, are easiest to keep track of, but since I bring in so many other series in the middle of writing these books, it does get a bit confusing.

So here we go. And as always, I love to hear feed-back from you. After all, I can't do this job, can't write these fantastic stories, and can't live in my dream world, without your support. You make the magic happen. You give me a voice to put onto paper, and you make my dreams come true. If the order is at all messed up, then please let me know and we'll adjust.

I have a fantastic team I work with, and we're constantly changing and fixing things. It's amazing this digital world we now have, that we can fix things so easily. Before the world of epublishing, if there was a mistake, it couldn't get fixed until the next set of books were printed. Now, it's just a few hits on the keyboard, and viola, we're good to go again.

Thank you so much for your support. And I hope you are well, are enjoying these stories, and are making magic happen in this crazy world we've found ourselves in in the parallel universe that some call 2020.

Read Order for The Anderson Empire

Billionaire Bachelors
1. The Billionaire Wins the Game
2. The Billionaire's Dance
3. The Billionaire Falls
4. The Billionaire's Marriage Proposal
5. Blackmailing the Billionaire
6. Runaway Heiress
7. The Billionaire's Final Stand
8. Unexpected Treasure
9. Hidden Treasure
10. Holiday Treasure
11. Priceless Treasure
12. The Ultimate Treasure

Now, you can read the Tycoon Series, which Joseph's in, but only one of the books is truly relevant to the continuation of the Anderson's stories. I'll list all of the Tycoon books here, but highlight Damien's story, which will come up later on in a twist for *The Billionaire* Andersons listed below.

Billionaire Bachelors
Book One: The Tycoon's Revenge
Book Two: The Tycoon's Vacation
Book Three: The Tycoon's Proposal
13. Book Four: The Tycoon's Secret
Book Five: The lost Tycoon
Book Six: Rescue me

And here we go again, with another insert. So, Joseph next appears in my Heroes Series. We have a visit from *Dr. Spence Whitman* in this book you've just read, which is in this series. You can read this series next to know Spence's story, but you won't be lost if you don't. So I'll list the entire series here, and again highlight the story that has Spence in it, adding it to the list. All of these books can stand alone, but I do bring my characters in and out of most of my series because I can't let them go. So if you read *Her Hometown Hero*, it's a complete story, but the brothers will all be throughout it.

Heroes Series
Pre-Book: Safe in his arms (in an Anthology called
    Baby it's Cold Outside)

And now, we come to Sherman, who will play a big roll in this series. Sherman's another of those characters I seriously love! When I came up with Bobbi, Avery's mother, I knew right then and there, she was going to be a match for Sherman. By the way, Bobbi is named after my best friend's mother, who I absolutely adore! She mirrors some of her character traits too, and we'll be seeing a lot more of her. In real life she's married to Hal, who happens to be a fantastic man.

After I wrote the Bobbi character, I was telling the real Bobbi what she's saying and doing, and I might've made her blush. Hal's okay with it though. If he's gonna lose his wife, at least it's to Sherman, who happens to be a pretty great guy. We just spent a long weekend at their house in Northern Cali, and had a refreshing, fantastic time. But I was also putting them under the microscope for my upcoming stories. I use real life in my books all of the time because family events are definitely story worthy. So, Bobbi, beware because I'm gonna have fun with this character.

I list the Billionaire Aviators next, but don't number them because you don't have to read these to read all the rest, but if you want to get to know Sherman, then I'd dive on in. This series was one of my fav to write, because I love the characters, love the journey, and I was really growing in my writing at this point, getting a little more courageous with what I was doing within my fantasy worlds.

Billionaire Aviators
Book One: Turbulent Intentions
Book Two: Turbulent Desires
Book Three: Turbulent Waters
Book Four: Turbulent Intrigue

Joseph and other Andersons appear in my Undercover Billionaire world, where I started adding more suspense into my writing. Some of these characters will pop in and out of this world as well, because, like I said, I love to bring these characters into each world. So you can read this series, but again, won't be lost if you don't, so I won't number them.

On a side note. *Owen* is my *favorite* book I've ever written. I lost my dad in 2018, and it nearly killed me. I write men like Joseph, George, Sherman, and more because I'm a daddy's girl, through and through. He raised me with so much more love than I can even begin to explain, and he also taught me how to be independent and strong. He's the reason I'm an author, the reason I'm so strong, and the reason I still cry because I miss him so much.

He LOVED UFO stories, and when all of the news broke that they were releasing the government files on UFOs, my heart was breaking again, because he would've been so excited and absolutely glued to the internet. I know he's up in Heaven laughing because he has all of the answers now, but I sure would love him to be here with me so we could talk and wonder, and laugh . . . and so his arms could be wrapped around me.

My heroine loses her dad in Owen, which I'd begun writing before I lost my dad. I had to stop, and when I came back to the book, I cried my way through a lot of it. A lot of the lines she uses when she's talking about her father were things I asked and said. I was so lost for a long time after losing him. Writing Owen helped me heal. My heart will never be truly full again, but my dad loved me, and I love him, and I know he'd kick my butt if I didn't live my life with love, laughter, and triumph. He raised me to be a powerful woman, and I won't dishonor him by being anything less than that. So I'm gonna highlight Owen, not because it's needed for the Andersons, but because it's needed for my soul. ☺

Undercover Billionaires
Book One: Kian
Book Two: Arden
Book Three: Owen
Book Four: Declan

Now it gets a bit more confusing as I'm finishing out my Montlake series at the same time as we're writing *The Anderson Black Ops* series, so you get to go back and forth a bit if you want to stay exactly in the timeline. We're finally making it to the end . . . for now. But I guess I'll have to stay on top of this because I have no doubt that the Anderson world will continue to grow and grow and grow, even as I take time to visit other worlds in between. Thank you again for all you do. I hope you fall in love with these characters over and over again, just as I do each time I dive back into the Anderson Universe.

The Billionaire Andersons
15. Book One: Finn
16. Book Two: Noah

Anderson Black Ops
17. Book One: Shadows

The Billionaire Andersons
18. Book Three: Brandon

Anderson Black Ops
19. Book Two: Rising

The Billionaire Andersons
20. Book Four Hudson
21. Book Five: Crew

Anderson Black Ops
22. Book Three: Barriers
23. Book Four: Shattered
24. Book Five: Reborn

The Story Continues with this new series With Jasmine Anderson now working in Miami for the FBI

Truth In Lies
25. One Too Many
26. Two Secrets Kept

About the Author

Melody Anne is a NYT best selling author of more than 65 books including contemporary romance, erotic romance, young adult, and thriller books.

As an aspiring author, she wrote for years, then officially published in 2011, finding her true calling, and a love of writing. Holding a Bachelor's Degree in business, she loves to write about strong, powerful businessmen and the corporate world.

When not writing, she spends time with family, friends, and her pets. A country girl at heart, she loves the small town and strong community she lives in and is involved in community projects.

To date, she has over 10 million book sales and has earned multiple placement on varying best seller lists, including NYT's, USA Today, and WSJ, being an amazon top 100 bestselling author for 3 years in a row, as well as a Kobo and iBooks best-seller. But beyond that, she loves getting to do what makes her happy—living in a fantasy world 95% of the time.

See her website and subscribe to her newsletter at: www.melodyanne.com. She makes it a point to respond to her fans. You can also join her on her official facebook page: www.facebook.com/melodyanneauthor, or on instagram @authormelodyanne.

She looks forward to hearing from you and wants to thank you for your continued interest in her stories.

Made in the USA
Middletown, DE
19 April 2022

64475285R00179